DON'T ANSWER THE PHONE

MIRANDA RIJKS

INKUBATOR
BOOKS

Published by Inkubator Books
www.inkubatorbooks.com

ISBN (eBook): 978-1-83756-715-7
ISBN (Paperback): 978-1-83756-716-4
ISBN (Hardback): 978-1-83756-717-1

For Pippa Bugby, who made our house a home. I couldn't have got through the past year without you!

PROLOGUE

THEN

'Mom, what's that on your arm?'

I tug my sleeve down over my wrist to cover the livid bruise, even though it's much too hot to be wearing a long-sleeved dress.

'Nothing,' I say. 'The iron fell on me earlier.' We think we can kid our children, but we can't. Not really. Sometimes I wonder whether mine were born with an innate wisdom, because they know things I've never taught them. I gaze at my family—my perfect family. My husband sits in his deckchair, reading *The Boston Globe*, his starched white shirt open to expose his hairy stomach. My three cherubic children, two of them playing contentedly in our secluded garden, one fast asleep in her bassinet, shaded under an umbrella. The fairytale treehouse in the middle of the lawn, constructed around the beech tree, with its turrets and little windows and narrow steps that wind up and around the trunk, so high above the ground.

I am lucky, I tell myself. So very lucky.

I need to remind myself of that.

'Mommy, will you play with us?'

I smile at my eight-year-old daughter with her cherubic smile and creamy porcelain skin. At least she is never marked with bruises.

'Play with your brother, darling.'

My husband lowers the newspaper and scowls at me, opening his mouth as if to say something. Except then the phone rings.

'Don't answer the phone,' he mutters. 'Concentrate on the cooking. I'm starving.'

I hurry inside, and I do answer the phone. Except all I hear is static.

'Who's there?' I ask.

No one answers.

I'm about to ask again when there's a scream.

A terrible, ear-piercing scream. Coming from our garden.

I drop the phone, leaving it to dangle, and race through the house into the garden.

My scream mingles with theirs. For a moment, I can't make sense of what I'm seeing, except I know that our lives will never be the same again. How is that terrible things can happen on such a beautiful summer's day?

'No!' I shout as I rush forward, falling to my knees, reaching for her. My broken baby, her head lolling to one side, her perfect almond-shaped eyes staring at the azure blue sky. Unseeing.

I pull her into my arms, knowing it's too late. The best first aid skills in the world won't bring her back to me.

'Which one of you did this?' I screech, staring up at them.

'Don't be so stupid. It was an accident.'

Except I know it wasn't. I only have to look at their faces.

CHAPTER ONE

DANIELLA

'I'll see you at the counseling session,' I say to Grant as he picks up his worn leather satchel and strides out of the kitchen.

'Yes, Daniella.' He adds an exaggerated sigh. 'How can I possibly forget?'

'Sorry,' I mutter, because even I realize I've reminded my husband at least five times during the past twenty-four hours. And Grant isn't the sort of man to forget any appointment. In fact, he has the memory of an elephant.

'Who's going to counseling?' Arlyse makes me start as she pads silently into the room just as the sound of Grant closing the front door and leaving the house echoes down the hallway. She's the older of our non-identical twins by a minute or so.

Damn. I didn't want either of the girls to overhear that, but then again, we've always preached about honesty.

'Dad and I are going to couples counseling. It's a big deal when your kids fly the nest, and our lives are going to be very different without you and Tasia here.'

'You're not getting a divorce or anything, are you?' She's scantily dressed in a long T-shirt and wraps her skinny arms around herself. 'Both Candy's and Brooklyn's parents waited until they'd left home, and now they're divorcing. Turns out Candy's dad has been having an affair for years.'

'Absolutely not. Dad and I love each other, and the best decision I ever made was marrying him. This is just to help us through the next stage of our lives.'

'It's just that you've never been into therapy. You've always been... I dunno, scathing about it.'

'True, but I think it will be useful for us now that we're going to be empty-nesters, and Dad agrees.'

Arlyse knots her eyebrows together.

'You've got nothing to worry about,' I reassure her.

'I don't believe in marriage anyway,' she says, turning from me and reaching for a mug from a high cupboard.

'Nor do I,' Tasia says as she walks into the kitchen. She is fully dressed in jeans and a crop top, her wet hair piled on top of her head. 'It's a social construct, and anyway, why are we as a species so hung up on monogamy? It's useful for governments to control us, a way to make society operate. You're less likely to be hurt as well if you're not in a monogamous relationship.'

'Well, that's very cynical of you,' I say. 'And I'm not sure it works that way.'

'Love doesn't mean you need to be together forever, and it certainly doesn't have to lead to marriage,' Arlyse says.

'What do you know about love?' Tasia asks. 'You've only ever had one boyfriend.'

'This is not a conversation for now.' Arlyse speaks through clenched teeth. Their banter surprises me, especially as I wasn't aware that Arlyse had—or possibly has—a boyfriend, and it strikes me how little I know about their lives these days.

'Just concentrate on all the exciting things that will happen over the next few months. Anyway,' I say, changing the subject, 'how are you both getting on with ticking things off the packing list?'

'God, Mom, we're not going for weeks. Stop stressing.' Tasia is rooting around in the pantry cupboard. 'Is there any more granola?'

'Top shelf. But you'd better eat up. You don't want to be late for work.'

'Stop with the bugging. We'll be on time,' Arlyse says. They can both be quite cutting, and sometimes I take them to task on it, but this morning I haven't got the energy. I'm proud of our girls. They're currently working to save money for their forthcoming trip to South America. Arlyse is going to study medicine at college, and she's chosen to volunteer in a remote clinic in Belize, hoping to get first-hand experience with public health in rural communities. Tasia is enrolled in a marine conservation program in Costa Rica. This will be the first time the girls have been separated, and it's a big deal for all of us, but a vital trial run, as they will attend different colleges. They're really close, and I'm concerned about how they'll cope away from each other. Sometimes when we're seated at our big kitchen table, I look at my family and wonder how I've gotten here. The three of them are Bostonians through and through, whereas I have never lost my British accent and will always be a foreigner in this land.

Half an hour later, they leave the house in a noisy, messy clatter, one that I despair of but know I'm going to miss horribly. I've got an hour before I need to leave, and I'm getting increasingly nervous. It's not like our marriage is in trouble, at least I hope it's not. I still love Grant after two decades together, and I'm pretty sure he still loves me; not that he remembers to tell me that. But we have a lack of intimacy. I mean a huge lack of intimacy. When I read articles about mid- and late-life sex, time gaps are measured in weeks or months. We're talking years. It's not like I woke up one morning and realized I might never have sex again, it's been a creeping realization over the past decade, and I'm fearful it's going to break us. Well, break me, anyway. Somehow, I've persuaded Grant that we need to go to couples therapy, and this morning is our first session. I know he's dreading it and only agreed to go because he loves me, and now that it's practically upon us, I'm getting second thoughts too.

I busy myself by responding to emails and cleaning up the kitchen, trying not to think about how embarrassing it's going to be to vocalize the fact that Grant and I haven't had sex in so long, and then realize it's time to go.

It's a beautiful winter's day—a clear blue sky, the trees bare of leaves—so I wrap up warmly with my hand-knitted, matching burgundy hat, scarf, and gloves and choose to cycle.

I love my bike. It's spearmint green with a large basket at the front and a tiny Union Jack flag on the bumper to remind me I'm still British at heart. I turn out of our driveway onto the quiet residential street. We're so lucky to be living here in Brookline, a smart road with large houses and bigger gardens, so we never actually see or hear our neighbors. Of course, I know a few of them, but it's one of those neighborhoods where we get together maybe once a year if someone feels inclined to throw a Christmas party. I couldn't even tell you what cars my nearest neighbors drive, and sometimes I think that's a shame. But this morning my mind is focused on how I'm going to share my concerns with the therapist without making Grant feel bad, and I'm not really concentrating on my familiar surroundings.

I GET to the junction with Ivy Street and glance right and do a double take, slamming the brakes on the bike, jamming my trainers onto the tarmac to stop myself from going over the handlebars. It looks like two people are fighting just fifty or so yards away from me.

Without thinking, I'm off the bike, letting it fall onto the soft grass next to the sidewalk. I stand still for a moment, appraising the situation. It doesn't look good, and my heart is hammering in my chest.

'Hey!' I shout, wondering if this is even the right thing to do. I take a few steps towards them and realize there's a person on the ground. A man stands up and glances towards me, but he's too far away to make out his features. He's wearing a black hoodie pulled low over his face and black trousers. This is not good.

'What's going on?' I yell and just pray that he doesn't have a knife or a gun. But then he turns around and runs at full speed in the opposite direction, a dark figure disappearing around the corner in a blur. Without thinking, I race towards the person lying on the ground. As I approach, I realize it's a woman. She's wearing a wool skirt that's hitched up above her knees, her stockinged legs lying at a strange angle, flat pumps discarded to her side. She's not even wearing a coat.

'Oh, my goodness! Are you alright?' I ask as I crouch down next to her. She has light gray curly hair and the beginnings of a livid bruise over one eye, blood dripping from a split lip. What bastard would do this to an older woman? Her eyes flicker open; she opens her mouth as if to talk to me, but just lets out a whimper.

'It's alright,' I say, grabbing her hand and squeezing it gently. 'I'm calling the police right now, and we'll get you to the hospital.'

I dial 911 and explain the urgency of the situation. The lady is shivering, so I take off my coat and lay it over her, using my scarf to fashion a pillow under her head. I'm nervous about moving her in case she has broken bones or a neck injury. I take off my gloves and try to pull them over her fingers, and I lay my hat over her head.

'You're going to be alright,' I murmur. 'The paramedics won't be long now.' I hope that I'm correct. 'Can I do anything to make you more comfortable?'

'I'm alright,' she says in a whisper, although it's clear she's not. 'You're very kind,' she says. 'It's just a bit of a shock.'

Her voice is faint, but I'm relieved that she's able to talk properly.

'What's your name?' I ask as I stroke the back of her hand with my fingers.

'Margaret Denman,' she whispers.

'Margaret,' I say, 'my name is Daniella, and I live on the next street over.'

'My friends call me Peggy,' she adds.

'Are you in a lot of pain, Peggy?'

'Yes, but I'm made of sturdy stuff.'

I smile. Her right eye is very swollen now, and her breathing rather shallow. I need to keep her talking.

'Do you know what happened, Peggy?'

'I got mugged,' she murmurs.

'Do you live around here?'

'That's my house.' She tries to move but winces with pain.

'Best keep still until the paramedics arrive,' I say as I glance up at the house to our left. It's old-style clapboard and looks like it could do with a lick of paint and a general spruce-up. The house is smaller than most on this street, and I imagine developers offering her millions to sell so they can knock it down to rebuild a mansion or two. I see her mailbox is open and suppose she was just popping out to collect her mail.

'How long have you lived here?' I ask.

'Ever since I was married, fifty years ago.' That must make her at least early seventies.

'And your husband?' I ask.

She gently shakes her head, so I don't question her anymore, and then her eyes close, and it looks like she's slipping into unconsciousness. To my relief, I hear the faint sounds of sirens that grow increasingly louder.

An ambulance and a police car arrive within seconds of each other, and the paramedics rush over.

'Please stand to one side, ma'am,' they instruct me.

Two police officers jump out of their car and pace towards me. 'What happened?' the taller man asks. I explain that it looked like Peggy was the victim of a mugging and that I just happened to be passing by when I saw the scuffle. Meanwhile, the paramedics get a gurney out of the ambulance. I stand to one side as they treat her, wondering if I should leave or stay.

'Mrs. Denman wants to talk to you.' A paramedic beckons to me. I'm relieved that she's come to.

'Hey, Peggy.' I crouch down next to her.

Her voice is very faint. 'They want to take me to the hospital. Will you come with me?'

For the first time, I glance at my watch and realize that nearly forty-five minutes have passed, making me over twenty minutes late for the counseling session. Nothing I can do about that now.

'Of course,' I say, and Peggy tries to smile.

'Ma'am, we need to take your statement,' a police officer says. He's a large man, and my breathing speeds up even though I've done nothing wrong. 'Could you talk us through what happened here?'

I explain what I saw, which in reality wasn't enough to give a description of the man.

'What will happen next?'

'We'll investigate as best we can; look for any camera footage in the area. Find out if the lady recognized her attacker.'

'Have you checked if someone has gotten into her house? She says she lives right there.' I point to the house behind us. 'I was wondering if it was a burglary gone wrong, because who would mug someone at their mailbox?'

'Members of the team will search the property. Thank you for your help.'

Clearly, I'm being dismissed. 'Will you keep me posted?'

'We'll do our best.'

That doesn't sound hopeful.

It takes another few minutes to get Peggy onto the gurney and comfortable in the ambulance. By the time they're ready for me to join her, she's hooked up to an IV. I sit down on a bench in the back of the ambulance. The engine starts, and then Peggy turns her face towards me with a little gasp. A female paramedic is seated next to her.

'Everything's alright, Peggy,' she says. 'We'll have you at the hospital in no time.'

'But what about Bippie? There's no one to look after Bippie!' Her voice sounds panicked.

'Who's Bippie?' I ask.

'My dog. He's trapped in the house.'

'Don't worry about him,' I promise before really thinking through the implications. 'Has a neighbor got a key?'

'My son does,' Peggy mutters.

She's quiet for a short while and then says, 'You're English, aren't you?'

'Yes.' I chuckle. 'I've been in Boston for over twenty years but seem incapable of losing the accent.'

'My mother was British. Such a lovely woman. She came from a seaside town called Hove. Do you know it?'

'I do,' I say with a grin. 'I was brought up in south London, and we used to go to the seaside at Hove, and then, when I was a bit older, I hung around Brighton a lot.'

'What a small world,' she says.

When we arrive at the hospital, Peggy seems more distressed. 'You won't leave me,' she cries, stretching out her arm towards me, her voice quivering.

'Who should we call to say you're here, ma'am?' the paramedic asks.

'My son, Lucas. You need to tell Lucas. But I don't want this kind lady to leave me.'

'I won't,' I reassure her, giving her hand another gentle squeeze.

They wheel Peggy into the hospital, down a long corridor and into a small curtained cubicle. 'A doctor will be along shortly to examine you, Peggy. Can you give us your son's telephone number?'

Fortunately, Peggy is lucid enough to reel off the number. I suppose if she just nipped out of the house for her mail, her handbag and belongings will be in her house. I hope she didn't leave her door open, that no intruder has gotten inside. I wonder what the police have found, if anything. What heartless thief would attack an older lady right outside her home?

'Louise, is that you?' Peggy asks, her voice faint now.

I stroke her hand. 'It's me, Daniella. I'm the person who found you.' Her eyes flutter closed, and I glance at my watch. I really need to call Grant.

Peggy's eyes open again, and she turns to look at me. She tries to smile, but with her bruised and swollen face, it looks more like a grimace.

'Peggy, I need to call my husband. I should have been at an appointment with him, and he'll be worried about me,' I say.

'You don't have a husband, love,' she murmurs, her eyes still closed. 'You're too young.'

I look at her and realize she must assume I'm someone else, maybe this Louise she called out to earlier. I pat her wrinkled hand and tell her I'll be back in a moment. Then I emerge out of the cubicle and walk down the corridor towards the exit. I take my cell from my purse and see that I've got three missed calls, all from Grant. I don't bother listening to the messages before I call him.

'I'm so sorry,' I say before Grant can talk. 'A lady was mugged on Ivy Street, and I stopped to help her, then she wanted me to go with her to the hospital, so I'm here now.'

There's a pause before Grant speaks, his voice taut. 'Are you hurt?'

'No. The mugger ran away when I shouted, but I couldn't leave her alone.'

'We've missed the therapy session,' Grant says. 'And I've returned to work.'

'I'm so sorry,' I murmur.

'Yes, well,' Grant says, 'you always need to sort out other people's problems, don't you, Daniella? Anyway, see you later.' He hangs up.

That was uncalled for and leaves me with a bitter taste. Grant rarely makes barbed comments towards me; if anything, he's normally too nice. I head back to Peggy's cubicle, where she still hasn't been assessed by a doctor. I sit down next to her.

'I'm so sorry I didn't protect you more,' she says. Her voice is quiet and tremulous, and with her eyes closed, the swelling on her face is livid now.

'It's me, Daniella,' I say gently. 'I met you for the first time today.'

'I really love you, you know that,' Peggy murmurs, and for sure she thinks I'm someone else. 'You're such a good girl. My girl.'

I wonder if she's talking about the dog.

'Are you worried about your dog, Bippie?' I ask.

'You'll look after Bippie, won't you?'

Before I can ask anything further, the curtain is swept back, and a doctor walks in wearing a white coat with a stethoscope around her neck. If she weren't dressed like that, I'd assume she was still in medical school; she looks impossibly young.

'Mrs. Denman,' she says, lifting up Peggy's hand. 'Are you a relative?' she asks me.

'No, I found Peggy. I don't know her.'

'Right. If you wouldn't mind stepping outside,' she says.

I do as I'm told.

Five minutes later, I'm pacing the corridor, wondering if I should leave or stay. A man runs past me and rushes to the desk where a group of nurses are typing into computers and talking in hushed voices.

'Margaret Denman,' he says breathlessly. 'I'm her son. She's been brought in here.'

One of the nurses looks up, and her cheeks flush slightly. 'Yes. She's being assessed by the doctor at the moment. She's in cubicle six.'

'Can I see her?' he asks.

'When the doctor has finished. If you wouldn't mind just waiting outside the cubicle.'

He turns around, his fingers clenched. I walk over to him.

'Hello. I'm Daniella Morris. I found your mother and called 911.'

He swivels around to face me, and for a moment I'm speechless. Peggy's son is quite possibly the handsomest man I've ever laid eyes on. He has thick, sandy blond hair, startling green eyes set under dark brows, a square jaw, and broad shoulders. There are wrinkles around his eyes and his mouth, and I suspect he looks younger than he really is. At a little over six feet, he's broad, with muscles evident through the white button-down shirt he's wearing, an overcoat casually hanging from one arm. His pupils enlarge as he looks down at me, and his gaze sweeps from my face down my body and back up again.

'I have a lot to thank you for,' he says, reaching for my hand. We shake hands awkwardly, and when he puts his left hand over the top of mine, a surge of warmth sweeps right through me. For the first time in my life, I understand the word swoon. He holds onto me for several seconds too long.

The curtain opens, and the young doctor emerges. Peggy's son lets go of my hand and steps forward. I see he has the same effect on most women based on the doctor's sudden color rising up her neck, but she's more professional than me and looks down at the clipboard in her hand.

'I'm Lucas Denman, Peggy's son,' he says. 'How is she?'

'She's battered, bruised, and in shock, and I suspect her ankle might be broken. I'm going to send her for an X-ray, and then we'll reassess. Even if it isn't broken, because of her age, diabetes, and high blood pressure, I'm going to admit her to the hospital for observation.'

'Can I see her?'

'Of course. But keep it short, as I want to get her more comfortable. If you leave your phone number, we'll be in touch once the X-ray results have been assessed.'

'Right.'

Lucas disappears into the cubicle, and I wait for a moment, wondering whether I should just slip away. But a couple of seconds later, two nurses have swept back the curtains and are wheeling Peggy away.

Lucas turns towards me. 'They said you accompanied Mom in the ambulance.'

'Yes, that's right.'

'Where did you leave your car?'

'I was on my bike, actually.' I hope it's still lying on the grass where I dumped it.

'I really can't thank you enough. Can I give you a lift home or to get your bike?'

'Your mother was very concerned about her dog. Bippie, is it?'

'Yes, the dog. I'll take care of him. Look, I'd really like to give you a lift to get your bike or take you home.'

I hesitate for a moment. Should I go with this handsome stranger? I can hear Grant's voice in my head. It's not safe. Except I know who this man is, and I know where Peggy lives.

'Come on,' Lucas says, briefly touching my hand and sending a shiver up my arm. 'It's the least I can do.'

LUCAS'S CAR doesn't match his debonair image. It's an old Honda CR-V, silver with dents along the rear and front bumpers. I wonder if it's his mother's car but say nothing as I slip into the passenger seat. At least it's scrupulously clean on the inside.

'You know, I really can't thank you enough,' he says as the engine coughs to a start. 'I hate to think what would have happened if you hadn't turned up when you did.'

'I'm just shocked that someone would beat up an older lady right outside her home. I thought we lived in a safe area.'

Lucas nods. 'Crime has gotten really out of control in this city. It's terrible. I hate that Mom is going to feel nervous living there now. Fortunately, I visit a lot, but I'll certainly be installing some cameras.'

'Good idea,' I say.

'And where does our good Samaritan live?'

I give a little laugh. 'Just around the corner on Amory Street,' I say.

'Well, that's great news.' Lucas glances at me with a dazzling smile. 'You'll be able to pop over and say hello to Mom when she's out of the hospital. Actually, I have a friend who lives at 2040. I think that's the number, but I might be wrong. Is that near you?'

'We're at 2011. I'm afraid to say despite living there for years, we don't know many of our neighbors.'

'That seems to be increasingly the way. It's a shame we no longer make the effort,' he says.

'So, what sort of dog is Bippie?' I ask as Lucas navigates the car along Boston's busy streets.

'A big, brown Labrador, much too large for Mom, but she loves him. And I guess he keeps her fit too because she walks him twice a day. Refuses to have a dog walker.'

We make small talk all the way home. It's easy conversation that flows seamlessly from one topic to the next, and before I know it, Lucas is pulling into his mother's driveway. To my great relief, I spot my bike still lying on the grass.

When I get out of the car, Lucas walks around towards me. His eyes are so stunning I feel awkward looking at them. 'You know, I really can't thank you enough. Could I have your number so I can call when Mom is out of the hospital?'

It seems churlish not to give it to him. We say our goodbyes, but as I walk towards my bike, I feel Lucas's eyes on my back. When I wheel the bike over the sidewalk and onto the road, I turn to look at Peggy's drive. Lucas is still standing there looking at me. He raises a hand as I cycle away.

I DECIDE to go into work, hoping it'll take my mind off the shock of the morning. I run a faux-flower business called the Silken Stem with my friend Lesley. Some people roll their eyes when I say we sell artificial flowers. Not very environmentally friendly, they murmur, oh so full of judgment. Except when you think of the air miles that real flowers travel, flowers that only last a few days, then it puts things into perspective. Our flowers last for years, need no upkeep, and require a careful eye to tell the difference between the real and fake versions. Yes, some of our flowers are made in China, but we're very selective whom we buy from and make sure that they are ethically produced. Lesley has visited the factories in China twice. Our business is small but successful. We have a lovely little boutique in Brookline where customers can buy ready-made arrangements in pots and vases, or single stems to make up their own arrangements. And a large percentage of our business is online.

As I walk into the shop, Lesley peers at me. 'You look... was the therapy session that bad?' she asks. She knows me too well, which isn't surprising considering how long we've been friends. We were at school together in Croydon back in England. In her early twenties, she fell in love with a square-jawed, blue-eyed American, married him within three months of meeting and moved to Boston. I assumed we would rarely see each other, except through her, I met Grant, and as they say, the rest is history, including the blue-eyed American.

'I didn't make the therapy session,' I tell Lesley. 'I rescued a woman from a mugging.' While she makes me a strong cup of tea, I explain what happened. I'm grateful to be around another Brit who shares my weird, wry sense of humor and understands my compulsive need to drink tea.

A message pings on my phone.

Lucas here. Hope to see you again soon.

My face must flush slightly because Lesley asks, 'What's the message?'

'Oh, just from the son of the woman I rescued.'

She raises an eyebrow but quickly returns to the spreadsheet on her laptop. Meanwhile, I'm feeling simultaneously restless and tired. The earlier adrenaline rush has morphed into an unsettling sensation. How fortuitous it was that I was passing at that very moment, how I might have saved Peggy but how I also put myself in potential danger. I busy myself fashioning some faux foliage into a wreath, but images of Lucas's face flash in my mind. I tell myself I'm being ridiculous. I'm married, fifty-two years old, and menopausal. Why on earth am I fantasizing about a handsome stranger? The wreath isn't up to my normal standard, so I leave it behind the sales counter and head home.

BY THE TIME Grant returns home from work, I'm bone-weary exhausted, and I've achieved next to nothing this afternoon.

'What exactly happened this morning?' Grant asks as he walks into the kitchen. We have a beautiful kitchen, large and airy, with white marble countertops and a pale oak table big enough to seat ten. Double patio doors open out onto the terrace and the verdant garden beyond. It's easy to forget that we live in a big city.

I pour both of us a glass of wine, and Grant sits at the table while I recount the events of the day, omitting any details about charismatic Lucas.

I don't notice Arlyse standing in the doorway until Grant raises his hand at her.

'God, Mom. I never had you down as an action hero,' she says as she strides into the room. Both girls have an array of part-time jobs, and I've lost track of what they're doing when. 'I wish I'd been there. I could have gotten real-life practice.'

'Plenty of time for that,' I say, still buzzing with pride that she's gotten into medical school.

'Honestly, Daniella. Why did you even get involved?' Grant says. 'You could have been seriously hurt. That guy could have hit you or even pulled a gun. You should have called the police from a distance when you were out of danger.'

'The guy had gone by the time I reached Peggy, and I only did what any decent person would do,' I say, feeling resentment towards Grant. I thought he might have praised me for my bravery, not that that crossed my mind at the time. I acted purely on impulse.

'I'm proud of you,' Arlyse says, placing an unexpected and very welcome kiss on the side of my cheek. She grabs a soda from the fridge before leaving the room.

I wait until I'm sure I won't be overheard and take a swig of wine. 'I'm sorry I missed the counseling session,' I murmur.

'I'm not,' Grant mutters into his glass.

CHAPTER TWO

LUCAS

I'm in my study in the brownstone, comfortable in the gaming chair that Jade bought a few months ago. The phone rings, and I'm almost tempted not to answer it except it's from a withheld number.

'Yes,' I say impatiently.

'Good afternoon. Is this Mr. Denman?'

'Yes, that's me.'

'I'm calling from the hospital where we're looking after your mother.'

'Shall I come and get her?' I glance at my watch. If I go now, I can be back here in just over an hour, in time for dinner, which Jade will pick up from some fancy store.

'Peggy hasn't broken any bones, but she's very bruised and fragile, so we'd like to monitor her overnight.'

'Right,' I say. 'Nothing too serious though?'

'No, but with her underlying health conditions and the shock, we'd like to be sure. We'll contact you tomorrow.'

A knot of unease sits in my stomach. I hope Mom is okay. I might be a grown man, but I struggle to imagine life without her. And then I remember Bippie and groan. This means I'm going to have to look after the damn dog. I can't have him at our place because Jade is allergic to dogs, so that means I've either got to stay at Mom's or leave him alone overnight. I growl with annoyance and decide I'll stay at Mom's tonight.

If I had to have a pet, I'd choose a cat. I respect their independence, the way they can see in the dark and prowl through the night, how they move stealthily, hopping up onto surfaces with a mind of their own. Dogs, on the other hand, are a pain. They need feeding and walking and crave affection. Mom adores Bippie, but then he's her constant companion, and he forces her to be active and look after her health. I've been saying for ages that she needs a dog walker, but Mom refuses to countenance anyone else looking after her beloved pooch.

I could wait for Jade to get back, except the dog will have been alone for hours already, and I can't face the thought of having to clean up its muck. Chucking a few things in an overnight bag, I return to the car and head back to Ivy Street. Some sickly-sweet romantic song that I don't know the name of plays on the radio, and for some reason it makes me think of Daniella. Actually, it's not just the song; I've been thinking of her pretty much nonstop ever since I dropped her off.

I've never believed in love at first sight. It's a ridiculous notion devised by authors of old to get us to buy into monogamy and romance. Physical attraction, though, is another matter. Whether it's some base chemical fusion or just the fulfillment of our ideal of beauty, I don't know. I've been hit by it a few times, but none more powerfully than when I laid eyes on Daniella. Sure, she's an attractive woman with thick dark hair and large mahogany eyes, but she's not model gorgeous. Not like Jade or several of the women who came before Jade. And she's certainly older than the women I normally go for. I could try to analyze what makes my nerve endings tingle when I think about her or why I literally had to restrain my fingers from stroking her face, except what's the point? I want Daniella. No, I need Daniella. I try to tell myself I'm being ridiculous. I've spent mere minutes in her company, and I know absolutely nothing about the woman. She might be a complete bitch. Although that's unlikely, because if she were, she wouldn't have rescued Mom. All I know is that I have to see Daniella again.

THE DOG HAS LEFT a great big puddle of urine in the kitchen. I'm tempted to shove his nose in it so he learns a lesson, but occasionally I think Bippie is so bright, he might tell Mom. It's almost as if they have this secret language, intuition or something, so they know what each other is thinking. A ridiculous concept, I know. I clean up the mess, muttering expletives under my breath. Jade calls me, and I ignore the call. A message pings through.

Where are u?

It drives me insane that she uses teenage text speak. How much more effort does it take to type three letters rather than one? I don't feel like answering, except I know she'll get all mouthy, so I reply.

Staying the night at Mom's.

I don't sleep well. I never do in this house. Too many memories, I guess. The only thing that keeps me here is the thought that I'm only a couple of streets away from Daniella's house. When sleep evades me, I slip out of bed, pull on my clothes and head downstairs. Bippie wakes up too, so I grab his lead.

'Let's go for a walk,' I say, pleased with myself that walking a dog will prevent me from looking suspicious at 2:03 a.m.

We walk briskly along the darkened roads. Everything is silent—no cars, no birds, no wind. The only noise is the sound of my sneakers squeaking on the sidewalk. I stop at the top of Daniella's drive. 2011 Amory Street. It wasn't difficult getting that information out of Daniella. The house is completely dark. I stare at the windows on the upper floor, wondering which is her bedroom, or perhaps she sleeps at the back. It's a sprawling house, difficult to make out its features in the dark, but I'm pretty sure it's the type of property to have security lights. I restrain myself from walking down the driveway or creeping around the backyard. Instead, I console myself that she's in there, quite possibly dreaming about me. After about fifteen minutes, I'm getting cold, so we head back home.

The next morning, I get another call from the hospital to say that Mom can come home. Good news. I'm just heading out to the car when my phone pings with an incoming text. A wide grin curls across my lips. It's from Daniella.

Just wondering how Peggy is doing.

I reply immediately.

Thank you so much for asking. She's doing well. No broken bones, and she's being released from hospital. The only problem is Bippie her dog. I'm got meetings this week and need to find a dog walker to help when I'm not able to make it over. Do you know of one?

I wait impatiently as the little dots turn into a message.

I'd be happy to help for a few days until you find someone else. I could walk her before and after work. Would you like me to pop by later?

I do a fist pump. Hook, line, and sinker.

MOM LOOKS LIKE A MESS. Her face is one big bruise, and her eye is so swollen she can't see out of it. Her ankle is badly sprained, and according to the nurse, she's black and blue down her left side. She's discharged in a wheelchair with a big bottle of painkillers. But Mom being Mom is ridiculously cheery.

'Just happy to still be here,' she says as I wheel her towards the car.

'What are the police doing to find the person who attacked you?' I ask.

'No idea, Lucas. I can't see a mugging being a top priority. It's not like the man even took anything. I'd only walked down the driveway to check the mailbox, and my house key was still in my pocket. All that hassle for nothing.'

I give her shoulder a gentle squeeze, and she flinches. 'Sorry,' I mutter.

It takes a while to get her into the car and even longer to get her back out again and into the loaned wheelchair. I try to be gentle with Mom, but her house isn't designed for wheelchair access, and every jolt and step clearly ricochets her with pain.

I settle Mom in the living room and offer her a drink, but all she's interested in is Bippie, cuddling the dog and telling him how much she's missed him. I can see the next few days are going to be hard. Mom will be relying on me for everything, and as much as I love her, I'm no nurse. I wonder for a moment if I should employ someone.

'I'd like to see that lovely lady who helped me,' Mom says as I hand her a cheese sandwich. 'I want to thank her. Did you get her contact details?'

'Indeed, I did,' I say, a sensation of warmth fluttering through me. 'She's already offered to walk Bippie.'

'Has she?' Mom sounds surprised.

'In fact, she's coming later this afternoon after she's finished work.'

Mom dozes off to sleep in her wheelchair, and I debate leaving her and stopping in later, except I don't want to take the risk of missing Daniella. She didn't say when she finishes work, and I need to be here.

The doorbell rings at 3:43 p.m. When I swing the front door open and see Daniella standing there, that magnetic pull is so strong I literally have to stop myself from pulling her into my arms. A slight flush appears on her cheeks, and her eyes widen involuntarily. What a relief to know that she feels it as well. I'm silent, smiling at her for a little too long, and I'm startled when she asks, 'Is Bippie ready for his walk?'

'Sorry,' I say, feeling awkward for the first time in years. 'Please come in. Mom wants to see you.'

She throws me a half smile and follows me inside.

'Got a visitor for you,' I say as I lead Daniella into the living room. Bippie does a stupid little bark and then scurries towards Mom. I see the space through Daniella's eyes. Everything is threadbare, the furniture is mid-century modern, I think they call it, but to me it just looks unappealing. There's too much orange and brown, and the room hasn't changed since Dad died, which reminds me of him.

'Daniella!' Mom exclaims, her face lighting up.

'How are you feeling?' Daniella walks towards Mom. She produces a small bouquet of flowers and hands them to Mom. I hadn't even noticed her holding them, I was so transfixed by her face. 'They're from my shop. They're faux flowers, so they'll last forever.'

The swelling and bruises hide Mom's expression, but I know she won't approve. Mom likes fresh flowers.

'Thank you, my dear,' Mom says, holding onto Daniella's hand as if she were some long-lost relative. 'You saved my life, and I am deeply grateful.'

'I only did what anyone would have done in the situation,' Daniella says, flushing slightly. We all know that isn't true. Daniella is a brave and selfless woman.

'Lucas, you haven't offered our guest a drink!' Mom chastises me.

'You're right. Forgive me, Daniella,' I say involuntarily, bowing my head slightly. 'What can I get you?'

'A cup of tea if you have it.' She grins. 'I'm still very British in that respect.'

'Of course we have tea,' Mom says. That's my cue to disappear into the kitchen to make it. Under normal circumstances, I might be annoyed, but I'd bake a damned cake for Daniella if she asked for one.

When the drinks are made, I put everything onto a tray and return to the living room. Daniella is seated on the upright beige chair that used to belong to Dad, and she's deep in conversation with Mom. She sits back and smiles at me as I place the tray on the coffee table.

'So, what do you do, Lucas?' she asks. 'Have you had to take time off work to look after Peggy?'

I tense for a moment because why does my work actually matter? But Daniella is staring at me with those big brown eyes, and I force a smile. 'I'm in property. I have a portfolio of developments, and I'm also a personal trainer on the side. I love sharing my passion for keeping fit.' I keep my eyes averted from Mom, once again glad that her swollen face is unlikely to give away her true thoughts. 'You have a shop?' I ask, keen to divert the conversation away from me.

'Yes, I have a business called the Silken Stem. We sell top-quality artificial flowers.'

'I know the one,' Mom says. 'I've walked past it many times and admired all the displays. You have beautiful arrangements. I was quite shocked when I realized they weren't the real thing.'

Daniella laughs. 'Yes, we fool most people. The difference is our flowers last forever.'

If it weren't Daniella talking, I'd scoff. Plastic flowers from China aren't my idea of beauty.

'Do you have any children, Daniella?' Mom asks. She slurps her cup of tea, and a dribble slops down her blouse, soaking into the fabric. She doesn't seem to notice, but I have to repress a shiver of disgust. I try not to think about what's going to happen when Mom is too old and infirm to look after herself.

'Yes. We've got twin girls. They're shortly turning eighteen.'

'You don't look old enough,' Mom says.

Daniella laughs, but my attention has fallen on the word 'we'. Stupidly, it never crossed my mind that Daniella might be married—and yet, of course she is. I glance at her left hand. She's wearing a cluster of three diamond rings, so I assume she's still with the father of her girls. But eighteen-plus years is a long marriage. Perhaps she's bored, perhaps theirs is a marriage of convenience, or perhaps the husband is dead. Looking on the bright side, it's better she's in a long-term relationship rather than newly wed and in the initial throes of love. I saw how she looked at me, and I reckon I have a very good chance.

CHAPTER THREE

DANIELLA

I rearranged our couples therapy, and now we're here to see Linda Gibson. The practice was recommended by a friend of Lesley's, and I chose Linda from the list of therapists because she specializes in marriage counseling and intimacy issues. She also has a long list of qualifications and many letters after her name.

Grant and I are sitting in the waiting room of the brownstone, our knees touching, but we're not looking at each other. Grant is scrolling through something on his phone, probably a recent research paper, and I'm flicking through a home and garden magazine that was at the top of the pile on the coffee table. I'm on edge, wondering whether I'm opening a can of worms by being here.

My husband is a brilliant professor who teaches at MIT. Grant's specialism is astrodynamics, and yes, I had absolutely no idea what that meant when I first met him. Even today, the extent of my understanding is that he researches and teaches how artificial objects—such as satellites and spacecrafts—move through space, and that he and his team analyze the launch trajectories of rockets. I frequently wonder why this genius American man chose to marry me, an ordinary woman from South London with a diploma in floristry. Despite the obvious differences in our intellectual capacities, our marriage of almost two decades has been a contented one. It's just now that I'm facing an empty nest, I'm wanting more.

'Mr. and Mrs. Morris?'

With his PhD, Grant is officially Dr. Morris, although neither of us corrects her. We both stand up.

'Good morning, I'm Linda Gibson.'

Although she must be in her late thirties, she looks barely older than our girls. She strides towards us with an outstretched hand and a warm smile, reaching for my hand first. Her auburn hair is cropped very short, and she wears thick-rimmed oval glasses that are too large for her small, round face.

'It's a pleasure to meet you both. Please follow me.' Linda Gibson is wearing a forest green sweater and cropped navy jeans, her legs bare above chunky black boots.

We walk in silence along a narrow corridor, and then she pushes open a door and indicates for us to enter. It's a cozy room, designed to look more like someone's living room than an office, with a large cream sofa covered with a couple of pale gray mohair throws and cushions in raspberry boucle fabric. Linda takes a seat in the armchair, leaving us the sofa. I wonder how close Grant and I should sit next to each other, whether she's judging us as we make ourselves comfortable.

She smiles warmly. 'Perhaps you'd like to tell me why you chose to come here today.'

Grant and I glance at each other, and he nods at me, indicating he wants me to speak. Fair enough, since it was me who pushed for this session.

'I want to start by saying that I love my husband very much, and that's the reason I asked him to do counseling.' I reach for his hand and squeeze it. 'The thing is, the physical side of our relationship is pretty much nonexistent, and I would like to get it back.'

'Alright. Before we discuss the specifics, I want to emphasize that this is a safe space for both of you to share without judgment. My job is to help you communicate more effectively and reconnect. I'd like you to focus on your own feelings and experiences rather than blaming or accusing your partner. Grant, how do you feel about coming for couples therapy?'

Grant shrugs. 'Obviously, I want to have a happy marriage. The intimacy doesn't bother me, so I don't really have a problem.'

Linda asks questions about our current life, and I try hard to take on board her instructions not to blame Grant in any way. Except the more questions she asks, the more I realize there's so much I can't share because if I told Grant the truth, I might really destroy our marriage.

Grant and I met, got engaged and married within a year of meeting. It was an exciting whirlwind, and although I was absolutely sure I wanted to be married to him, the issue of my green card was very much at the forefront of both of our minds. Perhaps if there had been no visa issue, we might have taken the relationship more slowly. But we were both in love, and why wait? About a year into our marriage, that intense physical desire had fizzled out. We held hands when we went out, we went to sleep in each other's arms, and I tried not to miss any further intimacy because our lives were frenetic with work and weekends away and moving into a new house. But one day at Trader Joe's, I dropped a bag of groceries, and as I knelt down to gather up the rolling apples, I came face-to-face with a man who had the most intense blue eyes I'd ever seen. When his fingers grazed mine, a jolt ran through the whole of my body. I picked up my groceries, mortified by the box of tampons and cheap shampoo. When we both stood, his gaze was electrifying.

'Would you like a coffee?' he asked.

Bizarrely, I was rendered mute. I desperately wanted to say yes, but I knew I needed to say no. And then I muttered, 'Sorry, I've got to go.' I literally ran out of the store.

Of course, I couldn't stop thinking about my handsome stranger, and that made me feel terrible, like I was betraying Grant even though I hadn't done anything. The lack of sex with Grant just compounded my imaginary narrative that the man in the grocery store was my soulmate whom I'd allowed to get away. I talked for hours with Lesley, and she said if I had doubts, better to act now rather than once Grant and I had kids. We'd talked about starting a family, sooner rather than later, because both of us wanted to be young parents.

With hindsight, it was both ridiculous and perhaps fortuitous. I told Grant that I wasn't sure about our marriage. He sobbed for hours, and eventually, I suggested that I move out of our house for a couple of weeks to take stock. I went to stay with Lesley, and during my free time, I hung around Trader Joe's. But I never saw Mr. Handsome again. What I did realize was I missed Grant. Terribly. I loved his silly sense of humor, the way he brought me tea in bed every morning, our chats about what our children might look like—his straight nose, my wide eyes—where we wanted to visit when we were old and retired. Grant offered me everything I'd ever dreamed of. Security, love, kindness, interesting conversation, and humor. I was about to blow that apart, and, to boot, I would have to return to the UK, my tail between my legs.

A week to the day after I left, I turned up at our house, took one look at Grant and threw my arms around him, sobbing. I apologized profusely, telling him it was a blip, a blip I promised would never happen again.

I know that I made the right decision. Grant has been a wonderful husband and father. We've had a great couple of decades blessed with health and wealth. I've accepted the lack of intimacy, that we're mismatched in the bedroom, and instead, secretly fantasize about unattainable movie stars and romantic heroes in novels. And I honestly thought that I could carry on like this for the rest of my life. Except with the girls about to leave home, my future life seems empty, and that longing for more has been growing over the past few months until it's become a bit of an obsession.

And to compound it all, I met Lucas. He looks nothing like the man from the store, but when he touched me, that shiver was exactly the same. The deep tingling desire that I thought would never resurface in my life showed up once again. And now, I can't banish thoughts of Lucas. I know it's a betrayal of my love for Grant, except I can't help myself. I wonder if it would have been fairer to have counseling alone today, because I can't be truthful.

'Daniella?' Linda Gibson peers at me, and I realize I

haven't been listening. She raises an eyebrow, and I mutter an apology.

'Come on, Daniella,' Grant says with a deep sigh.

'I'm sorry. This is a lot.'

'It was you who wanted to come.'

'I know. And I'm grateful you're here with me.'

'If you want to have sex, why don't you just initiate it?' he asks, his voice a little fractious.

'Because when I do, you're always too tired or not in the mood, and frankly, I don't see why it should always be me.' And to be blunt, I'm not sure I even find Grant attractive anymore. His once-full head of hair has fast receded, and he is carrying much too much weight around his middle.

'We're aiming for no blame, here,' Linda says. 'You've both stated that you love each other, so what we need to do is work out how to communicate better and understand what is causing this lack of intimacy.'

'I've started going to the gym,' Grant says, his eyes on the ground.

'That's great. Do you also go to the gym?' Linda asks me.

'No. I cycle everywhere, and I go to Pilates twice a week. I am lucky, as I don't really have to worry about my weight.'

'You know, all of this, it's really hurtful,' Grant says, waving his hands around.

'In what way is this hurtful to you?' Linda asks Grant.

'I suppose it's the implication that I'm not enough for Daniella. I dunno.' For a highly articulate man, Grant is hopelessly inarticulate when it comes to talking about feelings.

'Is that what you think, Daniella? That Grant isn't enough for you?'

'No, of course not. This makes me feel hurt too. I don't

want to hurt him. I love Grant and can't imagine my life without him.' I glance at my husband, who has tears in his eyes, and I fear I might be picking at a wound that needs to heal. Am I causing upset unnecessarily? But then Lucas's face flickers into my imagination, and I know I need to be here.

'What other changes do you wish to make to your life?' Linda asks.

'We've talked about selling our house and moving out of Boston when the girls go to college,' I say.

'And how do you feel about that?' Linda asks Grant.

'I'm up for considering it. I get that we need to consider changes to our lifestyle.'

The rest of the session involves us talking about our normal lives, how we never go on date nights, how we don't even touch each other in bed at night. Linda suggests that we give each other a hug every day, that perhaps we spoon in bed at night with zero expectations. Grant agrees to that, and I squeeze his hand. We talk about downsizing. Finally, we set a date for our next session.

GRANT HEADS BACK TO MIT, and I cycle to the Silken Stem. I love our shop. The area out front for the public is quite small, with shelving on one wall and small tables covered with our floral displays. It's the large workroom at the rear that gives me the most joy. There's nothing more exciting than receiving a delivery of silk flowers, unboxing them, and marveling at the delicate flowers and realistic foliage. Because then it's up to me to fashion them into arrangements that will sell. Mostly people have limited imagination, so I come up with the designs, selecting which stems to use dependent upon the time of year. I'm the one with the training in floristry, whereas Lesley is great at logistics, numbers, and procedures. She makes sure that our pricing is right, that we maintain the correct stock levels and ultimately turn a profit. We make a good team.

'Hello!' I shout as I enter through the back door.

'In here!' Lesley replies. I wander through the workroom into the shop. Lesley is behind the counter, ringing up a sale and chatting to a customer. I wait until they've finished and the woman has left. Lesley's black hair is braided and hangs low down her back, and she's wearing her Silken Stem overalls, which covers her long-sleeve black T-shirt and black jeans. Our brand colors are bronze and olive green, and she wears a bronze-colored rose behind her ear.

'How did it go?' Lesley asks. I feel guilty for even telling her that Grant and are doing therapy but then remind myself that everyone does it here; it's nothing to be ashamed of. It's not like I told her the real reason why.

I groan. 'I wonder if I'm causing unnecessary hurt to both of us.'

'Repression is never a good idea,' Lesley says, looking up from the laptop. 'Personally, I think counseling should be mandatory for all married couples. But then I'm hardly the right person to preach about marriage.'

I nudge her shoulder. Lesley's marriage breakdown was a disaster, but at least her visa situation was such that she didn't need to return home. And now she's a serial dater.

'Who's the latest, then?' I ask as I gather a few stems together.

'Honestly, he's the best lover I've ever had. He's not as handsome as some, but he's really successful, and, best of all, he has magical fingers and—'

I interrupt Lesley. 'I don't need to know the details!' I wonder if my laugh sounds a little strained. I'm sure Lesley doesn't mean to boast about the copious amount of sex she's having, but it does leave me feeling a bit jealous. No, not jealous but more unwanted and unseen. Dissatisfied, certainly.

CHAPTER FOUR

DANIELLA

I stop off at Peggy's on my way to work, happy that walking Bippie is forcing me to take regular walks. All the same, I'm conflicted. On the one hand, I desperately want to see Lucas again, but on the other, I feel like I'm playing with fire and betraying Grant, which is super hypocritical considering I've signed us up to therapy. I remind myself that nothing has happened and that the betrayal remains in my head. Perhaps most women dream about unattainable lovers? I wouldn't know because it's not the type of conversation I'd initiate with any of my friends in Boston, with the exception of Lesley perhaps. I ring Peggy's doorbell and wait. Bippie barks, and I can hear shuffling on the inside before the door eventually opens. Peggy is there, leaning on a cane, her face a patchwork of yellows and greens.

'Oh, Daniella. It's lovely to see you.'

Bippie bounds forwards and shoves his nose into my legs, his tail wagging so hard it almost whips Peggy. 'Hello, handsome,' I say, bending down to stroke the dog.

'Are you talking to me?' a male voice asks from behind Peggy.

I glance up and immediately feel my cheeks heat up. Lucas is standing on the second-to-bottom step, an eyebrow raised and a twinkle in his eye. He's wearing a white shirt and smart navy pants.

'Finished your call, then?' Peggy turns to ask him. 'Well, go and put the kettle on, Lucas. Daniella and I will have a cup of tea before she takes the dog for a walk. You do want one, don't you, dear?'

I'm not thirsty, but I don't want to be rude to Peggy, so I accept. I follow her into the living room and look on with concern while she winces with pain as she sits down.

'Are you still on painkillers?' I ask.

She waves her hand dismissively. 'I'm on all sorts of medication for diabetes, high blood pressure, pain relief. The joy of old age.'

'Can I do anything to help?'

'You've done quite enough, honey. Besides, Lucas is around a lot at the moment to help me. He's such a dear son. What have you been up to, Daniella?'

We make small talk about my shop and the delivery that we're expecting at the end of the week. Then I notice a bag of yarn and knitting needles tucked to the side of her chair.

'What are you knitting?' I ask.

'I knit for premature babies. An old woman's pursuit.'

'But it isn't!' I exclaim. 'I've been knitting since I was a teenager. In fact, I give the girls hand-knitted sweaters every Christmas.'

'And they like to wear them?' Peggy sounds surprised.

'Absolutely. And all their friends ask if they can have one too. I have cupboards stuffed full of yarn.'

'Me too!' Peggy laughs. 'You should go through my stash and take anything you'd like.'

But then Lucas walks in carrying a tray of mugs, a teapot and a milk pitcher. He places it down on the table.

'A drop of milk and no sugar,' he says. I'm impressed that he remembers.

When he hands me the mug, his fingers graze mine, but the heat from the mug is nothing in comparison to the burning that fires up my veins. He's looking straight into my eyes, his lips curling into a wry smile. For a moment, the worlds stands still as we both hold the mug, and it isn't until Peggy speaks again that he breaks away, and I realize the mug has actually burned my hand.

'Here you go, Mom,' he says, placing Peggy's mug on a small table next to her.

'Are you joining us?' Peggy asks.

'No,' Lucas replies, his eyes back on me. 'I've got work I need to catch up on.' He nods at me, and when he leaves the room, it's as if all the air is sucked out with him.

I don't stay long, telling Peggy that I need to get on with Bippie's walk, as I've got things I need to do at home. We walk for about twenty minutes, during which I wonder why I'm the one walking the dog when Lucas is around so much. Perhaps Peggy has asked for my help because she's lonely, or maybe Lucas is too busy to help further. On the one hand, I'm glad he's here, making me feel that flicker of excitement, literally giving me a spring to my step, but at the same time, I wish he weren't around every time I pop over. It's all so confusing, so disconcerting.

I've wanted a dog for years, but Grant used to be allergic to dogs, and although I think he's better these days, he's always resisted. Now that the girls are leaving home, I suggested getting a hypoallergenic puppy, but he wasn't keen. I'm dreading my empty nest, so I might push for it again in a few months, but for now, I need to pick my battles. That's another reason why I'm happy to take Bippie out, for the companionship.

We're wandering back along Ivy Street, Bippie snuffling around every tree trunk and post, while I'm enjoying the weak, early sunshine on my face, not paying much attention to my surroundings.

'Daniella!' The word is spoken in a low whisper, and my throat immediately constricts. This is almost the place where Peggy was mugged. I freeze.

But then Lucas appears from between two parked cars, giving me a second fright.

'Were you hiding?' I ask, my hand rushing to pat my chest in a vain attempt to stop my hammering heart.

'No.' He grins. 'I'm just on my way out and wanted to catch you.'

'Right,' I say. Bippie is pulling on the lead.

'Will you have dinner with me?'

'What!' I exclaim. 'No, of course not. I'm married.'

There's a beat of silence before he exclaims, 'Oh, no!' He barks a little laugh. 'I wasn't propositioning you; I just wanted to thank you for everything you're doing for Mom.'

My face burns with embarrassment. How utterly humiliating that I got it wrong. I want to bury my head in my hands, but if Lucas notices my embarrassment, he doesn't comment.

'There's a new restaurant that's opened downtown, and I want to try it. I thought we could go together.'

He reaches out and places his hand on mine, the one that's holding onto Bippie's lead. It sends tingles right up my arm, and I wonder if he can feel it too. I pull my hand away and fuss with Bippie's lead. When I glance up at Lucas, his eyes are once again locked on mine. They're the color of pine needles, an unusually dark green with amber flecks in the pale morning light, and his lashes are dark, giving the impression that his eyes have been highlighted with a dark pencil. I find it almost impossible to look away. I wonder if the attraction is mutual, or it's just me having this completely inappropriate reaction.

Can I say yes to dinner? I desperately want to. His aftershave is as alluring as his eyes, and the scent of cedar wood along with a spice I can't identify makes me want to breathe this man in. He's looking at me, his eyebrows raised, an expectant look on his face.

'Dinner?' he says.

'Alright, yes. Thank you.'

There's a look of amusement on his face. 'This is purely between friends, and you can trust me. When are you free?'

'Um, I'm not sure.'

'Could you check your calendar? On your phone, I assume?' he asks gently, his head slightly cocked to one side, his eyes glinting.

'Sure,' I say, fumbling to take my phone out of my cross-body bag while holding onto Bippie's lead.

'Let me help.' He reaches for the lead. Our fingers touch again, and I have to suppress another shiver. This is ridiculous. I'm a grown woman, married, and I should not be feeling raw lust. I rummage in my bag and find my phone, having to hold it with both hands to stop it from shaking. I'm not even sure why I'm looking, as I know I have nothing in my calendar other than a cocktail party at MIT in a fortnight.

'When were you thinking?' I ask.

'Tonight, tomorrow, Thursday, Friday. You choose.'

But what am I going to tell Grant? I'll worry about that later and select Thursday evening, as Grant is always home late on Thursdays.

'I'll text you the address,' Lucas says. 'Looking forward to it.' He passes me back Bippie's lead, and then, completely taking me off guard, he places a quick kiss on my cheek. Before I can respond, he's striding away down the street. I try to compose myself and hurry up Peggy's driveway.

I'M PLAYING WITH FIRE. I know it, and it terrifies me, but there's something so magnetic about Lucas, I feel almost incapable of staying away from him. Is it because Grant is distant and I'm flattered by Lucas? Of course it's purely physical, reawakening that need to be wanted. It's so gratifying, seeing a man's pupils widen with desire, how his lips part slightly and his gaze doesn't waver from mine. After securing the bike at the back of the shop, I walk through the rear door and straight into Lesley.

'Sorry,' I mumble.

'You look like you're miles away,' she says.

'Yes, I probably am. Anyway, how are you this morning?' We amble together into the rear workroom.

'So, you know I told you about Matt?' she says, her expression bright.

'Matt?'

'My new man. The one with the magic fingers.'

'Ah, yes,' I reply.

'He's this mega business hot shot, and I told him about the Silken Stem, and he's really interested.'

'Interested in what?' I frown.

'I'm not sure exactly, but he might be a possible investor.'

'Do we need investment?'

'We do if we want to expand. But anyway, I'm going to have lunch with him, and I'll see what he says.'

'Is he a boyfriend or a business contact?'

'Well, kind of both. I really like him, and I think you will too. He's super bright.'

She must note my frown of concern.

'Don't worry. I won't do anything without your say-so. We're equal partners in the Silken Stem, Daniella. Anyway, why do you look as if you've been struck by lightning?'

It's annoying how insightful Lesley is, but I guess that comes from knowing each other for so many years. As Lesley boils the kettle to make us both our morning cups of tea, I debate whether to tell her. I'm fiddling with a stem of eucalyptus when she plops the mug in front of me.

'Spit it out, Danni,' she says, opening our biscuit tin—I've never learned to call them cookies—and shoving it towards me. 'I know there's something going on with you.'

'It's Lucas, Peggy's son.'

'Peggy being the lady you saved?'

'Well, yes.'

'What about him?'

'He's invited me out for dinner.'

'Okay,' Lesley says, drawing out the word. 'And I'm assuming this isn't an invitation for you *and* Grant?'

'No. He's gorgeous, Les. I mean, probably the most handsome man I've ever spoken to.'

'And he likes you? Like that?'

'I think so. But obviously I've told him I'm married, and

we're only meeting as friends. I've agreed to see him on Thursday evening.'

I expect to see disapproval or confusion on Lesley's face, but she startles me by clapping her hands together. 'Go for it, girl!' she says. 'And you can use me as your excuse.'

'Really?' I ask. 'But I feel terrible. It's like I'm knowingly cheating on Grant. I don't want to destroy our marriage.'

'First of all, you haven't done anything. And frankly, if Grant isn't giving you what you want, then you need to get it elsewhere. Why should you be celibate for the rest of your life?'

I feel myself flush. I've never told Lesley in so many words that Grant and I don't have sex, but she's correctly surmised the truth. Is it really that obvious?

'Maybe a hookup with someone else is exactly what's needed to reinvigorate your marriage,' she adds. 'That's the reason French women have affairs, isn't it?'

'But I've never cheated on Grant.'

'You might never have cheated on him, but can you be so sure that he's never cheated on you?'

That startles me and makes me wonder if Lesley knows something I don't. Could Grant be having sex with someone else, just not me? But then I check myself. This is Grant we're talking about, my lovely Grant, who is everyone's brilliant best friend and honest to the core. Of course he hasn't cheated on me. Maybe he doesn't fancy me anymore?

'Sex doesn't mean anything these days, anyway. It'll do you good to have a fling.'

'I'm not sure Grant would agree with that. And what if I fall for Lucas? Or what if Grant finds out?'

'It's sex,' Lesley says. 'This man is taking you out for

dinner; you may or may not sleep with him. He's not asking you to divorce your husband and marry him, is he?'

I shake my head. 'He's said he won't do anything inappropriate, anyway.'

Lesley harrumphs. 'Yeah, right. Honestly, Dani, this will be good for you. And I'll cover for you.' She turns away from me, picks up her mug and walks through to the shop.

THURSDAY ARRIVES ALL TOO SOON. I tell Grant that I'm going out with Lesley tonight, and of course, my trusting husband doesn't question it.

'Have fun later,' he says as he leaves the house that morning.

It makes me feel terrible. I spend ages deciding what to wear, and in the end, I select a pair of smart jeans and a cashmere V-neck sweater in a soft baby blue, teaming it with a turquoise necklace I bought in Vermont years ago. It's casual and comfortable, and I certainly don't look like I'm dressed up to go on a hot date.

The restaurant is off Washington Street. It's small, with the air of a London club: dark paneled walls, vintage hardback books on shelves, and oil paintings in heavy golden frames. Lucas is already there, dressed in a blue open shirt and navy pants with sharp creases down the front, and he jumps up as the server guides me towards our table.

'Daniella,' he says, grasping both of my hands and kissing me on each cheek. He then moves quickly to my side of the table.

'I'll take it from here,' he instructs the server as he pulls out my chair.

It's all a bit strange, but I sink into the plush chair as he returns to his side of the table. 'You're looking stunning,' Lucas says. 'And that blue complements your complexion perfectly. So, how are you?'

'Good, thanks,' I reply, feeling extremely awkward. I glance around at the tables set with sparkling crystal ware and silver cutlery. We're early, and only a couple of tables are occupied.

'Do you drink champagne?' Lucas asks.

'Yes, but—'

He interrupts me. 'Good, because I've ordered us a bottle.'

A moment later, the server arrives, pours us both a glass, and puts the opened bottle in a silver cooler. He hands us each a leather menu.

Lucas picks up his champagne glass and holds it in the air. 'To you. Beautiful Daniella.' Once again, those startling eyes are fixed on mine. My smile feels crooked, but I take a sip. It's delicious, so I take another couple of sips to ease my nerves.

'Tell me all about you,' he says.

'Um, there's nothing much to tell.'

'I don't believe that for one second. What about your business?'

I tell him about the Silken Stem, and we start talking. He is so easy to converse with, asking insightful questions, interspersing them with compliments, and, as the restaurant fills up, his gaze never leaves mine. It's as if I'm the only person in the room, and my word, it makes me feel great. Not once does he ask me about Grant or the girls, and I realize with some shame that for tonight, it's as if they don't exist. It isn't until we both order coffee that I glance at my watch. We've been here for over three hours, and although the food was good, the company was better.

'I'm going to need to head off,' I say.

'And as much as I'd love to, I won't stop you,' Lucas replies. 'I'll order an Uber and drop you off. It's on my way.'

'Are you staying at Peggy's tonight?' I ask.

He shakes his head as he's fiddling with the Uber app. 'No, I need to get home.'

It's only then that I wonder whether perhaps Lucas also has a wife and children. He's not wearing a wedding band, but that means nothing. Perhaps he really was being genuine when he said this dinner was just a way of thanking me.

Lucas insists on paying the bill, and then we walk out of the restaurant, wrapped in coats, into the chilly night air. He looks at his phone and then waves at a silver Nissan Leaf that pulls up to the sidewalk.

'Here's our Uber,' he says.

He opens the rear door, and we both slip into the back seat. I'm feeling warm and slightly tipsy, so when he holds my hand, I don't pull it away. His thumb is gently, ever so gently, stroking my palm, as light as a butterfly's wings. It's inappropriate and gives me the shivers, rendering me speechless. Neither of us says a word. When the Uber turns onto Amory Street, Lucas leans forwards. 'Just drop us here, please,' he says.

I frown, but Lucas is out of the car and opening my door for me. I have no choice but to get out.

'I live a little further up,' I say.

'I know.' Lucas's eyes glint in the low light. 'I wanted to walk you home the last few yards.'

'Aren't you going to get the Uber to take you home?' I ask, a flutter of nerves in my stomach.

'I'll pop in on Mom first,' he says. I turn as if to walk, but he reaches out for me, placing both hands on my shoulders. He's pushing me backwards, ever so gently, until I'm standing in the shadow of a large eastern white pine tree. And then one hand cups the back of my head, and he's lowering his lips onto mine. I want this. My body craves this. As he kisses me more deeply, I can't help but kiss him back.

But then a car glides past, its headlights illuminating us, and the reality of what I'm doing slams into me. I push Lucas away.

'No, I'm sorry. I can't do this,' I say, completely flustered.

'Hey, it's fine.' Lucas steps towards me. 'We just had a beautiful kiss. That's all it was. A kiss between two people who have a deep magnetic attraction.'

'I can't,' I say. 'I've never cheated on my husband, and I can't be with you. Dinner was lovely, but I can't see you again. I'm sorry.' My words tumble out.

'Daniella.' He speaks my name in a deep but mournful whisper. 'Thank you.'

What's he thanking me for? The kiss, the whole evening? 'It was a mistake,' I say.

'We all make mistakes, Daniella. We're only human.'

What the hell does that mean? 'Lucas, I can't see you again. Please don't be there when I visit Peggy. It'll be easier for both of us.'

He tilts his head and gives me puppy-dog eyes. 'Easier for who?'

'Please, Lucas. Thanks for dinner, but I really need to go now.'

I turn on my heel and almost run home. When I glance

over my shoulder before turning into our driveway, I see him still standing there, a faint shadow in the distance, lit up by a streetlight. He raises his arm in the air, and I turn away, racing up our driveway. I've crossed the line, and I feel terrible.

CHAPTER FIVE

LUCAS

Oh, Daniella. She leaves me feeling desolate. She is completely different to my previous lovers, most of whom have been decades younger than me. Unfortunately, their nubile bodies came with limited conversational skills and shallow values, so I'm excited that I'm attracted to someone of my age who is stunning and interesting. Beautiful Daniella has stronger willpower than me, and I admire her for it. I felt how she pressed her body against mine, how she longed for me as much as I longed for her. But she's letting her head rule her heart, and although I wish I could have pinned her up against the tree and taken her there and then, I would never do something like that. I respect her enough to wait. At least I know that she craves me. She'll come around, eventually. I walked away, and I'm proud of myself.

I don't go to see Mom. She'll be asleep by now, and frankly, I can't bear looking at her with her bruised face and new frailty. Mom has always been strong, and I've admired her for that. I don't like this new, broken old woman. It reminds me of mortality, something I choose not to think about. Instead, I take a long walk to clear my head.

An hour or so later, opening the door to my brownstone, I know what I need to do. It will be ugly, painful for Jade, but it has to happen. The walk back here has given me clarity.

Jade is asleep. She's one of those women who slathers cream on her face at night, wraps her hair in a silken scarf, and wears a matching silk eye mask. Heavens know why, since it's pitch black in the bedroom thanks to the heavy drapes and thick interlining. I stand at the bottom of the bed, looking at her as she sleeps, light from the hallway spilling into the bedroom. She's an attractive woman with an enhanced curvy figure and long, manicured nails. I guess she's at least a decade younger than Daniella, maybe even more, and in comparison, she seems vacuous and artificial. I realize how much I hate the breast implants and the filler-enhanced lips that make her look a little like Donald Duck.

'Wake up, Jade,' I bellow. I switch on the bedroom light and blink, not that it'll make much difference to Jade with her damned eye mask. Her hand emerges from under the cover, and I see she's wearing the sparkling ring I gave her. The engagement ring. I'll ask for it back.

'Jade, you need to wake up!' I lean close to her head, shouting into her left ear. She startles and pushes the eye mask up, blinking furiously.

'What's happened?' she asks breathlessly, levering herself up to a sitting position.

'We need to talk.'

She glances at the clock on her nightstand. 'But it's midnight.'

'It can't wait.'

'You're scaring me, Lucas.'

'It's over. You and me, it's over.'

She stares at me, her eyes appearing small without the fake eyelashes. 'What's over?'

'For God's sake, Jade. You and me. Our relationship. I can't do this anymore.'

'What?' she exclaims, her eyes glistening, her voice rising in pitch. 'But we're engaged. We're getting married.'

'Not anymore, we're not.' I start pacing around the room. 'I know I'll need to move out, but so be it.'

'You can't go!' she exclaims, pushing the duvet off and exposing those long, smooth brown legs.

I laugh. 'And how are you going to stop me?'

'I'm pregnant,' she says. 'I'm pregnant, Lucas. I was going to tell you at the weekend.'

'Oh yeah, right,' I say after a few beats of silence. I know this trick, and it's not going to work on me. 'I don't believe you.'

'But I am!' she replies, her voice trembling. Here come the tears, and frankly, it's pathetic. So melodramatic.

'You're saying you're pregnant because you don't want me to leave,' I say, walking towards the row of closets that stretch the full length of the wall.

'But I am pregnant!'

'Show me proof, then.' Although I wonder what I'll do if she really is pregnant. I won't stay, the bond between me and Daniella is too strong, and Jade is nothing in comparison.

Jade opens and closes her mouth. 'I left the pregnancy stick at work.'

I know she's lying.

'If you're really pregnant, get rid of it. I don't want to be a father, and I don't want to be with you.'

'You can't do this!' she wails, standing up and reaching towards me. I step backwards, and she slips, grabbing onto the side of the bed. What the hell did I see in her?

'We're getting married!'

'No longer.' I fling open the closet door and pull out my large duffel.

'Don't go! I love you!' Jade sobs. 'This is all some misunderstanding.'

'It's not, Jade. It's very simple—I don't want to be with you anymore.'

She stares at me, almost as if she doesn't understand, which frankly wouldn't surprise me, as she's not the brightest on the block.

'Is there someone else?'

I still. For a moment I wonder about telling her the truth, except I swiftly change my mind. If she thinks there's someone else, then she might try to sabotage my new relationship with Daniella. She and her bevy of friends can be quite the bitches. I can't risk it.

'No. I've just had an epiphany, and I know I can't be with you.'

'What have I done wrong?' she whimpers.

It's interesting how she's taking the blame, and for a moment, I admire the humility of it. But then I remember that she's the queen of emotional blackmail, except she doesn't have the brains to play that game well. I consider telling her I loathe her artifice, that she's dim and a lousy cook, sponging off her rich family. That she lacks a sense of humor, and although she thinks she's a seductress, she's actually very mediocre in bed. But that would be cruel, and I don't like to be cruel unless I really have to be. Instead, I say nothing.

As I shove my clothes into the bag, I realize my lovely standard of living will be going too. This is Jade's brownstone, and everything in it, except my paltry clothes, belongs to her or, more to the point, her rich daddy. That was one of her initial attractions; a ready-made home, plenty of spending money, a Range Rover and holidays in the Caribbean. I swear under my breath. Have I been too impulsive? Maybe I should stay, pretend this was all a mistake, except then I'd need to be with Jade, in her bed, pretending to go along with the engagement and the wedding plans. And play along with the ridiculous notion that she's pregnant; *we'd* be pregnant. No, I can't do that.

'Please don't go!' Jade is behind me now, her arms snaked around my waist. I shove her away. The desperation repulses me. Grabbing the straps of the duffel, I swing around, and it catches her in the stomach, sending her sprawling. She's sobbing pathetically, crumpled on the floor. I leave the bag and go into the bathroom to fetch my toiletries. All the while Jade is screeching, begging and crying. I hum under my breath to block out her noise. And then I return to the bedroom to zip up my bags.

'Can you take off the engagement ring? I ask. I expect she'll want to keep it, but that is not happening.

'You have to be joking!' Jade says.

I hold out my hand. 'Now, please.'

With tears pouring down her face, she removes the ring and throws it at me. I make a perfect catch.

I don't look back as I stride out of the bedroom and run down the stairs, slamming the front door behind me.

I stand on the sidewalk for a moment, the bags at my feet, and use my phone to call for an Uber. While I'm waiting, I turn to look at this handsome house where I've lived for the best part of a year, and an unexpected annoyance runs through me. Yes, I have been too impulsive. I've got nowhere to live now when I could have continued my life of luxury while courting Daniella. It would have been easy to lie to Jade, to tell her I was off traveling for weeks at a time.

The Uber arrives quickly, and the anger towards Jade and myself mounts the nearer we get to Mom's house. It's pitch black when I slide my key into Mom's lock. I switch on the hall light and stomp into the kitchen. I've got to live here again, and this place sickens me with its old-fashioned decor and stained butler's sink and Bippie, who wanders up to me, stretching out like a cat and then nuzzling me, expecting attention. A surge of anger courses through me, and I haven't got the energy to stop it. I curl my fingers into a fist and repeatedly slam it into the kitchen wall until my knuckles are bleeding and there's a hole in the plasterwork. I look at the fragments of plaster on the floor and grind them into the linoleum with the heel of my shoe.

'What's going on?' Mom shouts from upstairs. 'Is that you, Lucas?'

'Yes. Go back to sleep.' As the pain starts to throb in my hand, the fury eases. Jade made me do this. I should send her the bill for the repairs. I run my knuckle under the tap, watching the blood circle downwards until the water is clear; then I dry the wound with a clean tea towel and wrap it tightly with a bandage from Mom's first aid kit. I imagine Daniella gently holding my hand and cleaning the wound. She'd know what to do. The thought calms me, so I head to the utility room and take out the vacuum cleaner, getting rid of the mess the best I can. When I switch off the machine, I'm startled by a shadow behind me. I turn suddenly, adrenaline rushing through my veins. But it's only Mom.

She's looking at the hole in the wall, and for a second, I see a look of pity pass over her face. But then she steps forward, still leaning on her cane, her eyes on my bandaged hand.

'Would you like me to look at that for you, dear?' she asks.

CHAPTER SIX

DANIELLA

I've gotten into a regular rhythm of visiting Peggy twice a week to walk Bippie. I've worked out that I'm most likely to avoid seeing Lucas if I go in the middle of the day. It's not so convenient for me, because I'm often having to nip out from the shop during my lunch break and return to Ivy Street, but at least I have the flexibility to do so. Peggy is much improved. The bruising on her face has all but disappeared, and though she still uses a cane for support, her walking is also better. Today, when I bring Bippie home, she seems in a particularly talkative mood.

'Please stay for tea and cookies,' she urges.

'I really need to get back.' It's not strictly true, as Lesley has things under control in the shop, but I'm nervous about hanging around at Peggy's in case I see Lucas. The obsessive thoughts I've had about him have receded somewhat, and I'm eager to keep it that way.

'Humor me,' she says. 'Besides, I've baked some chocolate cookies, and I know they're your favorite.' She gives me a cheeky wink as I follow her into the kitchen. I have to admit that her cookies are delicious, and the scent of warm cookies makes my stomach growl.

We sit at her battered Formica kitchen table. She makes me a cup of tea while I savor a scrumptious cookie.

'You need to give me the recipe for these,' I say. 'The girls would love them.'

'With pleasure. Tell me about your family,' Peggy says as she sips from her mug. 'We never get time to have a proper chat.'

I tell her about Grant and the girls and how we're so proud of them, although I'm dreading them leaving for university.

'It'll be good for your marriage,' she says.

'I'm not so sure about that. I don't think we'll have anything to talk about.'

'It takes some adjusting, that's for sure. But it's worse when the men retire; then they're around the house all the time.'

'Is that what happened to you?'

Peggy snorts. 'Was a nightmare.'

'You don't talk about your husband,' I say, thinking of the sole photograph of Peggy, a rather debonaire man and a small boy, whom I assume is Lucas, displayed on the mantelpiece in the living room.

'He wasn't a good man. It's an awful thing to say, Daniella, but it was a relief when he passed.'

'I'm sorry to hear that,' I say, rather surprised.

'Whereas your Grant sounds like a good man. Kind, gentle.'

'Yes, I suppose he is,' I muse.

'So why don't you look happy?' Peggy asks.

I'm startled. *Don't I?*

'You can share with me. I'm just a silly old woman who doesn't pass judgment.'

'Thanks, Peggy,' I say. It's weird opening up to Peggy, and for a moment I stall, but then the words just seem to fall from my mouth. 'The only major thing wrong with my marriage is the lack of intimacy. There's none, and I miss it.'

She nods, a serious look on her face. 'Sounds like you and I have the opposite problem. My Jim insisted on his conjugal rights every single night of our marriage, in sickness and in health. He didn't care about me; I was just a vessel and someone on which to live out his cruel fantasies.' Peggy shivers.

That shocks me. 'I'm sorry,' I say. 'It must have been awful.'

'You learn how to switch off from it. How to disassociate from your feelings. You have to, otherwise you break, and I had to stay strong for Lucas.'

'Did you want to leave your husband?' I ask.

Peggy chortles. 'Of course I did, but I couldn't. It's not like today when women have rights and go out to work and can start all over again.'

I'm surprised she's saying this. Peggy isn't that old.

'Jim's family were wealthy and influential. They'd have taken Lucas away from me, and I'd have been left with nothing. His parents didn't want him to marry me in the first place, but Jim was determined. I was a pretty young thing back in the day and completely in awe of him. We should have listened to his parents. Do you know that his father waved a check for five hundred dollars in front of my nose if I promised to leave town and never see Jim again?'

'That's terrible,' I say.

'At the time I was affronted, and it made me want to be

with Jim even more. These days, I wonder whether he wasn't so much buying me off, but warning me. Perhaps that check was to help me start all over again far away from Boston, away from the clutches of his evil son. It was a lot of money back then.'

Bippie wanders into the room and sinks to the floor, placing his head over Peggy's feet.

I don't know what to say to Peggy. Her marriage sounds terrible.

'So the thing is, you might crave a bit of excitement, but you're so much better off with a man who expects nothing from you, rather than a cruel man like Jim. Sex really isn't very important, Daniella. Kindness is everything.'

She's right, of course.

'And enjoy your girls. Just because they're going off to college doesn't mean they still won't need their mom. It's a blessing being around young people. I'd love to meet them sometime.'

Impulsively, I say, 'Why don't you come over for Sunday lunch? Not this Sunday because the girls aren't around, but how about the following Sunday?'

Peggy claps her hands. 'I'd absolutely love to.'

IT'S FRIDAY LATE AFTERNOON, and we've had a busy day in the shop. Customers have been buying spring arrangements, wreaths and garlands covered in little snowdrops, anemones and narcissi, particularly. People need cheering up in this miserable, cold, gray winter, desperate for the gentle warmth of spring. As soon as I make up a new arrangement, it seems like someone buys it. Lesley is thrilled because it means we're going to, hopefully, have another year with a healthy profit. I'm lucky that I don't rely on the shop for my income. Grant has an excellent salary, and although I don't like to spend his money on myself, he never minds if I do. My husband has gone away for the weekend, attending some conference in Baltimore, and the girls are away with friends. I'm going to be all alone, and I'm rather looking forward to it. I intend to spend Saturday in the shop and Sunday lounging at home, perhaps in the company of Netflix.

It's cold outside, the air heavy, as if it might snow. I unchain my bike and then notice that the rear tire is completely flat. I'm too tired to deal with it now, so I wheel it into the back of the workshop and leave it there. Frustrated, I consider getting a cab home but decide the walk will do me good. En route, I stop off at Whole Foods and buy a few provisions for the weekend. The bag becomes increasingly heavier as I near home, and I regret walking after a long day. At last, I turn into our street but am startled by a familiar voice.

'Daniella!' I glance up ahead and see Lucas. In that fraction of a second, I'm both nervous about seeing him and ridiculously excited.

'Hey, Daniella,' he says as he strides towards me, his arms outstretched. 'How are you?' He's wrapped up in a navy wool coat and a red scarf, and his smile is dazzling.

'Fine, thanks. And you?' The exchange feels unsettling.

'Good. I really can't thank you enough for walking Bippie and keeping an eye on Mom. I've been so busy with work the past couple of weeks, it's been super helpful.'

I feel tongue-tied. That easy conservation we had over dinner has evaporated, yet Lucas doesn't seem to notice my awkwardness.

'Let me carry that bag,' he says, reaching for the bag. 'It looks really heavy.'

'It's fine,' I reply.

'I insist, Daniella. I'm a fitness instructor on the side, and these muscles need regular exercise.' He flexes his right arm and smiles broadly.

I hand the bag to him, and we start walking until I come to a halt at the bottom of our driveway. The house is dark.

'No one at home?' he asks.

'No, I'm alone for the weekend.' As soon as the words tumble from my mouth, I regret them. I shouldn't have said that, except on some level, I'm glad I did. There's a moment of uneasy hesitation as I realize he's expecting me to invite him in.

'If I'd known I was going to run into you, I'd have bought you flowers,' Lucas says. 'But instead, I can help you unpack your groceries.' His eyes crinkle, and he gives me that half grin that makes my insides melt.

I hesitate, knowing I should come up with a viable excuse that doesn't make me seem rude.

'I've got rather a lot of work to do,' I mumble.

'Well, if it's inconvenient...' He lets his words peter out. 'Although I could really do with a cup of tea to warm me up. That's what you Brits drink all day, isn't it?

I smile, unsure what to say or do now. His presence, so close to me, makes me feel weak and heady, the woody scent of his aftershave giving me a strange rush.

'I won't stay long, Daniella. I promise.'

It seems churlish to say no, so I smile at him and say, 'Follow me.'

LUCAS DOESN'T COMMENT on the house. He doesn't tell me I have a lovely kitchen or admire the view to the garden, as most people do when they visit here for the first time. Instead, he walks over to the large faux-flower arrangement I have on the dresser next to the kitchen table.

'Which of these flowers is your favorite?' he asks.

'The peonies,' I reply, a little taken aback.

He pulls out one of the peony stems and holds it out towards me. 'Please pretend that I haven't removed this from your arrangement, but I've brought it to give to you.'

'Okay,' I say hesitantly. This is weird, but I play along, placing the stem on the kitchen worktop. Lucas places my bag of groceries on the island and takes out a bag of lemons.

'Do these live in the fridge or on the side?' he asks.

'Oh, please don't worry. I'll unpack everything. Can I get you a drink?' I open the fridge to place the eggs inside. 'That cup of tea?'

'I spot a bottle of wine that's already opened,' he says, eying the bottle of white in the fridge door. 'Or is that too presumptuous?'

'No, it's fine,' I say. I pour us each a glass. He takes the glass from me, his fingers grazing mine, those extraordinary green eyes making my stomach flutter. I'm playing with fire here, and it's ridiculously exciting.

I lead Lucas into the living room. The light is fading, so I pull the drapes and switch on some of the table lights. He sits on the sofa facing the fireplace. 'Sit next to me,' he says. I hesitate but do as he suggests. It's as if I have two voices screaming in my head. One is shouting, *Danger, get away.* The other is saying, *You know you want it. You're alone in the house. Just do it.*

'Hey,' Lucas says. It's as if he can sense my internal

conflict. 'Don't overthink it.' And then he turns towards me, his fingers fluttering over my cheek, and he lowers his lips onto mine.

I try to push him away, I really do. Except I'm weak willed, and my body is craving his touch. It all happens so quickly, his mouth on mine, his hands tugging at my clothes, his murmuring of how beautiful I am, how much he wants me, me comfortable in the knowledge that I'm alone in the house. Within moments, he's on top of me, and my body is on fire. And I let him. I let him do everything that he wants, and oh my goodness, it feels utterly amazing.

I lose track of time. Maybe it lasted three hours, or it could have been twenty minutes. All I know is that I am a different person now to who I was earlier today. He rolls off me, and I feel tears trickling down my cheeks. The carpet is soft under my back, but I feel exposed and embarrassed. I grab for my clothes, eager to cover myself up, to get away from this man. But Lucas is gazing at me, a lazy smile on his face, and places a hand over mine to stop me from moving.

'You're beautiful, Daniella,' he says.

'I'm not,' I say, my voice sounding gruff. 'I'm a middle-aged mother with stretch marks and rolls of fat and graying hair.'

'Don't say that,' he says, his fingers wiping away the tears. 'You've lived. You've experienced the miracle of birthing, and the beauty and wisdom of years is so much more attractive than the conceit of youth.'

'You're just being kind.'

'Do you think I'd be here if I didn't have this overwhelming magnetic attraction to you? It's not my normal course of action to woo a married woman.'

I still for a moment, thoughts of Grant causing shame to course through my veins.

'You are quite extraordinary, Daniella Morris.'

'I've cheated on my husband,' I say, rolling away from him. This time I don't let him stop me, and I quickly get dressed, my back to him, all the while conscious that this stranger is lying naked on our living room floor. When I'm fully dressed, I stand up and throw him his clothes. He's staring at me, that cheeky grin on his face, and I try to stop my eyes from wandering down his muscled body.

'I'm sorry, but you need to leave,' I say.

'Oh, Daniella.' He groans. 'You're breaking me.' But he does as I want and gets dressed.

'When can I see you again?' he asks as he stands up.

'You can't, Lucas. We can't do this again. I'm happily married.'

There's a long pause, which he eventually breaks. 'Happily married women don't sleep with other men.'

I open my mouth to protest, but he holds up the palm of his hand. 'Let me finish. I'm sure you love your husband, but sometimes that isn't enough. A physical attraction like ours is visceral, and there's nothing we can do to stop it. We just have to let it run its course. That might be for a few days, a few months or a lifetime.'

'No,' I say.

'I'm not going to do anything to destroy your marriage. I'm no home wrecker,' Lucas says, glancing at his watch. 'What happens next will be up to you, but I just pray that we can do this again.'

'I think you need to leave now,' I say in a whisper.

He nods, a sad expression on his face. 'I just had one of the most exquisite hours of my life, Daniella, and for that I sincerely thank you.' He cups his hand around my cheek and gives me a heart-tugging, sad smile. Then he walks out of the room, with me on his heels.

'Don't worry, darling. I'll let myself out.' He doesn't turn, and I don't stop him. He opens the front door, steps outside and gently shuts it behind himself. I'm left in the hallway, feeling utterly desolate.

I am wretched. How could I have done that? How could I have betrayed Grant like that? I've never cheated on him, never even held another man's hand or kissed someone else —at least not since that first year of our marriage. I hate myself. I'm weak and a liar. And so deeply, deeply ashamed. I wish I could erase this afternoon. But at the same time, I agree with Lucas. I also had one of the most exquisite hours of my life. I take a burning hot shower, scrubbing myself until I'm red and raw, and then I sit on the end of our bed and burst into tears.

CHAPTER SEVEN

PEGGY

'Mom, we need to talk.'

Lucas strides into the living room, rubbing his hands together. 'God, this place stinks. You should open the windows, get some fresh air in here.'

I say nothing. Lucas is clearly in one of his moods, and bitter experience has shown me I shouldn't rile him. I'm worried about him, although that's nothing new. He seems to be sleeping here all the time, and when I asked him why he wasn't at Jade's, he just shrugged his shoulders and walked away. I hope everything is all right between them. And then there was the hole in the kitchen wall. He's patched it up with plaster and painted over it, but it was completely obvious he put his fist through the wall. I know better than to ask what prompted him to do that.

'Would you like a drink?' he asks. 'I could make you dinner if you want.'

Considering I've already made us dinner, and he's actually seen me at the stove, that seems like a strange thing to say.

'I'm fine, Lucas.' But I can sense he's not. He's pacing the room, straightening pictures on the walls, plumping up cushions. It's unnerving. 'What's up?' I ask eventually.

He stands stock-still. 'I need some more money. Another ten thousand will do for now.'

'Ten thousand dollars!' I gasp. 'I haven't got that sort of money lying around, Lucas.'

'It's in your savings account, and with interest rates as they are, it's not doing much good, is it? It's not like you're going to spend it.' He talks in a condescending tone, speaking low and slowly, as if I'm some idiot.

'Why do you need so much?' I ask.

'It's going to be mine anyway, so what's the big deal?'

I feel like saying, the big deal is you're a forty-eight-year-old man still living at home even though I thought you shared a house with your girlfriend, begging and borrowing off your mother, and goodness knows if you've actually got a job. Except I keep my lips firmly closed. Lucas has no idea how much I spend on the upkeep of this house and my medical bills. Especially my medical bills. I've got diabetes, and my doctor told me there could be further complications down the line. I assume I'll have to go into care at some point, and then where will the money come from? Maybe we should sell the house now to free up some cash. I can live in an apartment on the outskirts of the city, as I certainly don't need this big property. But then there'll be nothing at all for Lucas to inherit, and where will he go? I try not to think about the future, try not to be jealous of my friends whose children have families of their own, earn good money, and take care of their parents. I try not to look back through my bank statements at the thousands that Lucas has already siphoned off. We were rich once upon a time, but now the funds are dwindling. I can't just give him another ten thousand dollars.

'No,' I say, without meeting my son's eyes.

'No, what?' Lucas asks.

'No, I'm not giving you any more money.'

'Wrong answer, Mother.' He steps towards me, his lips thin and his eyes narrowed. The last time a substantial sum left my bank account, I knew that Lucas had forged my signature, but in these days of digital banking, it's actually harder for him to get access to my accounts. Some people might think I'm a doddery old woman, except I've taught myself to be digitally savvy. I change my passwords every couple of weeks, and I never write them down. I use voice and face recognition, and I keep my mobile phone on a chain around my neck. If he tries to get into my banking app, he'll fail.

'I need the money,' he says, his tone of voice menacing. I can feel my blood pressure rising as he walks closer to me, leaning over me now, his hands gripping the arms of the chair, his face just inches from mine. Lucas's face goes very pale when he's angry, and his voice becomes deeper.

'Sit down,' I say, except he doesn't move. He's scaring me because I know I can't physically stand up to him in the way I might have before the mugging. I've lost so much strength in my legs.

'Lucas, back off.' I try to put as much force into my voice as I can. I have an arsenal of tactics that I've used over the years to control my son's temper, but now I feel weak, and with weakness comes fear. And he's like a lion, I know that he can sense my fragility, and Lucas hates frailty. It disgusts him, winds him up even further, giving him permission to pounce. One of his hands shoots forwards and grabs my neck.

'Stop it!' I yell, and that breaks his trance. 'I'm your mother, and you will listen to me.' My heart is hammering as his hands drop to his sides, and he takes a step away from me. He turns to face the window.

'Have you lost your job again?' I ask, easing myself out of the chair.

'No,' he mutters. I'm pretty sure he's lying. And then he walks over to the mantelpiece and picks up the heavy silver candlestick. He swivels around, and his face is as pale as the white wax that has dripped onto the candlestick's base.

'I need the money,' he says, his voice low and foreboding. He holds the candlestick up in the air, his biceps bulging through his thin white shirt. My son has gotten so muscular. Not for the first time, I wonder if he's going to kill me. How would he make it look like an accident? Perhaps he'd drag me up the stairs and push me back down them again. Will it hurt? Probably. And then I think of Bippie, and my heart constricts. Who will look after my beloved dog? I know that Lucas won't. He only tolerates Bippie because of me. Besides, Lucas most likely won't get away with murdering me. He'll end up in prison, and there's no way my son will survive that. He pretends to be strong, but he's a fragile soul at heart.

'Alright, alright,' I say. I take the phone and punch in my code, fumbling arthritic fingers making the process slow. Eventually, I send him ten thousand dollars. Such a lot of money. His phone pings, and he uses his right hand to take the phone out of his pocket. A sly smile eases across his face, and very gently, he places the candlestick back on the mantelpiece.

'Thank you, Mother,' he says. 'That wasn't so hard, was it? Shall I get you a cup of coffee?' His smile is saccharine, as if nothing has just happened, and his callousness takes my breath away. I haven't seen this side of Lucas for a while, months even. I suppose this is why it's shocked me. I'm not an idiot. I know there's badness in my son, but I also know that he's desperate for my approval. At least, he used to be. And that's how I used to control him, by telling him how much I love him, how I'm so proud of him, even though—if I'm brutally honest—I'm not. He's an intelligent, handsome man, except he hasn't had the success he thinks he's owed, and I fear that's my fault. I've indulged him, tried to make up for his father's cruelty, tried to suppress so very much.

I close my eyes for a moment as I listen to him clattering around in the kitchen. When his footsteps re-enter the living room, I glance up. He's holding the little red tray, and on it is a mug of steaming coffee and a plate with three of my favorite cookies. Quite the loving son.

FIVE MINUTES LATER, Lucas goes out, and I let out a sigh of relief. He doesn't tell me where he's going or when he'll be home, and I don't ask. I get up from my chair, my legs even weaker than normal, and hobble into the kitchen. He's tidied up in here, placed my lunch things in the dishwasher and wiped the kitchen counters clean. Lucas is good like that. He likes order and cleanliness. Bippie is in the backyard, and he's pawing at the door to be let in. Thinking about it, I doubt Lucas would hurt me in the presence of my dog. Perhaps that's why he let him outside. Maybe I need Bippie around me as my protector.

When the doorbell rings, I'm startled, as is the dog, who lets out a low woof.

'Coming!' I shout as I walk slowly towards the front door, leaning heavily on my cane. Lucas tells me I should use a chain on the door rather than opening it, and in light of the mugging, I probably should. Except right now, the chain is off, and I open it anyway.

'Oh, hello, dear!' I say, surprised to see Jade. She looks awful, with her eyes bloodshot and acne on her normally flawless face.

'Hey, Peggy. Can I talk to you?'

'Of course, dear.' I hold the door open, and she walks in. Although Jade wasn't the woman I'd expected Lucas to settle down with, I was thankful he'd finally found someone. She's a pretty thing, not the brightest on the block, but if she can control him and make him happy, then that's fine by me. Just a shame about all the cosmetic enhancements, which make her look a bit ridiculous.

'Go straight through to the kitchen,' I say. 'I'll put the kettle on.'

Before I have the chance to fill up the kettle, Jade asks, 'Did Lucas tell you he split up with me?'

'Yes, he did. I'm sorry to hear that.' The lie comes easily, as it so often does when I'm talking about my son. It also doesn't surprise me, because Lucas has been staying here so much.

'Did he also tell you I'm pregnant?'

I lean against the kitchen units and let my hand slip off the kettle. That is a shock. A big shock. I honestly thought I'd never have grandchildren and had resigned myself to the fact. But Jade being pregnant... Did Lucas run away at the thought of responsibility?

Jade is staring at me expectantly.

'No, dear. He didn't tell me you were pregnant,' I admit.

With trembling hands, I fill up the kettle and remove some mugs from the cupboard.

'Could I have a glass of water, please? I'm avoiding caffeine,' Jade says.

I put one of the mugs away again.

'I want to keep the baby,' Jade adds. 'Whether Lucas wants to be involved or not.' There's a pause before she says, 'I suppose Lucas is seeing someone else.'

I don't answer, so Jade asks again.

'Please tell me the truth, Peggy. Is Lucas seeing someone else?'

'I don't know. I don't think so,' I say, but then Daniella's gentle face springs to mind. I'm not stupid. I've seen how Lucas looks at her, how her name seems to pop into our every conversation.

'Can you persuade Lucas to reconsider? We love each other, and now with a baby on the way... he'd make a wonderful father.'

I pause with my back to Jade. She's very wrong. I don't think Lucas would make a wonderful father. I fear what he would do when the baby won't settle. I fear what might happen to Jade when, after hours with a fretting baby, she hands the infant to Lucas to look after, because if he's tired after a long day at work and in a mood... it doesn't bear thinking about. I turn around to look at Jade, at her flawless skin and naïve eyes.

'I'll follow him and find out who the new woman is. It won't be hard,' she says.

I'm at a loss as to what to say, but I guess my silence speaks volumes. Jade stares at me, her filler-enhanced bottom lip dropping open. 'Don't you want me and Lucas to be together?' she asks, hurt evident in her voice. 'Don't you want to know your grandchild?'

'This is nothing personal,' I say. 'Look, I can give you money. I'll help you financially with the baby, but it's best not to involve Lucas. Believe me. Where is your family from? Was it Pittsburgh?'

Jade nods, her eyes moist with tears.

'Go back to your family. They'll give you the support you need during your pregnancy and afterwards, when your baby is born. Try to put as much distance as possible between yourself and Lucas. Find yourself another man. You're an attractive young woman. You'll find someone to look after you.'

'What are you saying?' Jade asks, shaking her head as if I'm speaking a foreign language.

I shrug.

She stands up now, pushing the chair away. 'Is this just an underhand way of saying I'm not good enough for him? Is it because you don't want your grandchildren to look like me?'

'Good heavens, no!' I exclaim, shocked to think she's accusing me of racism. 'You're a beautiful young woman. I just...' I'm getting my words tied up in knots, and I don't want to say out loud that I'm fearful of Lucas around a baby. 'I can give you money, Jade. Five thousand dollars should help buy you whatever you need for the baby.' It occurs to me that history might be repeating itself.

Jade throws me such a look of disdain, I realize I've got her wrong.

'I love Lucas,' Jade says. 'And I thought you and I... well, I got that wrong too, didn't I?'

'It's not personal,' I add, except the look on her face tells me nothing I can say now will make this right.

Jade storms towards the front door.

'If you change your mind about the money...' I shout after her.

'I know where you live,' she says in a taut voice. And then I hear the front door slam, and she's gone.

I sink back into my chair. I didn't handle that well, except hopefully I have achieved the right outcome. Lucas has a short attention span, and spending over a year with Jade is long for him. The girl did well, even if she doesn't realize it. But once Lucas has turned his attention elsewhere, there's no going back. I'm not stupid. I know he's got his eye on Daniella, and that would be a complete disaster.

WHEN LUCAS COMES HOME, I mull over what I'm going to tell him. I decide not to mention that Jade visited me, as that's unlikely to have a good outcome for her. But I do need to talk to him about the lovely Daniella.

I bake him his favorite fish pie.

'You're looking very debonair today,' I say. Lucas doesn't react. 'How's your personal training going? I'd love you to help me with a few rehabilitation exercises when you have time.'

'That physio isn't good?'

'She doesn't hold a candle to you, love. It makes you wonder what all those years of training were for. It's like you know instinctively what to do.' I've seen the local physio a few times, and she's excellent, but I'm not going to tell Lucas that.

His face brightens a little, as it always does when I flatter him, so I take a deep breath. 'I honestly don't know how I would have survived the mugging without you and Daniella. Such a lovely woman. You like her, don't you?'

He throws me a scornful look and carries on munching.

'You know she's married, that she has children,' I add. Lucas keeps his eyes on his food.

'So?' he asks eventually. 'What's that got to do with me?'

'Because I know you, son. I know when you've fallen for someone, and you've fallen hard for her, haven't you?'

He chucks his fork onto his plate, and splatters of food fly across the table. 'Butt out of my life, Mother,' he snaps.

'But Daniella has a family, and if you pursue her, you could cause untold damage.'

Lucas is silent now, cutting his meat aggressively.

'I don't want to interfere, but you're living in my home, so it's not that easy. You could cause untold damage if you pursue things with Daniella.'

'For God's sake, Mother. We're in love. Yes, I have fallen for her, and she's fallen for me. It's mutual.'

'Really?' The doubt is heavy in my voice because I've seen this before, when my son has become obsessed with someone.

'We've had sex.'

'You what?' I'm horrified. Absolutely horrified. Surely Daniella wouldn't do something as brazen as that?

'What? You don't believe me?'

'Well,' I bluster.

'You want me to describe it, because it was something else.'

'No, it's fine.' I see the cruelty in his eyes now, how they darken while his pupils become unnaturally wide.

'How could you do that?' I say. 'She's married, and I don't know, it just seems so out of character.'

'You don't know Daniella,' he says scornfully. 'But I do. And she's the love of my life. The woman I've been waiting for all these years.' His phone rings, but he silences it without even glancing at the screen.

'Oh, come on,' I say. I immediately regret it. Lucas's lips thin and turn pale. He pushes his plate away from him, and his fingers twitch as his breathing quickens, his chest puffing out. I've pushed him too far.

'It's alright, love,' I say, keeping my voice as level as I can. 'I've overstepped. It was just a surprise, that's all. Deep breaths, deep breaths.' I push my chair back, but my legs feel even wobblier than normal. I grab my cane and lever myself to standing. And I don't look at Lucas. It's like dealing with a wild animal. Don't make eye contact, back away; be very, very calm. I turn and head towards the bar cabinet, trying not to panic. Lucas scrapes his chair back, but I refuse to turn around. If I do, that might push him over the edge. Instead, I move steadily, five paces across the room. I take out a whiskey glass, but my hand is trembling. There are footsteps, and I hold my breath.

CHAPTER EIGHT

DANIELLA

However many times I've showered and washed my clothes on hot, I still feel dirty. Well, perhaps not dirty because it was exciting, possibly the most exciting thing that has happened to me in a decade. Illicit sex with a semi-stranger, and oh my, it was good. My body tingles whenever I think about Lucas's fingers stroking my skin. But then I get into a cycle of shame. How could I have betrayed Grant like that? Should I tell him the truth? Wouldn't that be a sure-fire way of destroying our marriage? He would never trust me again. Then again, what happens if he finds out? It would kill our marriage, and he would hate me, but worse than that, it would shatter the lives of our girls too. What sort of example am I setting, just as they're on the cusp of adulthood? These thoughts go around and around in my head, and I know that this is a shameful secret I will need to take to my grave.

I promised Peggy that I'd walk Bippie this morning, so I hurry to her house. As normal, I ring the old-fashioned doorbell and wait, expecting to hear her shuffling footsteps from the other side of the door. Except to my dismay, the door swings open almost immediately, and Lucas is standing there.

'Oh,' I say. 'I thought you'd be at work.'

He stares at me for a second, and then his face softens, and he throws me his dazzling smile. 'It's wonderful to see you.' He takes a step towards me, but then Bippie emerges from behind his legs, squeezing his way through the doorway, his bottom wiggling from side to side as he spots me.

I bend down to stroke the dog, who proceeds to lick my face.

'You give him a warmer welcome than me,' Lucas says. 'Do I get a kiss too?'

I look up at him, startled. 'It was a mistake,' I whisper, worried that Peggy might overhear this conversation.

'Don't worry, she's not here,' he replies. 'She's at an appointment.'

I stand up. 'I'm sorry, Lucas. But it can't happen again. I'm married, and it was a mistake.'

'But you and I are so good together. And I know you felt it too.' He leans forwards and strokes the side of my cheek. I take a step backwards, accidentally standing on Bippie's foot, who gives out a little yelp. 'You feel it, don't you, Daniella?' His voice is husky, and I wish it didn't make my insides melt. I crouch down again, encircling my arms around the soft head of the dog, creating a canine barrier between us. Still with my arms around Bippie, I look up at Lucas.

'I'm really sorry, but I'm not going to be able to walk Bippie anymore. I'll send Peggy a message to apologize for not being able to stop by, but it's for the best.'

'No,' Lucas says vehemently. 'This isn't Mom's fault.

Don't abandon her, please. She adores you, as does the dog.' He nudges his knee towards Bippie. 'Mom can pay you to help out.'

I stand up. 'Come on, Lucas. This isn't about the money, you know that. I enjoy walking Bippie and helping your mom. But—'

He cuts me off. 'She's becoming so forgetful, and she needs visitors. My work commitments are increasing, and I won't be here during the days. Mom has really perked up since you've been visiting her. If you or Mom tells me when you're coming over, I'll make sure I'm out of the house. I promise.'

I stand up, but Bippie puts a paw on my shoe, as if he can sense that I'm abandoning him. I run my fingers over his velvety ears.

'Let me think about it,' I say. 'But no promises.'

Although Lucas's expression is crestfallen, he nods.

'I'll take Bippie now for a quick walk,' I say. The dog's ears perk up, and he looks at me expectantly. Lucas reaches behind the door and hands me the lead, which I grab too quickly.

THERE'S an uncomfortable squirming sensation in my stomach. I've behaved terribly, and I feel like bashing my head in order to resettle all the confusing thoughts. It's as if Bippie can sense my discomfort because halfway to the park he turns around, looks at me with those soft brown eyes and starts trotting back the way we came. As normal, I ring Peggy's doorbell, dreading seeing Lucas again. Fortuitously, when he opens the door, he's on the phone and just mouths *thank you* to me as Bippie squeezes past him into the hallway beyond.

I'm still thinking about Lucas when I push open the door to the Silken Stem. To my surprise, Lesley is seated at our worktable, the laptop in front of her and a man I don't recognize at her side. He's wearing a dark gray suit with his white shirt open at the neckline. With his rectangular tortoiseshell glasses and dark stubble, he's more formally dressed than most of our normal suppliers.

'Danni!' Lesley exclaims, pushing her chair back. 'This is Matt.'

The man stands up and extends a hand towards me.

'Sorry, I, um...' I mutter. I have no idea who he is, yet they're both looking at me as if I should know him.

'Matt,' Lesley says. 'You know, I've told you about him. About us.' Lesley's cheeks redden, and she throws me big eyes.

'Oh yes, sorry!' I exclaim. 'The boyfriend.'

Lesley throws her hands over her face. I've clearly embarrassed her.

'I'm happy to be described as your boyfriend, your partner. Partner in life and business perhaps?' He's grinning at Lesley now, but this is super awkward.

'What's all this?' I ask, gesturing at the laptop and printouts of spreadsheets and charts scattered across the table.

'Shall I get us a coffee?' Lesley suggests. 'And Matt can explain the proposition.'

'Proposition?' I ask, pulling out a chair and picking up a piece of paper. It's headed *The Silken Stem* and shows projected growth for the next five years—growth far beyond anything we've ever achieved in the past.

'I'm so excited to share this with you,' Matt says, his blue eyes gleaming behind the glasses. 'Lesley has been telling me all about the Silken Stem, your achievements to date, and hopes for the future.'

I turn to look at Lesley because I'm not aware that we've discussed any plans for the future. We've mostly just muddled along. However, her back is to us as she pours coffee into mugs.

'The potential for expansion is enormous. The model you've created here is ideal for franchising, and that would enable rapid growth across the United States. Imagine a Silken Stem in every major city. That would bring your cost of sales down dramatically, and with increased purchasing power, your margins will increase exponentially. I can see you going public within five years.'

'I'm sorry, I'm not following,' I say, unable to keep up, but this stranger carries on talking.

'The Silken Stem would be the go-to brand of faux flowers across the US, supplying commercial properties such as offices and hotels, as well as upscaling your online business for domestic customers, and, of course, still doing B to B business via retailer outlets such as garden centers and gift shops. Your purchasing power may even be such that we could look at vertical integration and perhaps manufacture here in the States. That would mitigate your carbon footprint and reduce your reliance on foreign exchange rates and tariffs.' Matt picks up some of the pieces of paper and lets them flutter back onto the table.

Lesley places a mug of coffee in front of each of us.

'It's so exciting, isn't it, Daniella?' she says.

Everything Matt said makes sense superficially, but Lesley and I haven't even discussed opening another shop, let alone some crazy vast expansion plan across the country.

'And the timing is right, because Daniella's girls are flying the nest, so she'll have more time on her hands,' Lesley says.

I am completely blindsided by this talk. Earlier, all I could think about was Lucas and how I might have destroyed my family life, and now Lesley is suggesting we build an empire. They're talking between themselves, but I zone out.

'Daniella!' Lesley says. 'Are you listening?'

'Sorry.'

'I was just saying how all the traveling will be such fun. We can go to San Francisco, New Orleans, Miami—all the places I've dreamed of going to but have never gotten around to visiting.'

'I'm sure you'll easily find franchises across the States; however, there are other options too,' Matt adds. 'The most exciting thing is that this business is highly investable. We can either go the franchise route or raise money through private equity. Clearly, you will maintain greater control going down the franchise route, but the growth will be slower. Which do you prefer?'

'Please!' I interrupt, throwing my hands into the air. 'Please, can you hold fire. I'm not even sure I want to expand. I mean, Lesley and I haven't discussed it. Everything you're saying is... just too much.'

They both fall silent, and the only noise is the hum of traffic outside. Matt frowns and raises his eyebrow at Lesley.

'Alright,' Lesley says eventually. 'We haven't considered it per se, but we've talked about the future, obviously.' She turns back to look at me. 'What are your initial thoughts?'

'You can't expect me to have an opinion just like that,' I

say. The air is heavy with their disappointment, so I quickly ask, 'You said you have some printouts for me, explaining it all.'

Matt nods and pushes a thick folder towards me.

'I'll discuss it with Grant and let you know.' I pick up the folder and walk over to where my bag is hanging on the hook on the wall, shoving the folder inside. Then I take my mug and walk through to the front of the shop. I can hear Matt and Lesley talking in hushed whispers, but I don't try to listen. I'm uncomfortable. Why is Lesley being so influenced by this man? Why the hell hasn't she discussed all of this with me first?

After a few minutes, Lesley emerges into the shop.

'Sorry about that. I thought you'd be as excited as I am,' she mutters.

'It was a bolt out of the blue.'

'Anyway, think about it. This evening, Matt is going to introduce me to some of the business owners he's already helped.'

'I thought he was your boyfriend, not your business partner.'

'He might be both.'

'But I'm your business partner, Lesley,' I say.

'I know. I'm not trying to oust you or anything. I just thought it would be sensible for us to explore all options.'

IF I FELT uncomfortable about Lucas, now I feel equally uncomfortable about Matt and Lesley. I've got no desire to turn our lifestyle business into some great big conglomerate. The Silken Stem is profitable, and both Lesley and I make enough to fund our lifestyles, but I want an easier life, not a more complicated one. And it worries me that Lesley is being swept up by the ambition of a stranger. This is what happens with her: she falls for men so quickly, and nine times out of ten, it ends badly. How do we know that Matt is genuine, or whether he's any good at his job? This all feels wrong, yet I don't want to fall out with Lesley over it.

I'm relieved when the doorbell chimes and a customer walks in because it brings to a close the awkwardness of our conversation. She's a well-dressed woman, at a guess in her early thirties, wearing a camel-colored overcoat and a Prada crossbody bag. Her high-heeled boots click as she walks slowly around the shop. There's something about her that makes me uneasy, possibly the way she keeps on glancing at me rather than the arrangements on display. The phone rings, but by the time I reach it, Lesley has already answered on the other extension.

'Can I help you?' I ask the customer.

'Are you Daniella?' The woman keeps her eyes on me as she lets her fingers trail over our display units.

'Yes.'

'God, I thought you'd be younger, not bloody middle-aged!'

I recoil and step backwards, bashing a table and having to rescue a vase of faux roses from tumbling to the ground.

'Do I know you?' I ask, trying and failing to think where I could have met this woman.

'No.' She steps towards me, her arms crossed over her chest, tapping the toe of her right boot. 'But I know you, and you need to stay away from my man.'

It takes a long moment to get a word out of my mouth. *Stay away from her man?*

'I'm sorry, but I think you have the wrong person,' I say

eventually. 'I'm married, with two teenage daughters. In fact, I've been happily married for twenty years.'

She shakes her head, her expression one of disappointment. 'Don't lie to me, Daniella. I know you're after him.'

'After who?' I ask. I feel sick. What does this woman know?

'Lucas Denman. My name is Jade, and I'm Lucas's girlfriend, fiancée in fact. I'm pregnant with his child.'

I stare at her in horror as her words sink in. Then I shake my head and say, 'No. You've got it all wrong. I'm not interested in Lucas. In fact, I barely know him.' That, of course, is increasingly untrue. 'Lucas seems weirdly keen on me, but I can assure you it isn't reciprocated.'

'Don't lie to me!' Jade is shouting at me now.

Lesley appears from the back, glancing from me to Jade. 'Is everything alright here?'

'No, it's not!' Jade exclaims. 'Your colleague has been hitting on my boyfriend, and she needs to back off.' She stabs her finger in my direction. 'Find someone your own age, you old whore.'

I'm stunned. I'm not sure anyone has ever spoken to me like this, and frankly, I've no idea how to react. Fortunately, Lesley takes control.

'You need to leave,' she says, striding towards Jade. 'This is private property, and you're not welcome.'

'I wouldn't want to buy this fake trash anyway,' she says, flicking her head backwards. Her dark eyes are glistening with tears. 'Just stay away from Lucas, okay?' She gives me one last glowering look and then strides out of the shop.

'What the hell was that all about?' Lesley asks.

'That's the girlfriend of Lucas. The son of the woman I helped.'

'OMG! The guy you're having a fling with.' Her eyes are so wide, they're almost comical.

'I'm not having a fling!' I exclaim. Except Lesley tilts her head, bites her lower lip and raises an eyebrow.

'Don't forget that I know you,' she says ominously. 'Almost as well as I know myself.'

CHAPTER NINE

PEGGY

He didn't hit me. He didn't knock the door down. This time, at least. I wish I could improve my mobility faster. Sure, it's progressing, but my leg still aches, and I'm far from being back to my old self. I hate feeling dependent on other people, particularly Lucas. He's not a natural carer, my boy, but then again, who wants to look after their decrepit mother?

I count the days until Sunday. It's been a long while since I've been around a young family, and I'm ridiculously excited. With some difficulty, I put on my best silk blouse and black wool pants and even attempt to make up my face.

I'm waiting by the door when the lovely Daniella arrives. Even so, I'm a little nervous because although I don't believe that she and Lucas slept together, if she did, perhaps her demeanor will be changed somehow.

'Hello, Peggy. How are you doing?' she asks rather formally.

I notice straight away that there's something a bit off about her. Normally she's as warm as can be, but today she barely even strokes Bippie. It's as if she's slightly skittish, and instantly, it makes my stomach churn.

'I've been so looking forward to today,' I say too brightly.

'Actually, before we get in the car, I need to ask your opinion on something.'

My heart sinks. So she *is* going to ask me about Lucas, and I've no idea how to reply. Or maybe she's wanting to cancel lunch. If so, that would be a great disappointment.

'With pleasure,' I say politely. 'Shall we go into the living room?' She follows me into the room, and I wonder if I should remove my coat. I decide not to and lower myself onto my comfiest upright chair. Daniella sits opposite me on the sofa.

'This is a bit awkward,' she says, interlocking her fingers.

I wait because I find people always fill silences.

'A woman called Jade came to my shop the other day, and she was really angry with me.'

'Jade?' I ask, surprise in my voice.

'She said she's Lucas's girlfriend or fiancée, and she told me to back off. What was all that about?'

'Oh dear,' I reply. 'The thing is, Jade is out of the picture as far as Lucas is concerned, so there's really nothing to worry about. She's a fiery little thing, but I'm sure she won't trouble you again.'

'That's not the point, Peggy. I'm married. I'm not interested in Lucas, even though he seems rather keen on me.'

Oh, Lucas. What a mess he's making.

'Yes, I was worried he might be sweet on you. But you know what men are like. If you give him the cold shoulder, he'll move on soon enough. I'm glad you're sticking by your husband, because there's nothing more important in life than marriage and family.'

Daniella's shoulders drop, and I can tell my words have relaxed her.

'Do you want me to have a word with Lucas? He can get Jade to back off.'

'As much as I like Lucas, if he has feelings for me, they're really not appropriate. I need them both to leave me alone.'

I lean forwards, my hips creaking, and I try not to wince. 'You leave it with me, Daniella. I'm sorry if this has caused you any problems. Lucas is a good man, but when he falls in love, he falls hard. And Jade, well, she'll find someone else soon enough, a pretty girl like her.'

'Anyway, how are you doing?' Daniella asks, and I'm truly relieved that she's changed the subject.

'The mobility is improving, but I'm stuck in the house all day, and it's tough not getting out and seeing people.'

'I can imagine that.'

'It's shocking how quickly people drop you when you're incapacitated in any way. Before this blasted mugging, I'd have company most days, visiting my friends, wandering into the city. I'm not one for complaining, but it's making me feel very isolated.'

'I'm sorry to hear that.' She's quiet for a few long moments.

'Old age can be very lonely, Daniella, so make the most of your family while you have them around.'

'Well, I'm glad you're joining me and the girls for lunch.' She claps her hands together. 'We'd better get a move on before the food spoils.'

It cheers me up no end that lunch is still on. I stand up, a big grin on my face. 'I can't wait to meet them, and your husband.'

'Oh, Grant isn't here this weekend, so it's just me and the girls. And we need to bring Bippie. The twins love dogs.'

DANIELLA'S HOUSE IS BEAUTIFUL, as I expected it would be. Her kitchen is quite something, with pale cabinets and a lovely white marble countertop.

'I hope you like roast beef,' she says. 'I thought I'd do a full English roast with Yorkshire puddings and roast potatoes.'

'That sounds delicious. But remind me, what's a Yorkshire pudding?'

Daniella laughs. 'It's like a savory popover so really not a pudding at all. Can I pour you a glass of wine?'

'I won't say no,' I say.

She pours me a small glass of white wine, which I sip at slowly. And then I meet her children. Arlyse and Tasia aren't identical, and it's easy to tell them apart. Tasia wears her blonde curling locks in a messy bun. Arlyse has darker hair, and she smiles less. I don't recall how old they are—eighteen perhaps—but they're attractive young women, both the spitting image of their mother, and quite charming, of course. They help lay the table, and the girls clearly adore Bippie. I wonder why Daniella and her husband gave them such unusual names. I always think it's pretentious when people give their children strange first names, as if the run-of-the-mill names aren't good enough somehow. Yet that doesn't fit my opinion of Daniella, who seems down-to-earth.

'Does Bippie like to play with a ball?' Tasia asks.

'There's nothing he enjoys more,' I reply.

'Can we take him out to the backyard?' Arlyse adds.

Daniella looks at the clock on the wall. 'Twenty minutes until lunch.'

The girls and the dog rush outside. It warms my heart seeing this lovely family and knowing they've included me in it.

'It's so special to be around teenagers again,' I muse. 'You must be really proud of them.'

'I am,' Daniella says. 'I'm going to miss them terribly when they're away. They're leaving in three weeks.' She takes the meat out of the oven and sticks in one of those digital thermometers. Then she turns around and smiles at me. 'You mentioned something about Louise.'

I feel the blood drain from my face, and I have to concentrate really hard not to spill my wine as I shakily put it down on the table.

'Me?' I ask.

'Straight after you had your accident, when we were in the hospital. You were in and out of consciousness and mentioned Louise. I assumed she might be your daughter.'

'What did I say?' My voice sounds croaky, and the shock is making me dizzy.

'Nothing much.'

There's a long silence, and Daniella looks at me with her head slanted to one side, her eyes creased with concern. I need to pull myself together fast.

I sit up straighter and take a deep breath. 'She died,' I admit eventually. 'My daughter, Louise, died.'

'Oh, goodness!' Daniella's right hand swings up to cover her mouth. She looks genuinely shocked, so clearly I didn't tell her much. I have to believe that I didn't mention anything I shouldn't have. And then comes the question that I always dread.

'If you don't mind me asking, what happened?'

I'm trying to formulate an answer, but then Tasia rushes into the kitchen.

'Arlyse threw the ball too far, and it's gone into the bushes, and we can't find it,' she says breathlessly. 'Have you got another ball lying around somewhere?'

'I might have an old tennis ball in the utility room cupboards. You can have a look, but lunch is nearly ready.'

Fortunately, any discussion about my deceased daughter is halted.

Five minutes later, the four of us are helping ourselves to an array of delicious dishes. Daniella has cooked the beef perfectly, so it's pink in the middle, and her Yorkshire puddings are crispy on the outside and quite scrumptious. The girls talk excitedly about their forthcoming travels, and for a moment, I feel a pang of wistfulness. Why hasn't Lucas settled down and produced grandchildren for me? My life would be so different if I had a larger family. But I don't want to tarnish this lovely meal with thoughts of Lucas and of what might have been.

We're finishing off a smooth and creamy chocolate mousse when my phone starts ringing. For a while, I don't realize what's happening, because my phone is in my bag, and my hearing isn't as acute as it used to be.

'Is that your phone?' Daniella asks. By the time she brings me my bag and I fish out the cell phone, it's stopped ringing. Except then it rings again almost immediately.

'Oh,' I say, seeing Lucas's name come up on the screen. What does he want? He knows I'm here today, and I wonder if he's trying to jeopardize things. There's a flutter of foreboding in my chest, which I try to dismiss.

'Are you going to answer that?' Daniella asks with a smile.

'Sure,' I say, pressing the answer button.

'Hello.'

For a moment, I can't work out whether it's even my son on the other end. There's sobbing and strangulated words that I can't decipher. 'What's going on?' I ask, my heart beating a little too fast. More sobs and swallowing.

'Lucas, is that you?'

'Yes, Mom. Something terrible has happened.'

My heart plummets.

'It's Jade,' he says. Oh goodness, I think. I hope Lucas hasn't done anything stupid.

'She's dead, Mom. Jade is dead. She's taken her own life.'

CHAPTER TEN

DANIELLA

Peggy turns white, and although she's sitting down, I'm worried she might pass out. She drops her phone into her cavernous handbag. It's a few moments before she composes herself and turns to look at me.

'Jade is dead.'

'Jade? As in Lucas's ex?'

She nods.

'Oh my goodness. That's terrible. What happened?'

'I don't know,' Peggy says. The older woman is trembling, unable to bring her water glass up to her mouth.

'Girls,' I say, 'why don't you give Bippie some leftovers and take him into the garden?'

They clearly want to stay and listen to the drama, but I give them the raised eyebrow and a glower, and they reluctantly leave the table. When they are outside, I turn back to Peggy and take her trembling hand in mine.

'What did Lucas say?' I ask.

'He is terribly distressed. It was hard to make out what he was saying, but it seems that Jade has taken her own life.'

The shock leaves us both in silence. I wonder if Peggy is thinking the same thing—that Jade decided she couldn't live without Lucas. And if that is the case, it leaves me in some way responsible. If Jade found out that I slept with Lucas, it would be devastating. I'm not sure how to react, other than accept the sense of sadness for this woman that I met only the once. Then I recall how she said she was pregnant. She is way too young to die, and with a baby on the way too, it makes it so much worse.

Eventually, I make both of us tea with sugar. I'm not sure that it does much to console poor Peggy, who seems to have withdrawn into her own world. After a few sips, she turns to me.

'I'm sorry to cut short such a delightful day,' she says, 'but would you mind taking me home?'

'Of course.' We gather her belongings, and I tell the girls that Peggy and Bippie have to leave. Five minutes later, we're parked outside her house. I'm hoping she doesn't want me to come inside because I can't face seeing Lucas, but I ask anyway.

'Would you like me to come in?'

'No, dear. It's best if you don't.'

I nod with relief. I hope that Peggy doesn't think that I'm complicit in some way in Jade's death, but in my heart of hearts, I reckon I probably am. It's horribly unsettling.

I help her out of the car and watch as she trudges up the steps of her house and inserts the key into the front door. When she's inside, I get back into the car and look up at the house. I'm sure I see Lucas in an upstairs window, an expression of longing on his face, except when I blink and look again, he's gone. I turn the car around and head back home.

I've barely been home five minutes when my phone

rings. It's Lucas. Initially, I don't answer the phone and consider sending him to voicemail, but then I think about Jade. I accept the call.

'Lucas,' I say.

'It's Jade.'

'I know. Your mother told me.'

'She's taken her own life.'

'It's terrible,' I say.

'I found her.' His voice rises in pitch slightly. 'I found her dead at her house. Dead from an overdose. The worst thing is, she left a note saying she can't live without me.'

I reel. This is completely shocking and exactly as I feared.

'Jade's dead, Daniella. And it's my fault.'

'You couldn't have known she was going to do that,' I say. I only met the woman that once, and it wasn't a pleasant interaction, but she was young and beautiful, and it's horrendous that her life has been snuffed out at such a young age. And the thought of her taking her unborn baby with her too is truly awful.

'I'm not handling it very well,' he says, sniffing loudly. 'Could we go for a coffee or something?'

'I'm sorry, Lucas,' I say. 'I have my girls home, and it really isn't appropriate for us to meet up.'

He's silent for several long beats. 'I'm sorry,' I add again.

'Okay. Goodbye,' he says, rather formally, and hangs up.

GRANT ARRIVES HOME a couple of hours later, and I'm extremely happy to see him. I wish I could tell him about Lucas and Jade and Peggy, but I can't. Instead, I explain that the lady I helped after her mugging came for lunch, and then we talk about his weekend, and the girls provide a welcome distraction.

Later, when we're getting ready for bed, I tell Grant about Matt's proposition for the business.

'What's your gut reaction?' he asks. It always surprises me how my super-intelligent husband with his sharp, scientific analytical brain believes in God and listening to one's gut.

'That at worst he's a conman and at best a fantasist. To think that we can go from being a single shop to some mega-conglomerate in a matter of five years is crazy. We're not leading some dot com revolution. We're a brick-and-mortar shop making and arranging pretty fake flowers.'

'Harsh.' Grant laughs.

'I think that Lesley is being swept off her feet by this man, and even if he could pull off what he's suggesting, I don't want to be heading up some big business.'

'In which case, you've answered your own question. You need to let Lesley down gently. You're fifty percent partners, so either this Matt buys you out if he makes you an offer you're willing to accept, or otherwise, you just say no.'

'I'm happy with the business,' I say. 'And I don't want to have a fight with Lesley.'

'These things have a way of working themselves out. I wouldn't worry about it too much.'

I grind my teeth with irritation. Grant is so laid-back it grates. How can he tell me not to worry when Lesley is on track for tipping our business upside down? It feels as if I'm losing control of it, so of course I'm going to worry. As I brush my teeth, I realize that the issues with the business are being compounded by my thoughts about Lucas, but there's little I can do to stop the fears from coursing through my body.

SOMETIME LATER, we're lying in bed, doing the spooning exercise that Linda suggested, not that it's resulted in anything the slightest bit sexual. Frankly, I don't care. I'm not wanting anything more from Grant at the moment. Instead, I can't stop myself from imagining that it's Lucas's arms around me, his strong body pressing up against mine. I feel bad that I refused to see him earlier, but there is no way that we can have a repeat performance. All the same, it's confusing that I want him and don't want him at the same time.

'Don't get angry with me, but I've been thinking,' Grant says, jolting me awake just as I'm about to drift off to sleep. Unsurprisingly, I tense. 'I don't want to go to counseling again. I'm going to the gym three times a week and getting fit, and I really don't think picking over the past is helpful. To be honest, it's humiliating. Can't we just work through things by ourselves?'

I sigh and pull away from him. I can't force my husband to attend, although it makes me disappointed. I'm trying to be strong and not see Lucas, but at the same time, I need Grant to be supportive of me, of us.

'You were going to counseling for me,' I say, turning onto my back.

'I know, but it's too much. You could carry on going to see the woman and report back to me what I need to do.'

'I don't think it works like that.' Can't he even bring himself to call Linda by her name?

I sigh and fling the duvet back, pulling myself away from Grant and getting out of bed.

'You're pissed at me,' he says.

'A bit, but I can't force you to attend.'

'What about the house move?' he asks.

I stand still. 'What about it?'

'I think it will be good for us. A new start and all that. Have you started looking?'

'No,' I reply. 'But I will.'

AND SO IT is that I attend the next session with Linda Gibson alone.

'No Grant?' she asks as she collects me from the waiting room.

'He doesn't want to attend anymore.'

She raises an eyebrow.

When I'm settled on the sofa all alone, Linda asks, 'Did Grant explain why he didn't want to come?'

'He doesn't think it's necessary, and he doesn't like to pick through the past.'

'How does that make you feel?'

'To begin with, I was annoyed. It's like he's disrespectful of my feelings and can't be bothered to invest in our relationship. I paced the house for about an hour after he told me last night. But today, I think maybe it's a good thing,' I admit.

'Go on,' Linda says, her face frustratingly impassive.

I sigh. 'It means I can tell you what's really happening in my life.'

I search for a way to tell her about Lucas, to admit how I'm feeling, but the words don't come.

'This is a safe space, Daniella.'

'I know,' I say, squirming slightly. 'I've developed an attraction to another man, and I'm worried it's turning into an obsession.'

'An obsession?'

'I can't stop thinking about him. There's this intense

physical attraction, and it's mutual. He's made it very clear that he is into me, but I've tried to push him away.'

'And how does that make you feel?'

'In part, flattered. Well, obviously I'm flattered. It's been years since another man has wanted me.'

'And,' she prompts.

'And he's extremely good looking, so the attraction is mutual.'

'Is this a concern for you?'

'Of course,' I say, a little too harshly. 'It's a threat to my marriage. I feel this overwhelming magnetic attraction towards him, and I can't stop thinking about him, how he makes me feel, physically. You know...'

'And have you acted upon these feelings?'

'Yes, I mean no. To a small degree.' That's a blatant lie, and I assume my flaming cheeks are giving away my truth.

'How does that make you feel?'

Why does she keep asking me the same question? It's super annoying. I pause before replying.

'Wanted, desirable, honestly it makes me feel great. Except I'm riddled with guilt, and I don't want to destroy my marriage.'

'That makes sense. So what would you like the outcome to be?'

I sigh. 'To stop thinking about Lucas and to get intimate with Grant. Except, when I compare Grant to Lucas, I don't even fancy my husband.'

'Quite often in long marriages, the actual issue isn't about sex; it's about how we communicate with each other, how we make each other feel. It's about intimacy and being able to share our thoughts, feelings, and experiences. Of course, that means we have to allow ourselves to be vulnerable to our partners and share our thoughts and emotions openly and honestly. It's not just the physical intimacy of sexual relations but a sense of closeness, tenderness, and sharing. But first, we have to take personal responsibility, and I commend you for taking that initial step of being here today. We can't make our partners change, but you can change yourself. Tell me what intimacy means to you?'

I open and close my mouth, unsure how to respond. Linda goes on to elucidate.

'Think of the behaviors, things that a partner might do, or interactions that you have together that are intimate. What examples can you come up with?'

The next thirty minutes are difficult, requiring uncomfortable soul-searching, and when I leave Linda's, I feel utterly drained. Weirdly, I'm also struggling to recall exactly what we talked about. It's a discombobulating and not altogether comfortable sensation, as if my brain is experiencing a block. I'm heading towards the Silken Stem, but then decide I don't have the energy to go to work. I send Lesley a message asking if she can manage alone. When she reads the message but doesn't reply, I turn around and head home.

THAT NIGHT, Grant returns from the gym in a very upbeat mood. After his shower, he comes downstairs and throws his arms around me, his lips trailing over mine. I'm startled, and although I want to want my husband, I just don't. My body isn't feeling anything. Actually, a shiver of revulsion goes through me. Why don't I want to kiss him? Why don't I find this kind, brilliant man sexy? I try to recall what Linda and I discussed, how I defined intimacy, and I'm met with this weird fog.

'I need to get on with the food,' I say as I pull away from him.

'Are the girls here?'

'No. They're both out this evening.'

'Great,' he says. 'We have the evening to ourselves.'

I wonder what has gotten into Grant, and I'm not altogether sure I like it. I try to recall the last time Grant intimated he wanted to be alone with me, and honestly, I can't remember. Probably before the twins were born.

'What did Linda say?' he asks as we're digging into a butternut stew.

'I think she was disappointed you weren't there.'

He frowns. 'But was the session helpful for you?'

'Actually, yes,' I say. 'It made me realize what's important to me. Like when you hold my hand or pick up something from the store without me asking. Or notice what I'm wearing or clean up the kitchen just because.'

'None of that is very romantic,' he says.

'But it makes me feel seen. And I'm grateful that you're going to the gym and making an effort to lose weight.'

'You can thank my personal trainer for that.' He laughs. I struggle to smile. How can I tell my husband that I want him to look as sexy as Lucas? That Lucas's aftershave and gaze set my nerve endings on fire, and could Grant perhaps take some lessons from him? Except, of course he can't, they don't know each other, and long may that remain the case.

When we've finished, Grant says, 'I'll clear up. You go and put your feet up in the living room.'

I smile at my kind husband because, yes, he really is making an effort. But even so, there isn't even a glimmer of a sexual spark.

Later, when we're in bed, Grant tries again, and this time

I know that I can't reject him. It's the first time in years that Grant is taking the initiative in bed, and as Linda explained, I need to welcome it. Despite his greatest efforts, I find it impossible to relax. Eventually I let my mind wander and imagine that it's Lucas's hands on my breasts, his lips exploring my body. I hate myself for this pretense, but it works. I relax, and Grant climaxes quickly. I'm relieved when he gives me a quick kiss and heads out of bed to the bathroom. I turn over in bed, and by the time he returns, I've settled my breathing so it sounds like I'm asleep.

I'm being so unfair to Grant. I've betrayed my husband with a dangerous obsession with Lucas, and I don't know what to do about it.

CHAPTER ELEVEN

DANIELLA

The afternoon is busy with a regular flow of customers and several large online orders. At least it takes my mind off all the issues, helped by the fact that Lesley isn't around.

By the time I lock up and head home, it's dark outside, and I'm tired. The girls are both home, the beat of loud music blaring from their bedrooms. I go straight to the kitchen and pour myself a glass of red wine.

'Hey, sweetie,' Grant says as he bounds into the kitchen. I'm glad to see that he's dressed in his gym wear, and from the state of it, he's had a decent workout. 'I hope it's alright, but I've invited a friend home for supper. He's going through a rough time.'

'Sure,' I say. This isn't unusual. We regularly entertain Grant's professor colleagues as well as stray PhD students, particularly foreign students who don't have anywhere to go for Thanksgiving and Christmas.

'Who's coming?' I ask as I peer into the fridge, wondering what I can make with short notice. 'Do you want me to cook?'

'If you don't mind. I need a shower and a freshen-up.'

Grant and I take it in turns to do the cooking; another reason why I'm grateful for my husband.

'Any dietary requirements?' I ask.

'Whoops, I forgot to check, but I doubt it.'

'Not some fussy student, then?' I laugh.

'No. A friend from the gym.'

'You're such a collector of people.'

He grins at me and slips out of the room.

I listen to his heavy footsteps as he climbs the stairs. For a moment, I wonder what my life would be like without Grant. Despite feeling lonely in my marriage, I'd be lonelier in life. With most of my married friends, it's the women who organize their social lives, and the wives who introduce new people to their friendship group. With Grant and me, it's different. Everyone loves Grant, and I'm the spare part. He's the partner who regularly meets new people, who extends invitations and organizes social gatherings. And he enjoys cooking, so whenever we have dinner parties, it's Grant who plans the menu and cooks the food. Unlike some of his gauche academic colleagues, Grant is socially confident and funny. I've lost count of the number of times girlfriends have told me how lucky I am to be married to him. Of course, that makes everything that I've done so very much worse.

I make one of my staples: a chicken stew with dried apricots and wild rice. I'm in the middle of cooking when Grant appears, showered and dressed in jeans and a polo shirt despite the cold weather.

'Can I do anything to help?' he asks.

But before I can reply, the doorbell rings.

'You can answer that,' I say.

The kitchen fan is noisy, so I don't pay much attention to

the male voices in the hall. I'm holding a wooden spoon, stirring the pot, when Grant comes back into the kitchen.

'Sweetheart, I'd like you to meet my new gym buddy, Lucas.'

It's as if everything goes into slow motion. I swivel around, dropping the spoon into the pot, which splashes up burning liquid, scorching my forearm. Grant is staring at me expectantly, and I hope, in that very brief millisecond, that there is another Lucas. Except when I look up at the visitor in our kitchen, my Lucas is there, my husband's hand on his shoulder, and he's holding a bunch of flowers and a bottle of wine, a huge smile on his face.

IT TAKES a few long seconds for the burning on my arm to fire up my pain receptors.

'Are you alright?' Grant asks, hurrying to my side.

'It's nothing,' I say, dashing to the kitchen sink, where I run my arm under the cold tap. It gives me a few moments to compose myself, the chance to turn away from Grant, who hopefully will assume the shock on my face is because of my burned arm rather than his new friend.

'It's a pleasure to meet you,' Lucas says. 'Grant has told me so much about you.'

'Right,' I reply, wiping my arm down with a clean tea towel and searching in a drawer for the aloe vera gel.

So this is what we're doing. Pretending we don't know each other. Is that better than the alternative, or worse? I probably should have admitted I knew him, that I'd met him at Peggy's because he's her son. But it's too late now. Or is it? I could pretend that I didn't recognize him at first, but how would that play out?

'What can I get you to drink, buddy?' Grant asks. Nausea burns at the back of my throat as Grant calls Lucas that.

'A beer would be great. Thanks.'

'Daniella, what would you like?' Grant asks. 'Some more red wine?'

I want to scream, *I don't want any wine! I need you to get Lucas out of our house.* Except I don't. When I eventually speak, my voice sounds high and scratchy. 'Wine, please.'

I return to the stove, grateful that I don't need to look at either man. Grant puts some music on. It's slow and sensual and the last thing I want to listen to. What the hell am I going to do? This can't be a coincidence; it just can't.

'So where did you two meet?' I ask when I've composed myself sufficiently to use my voice.

'In the gym,' Grant replies. 'This man knows his stuff. You should see his muscles.' Grant laughs, and I die a little inside, because I know exactly what Lucas's muscles look and feel like.

'I'm a bit of a gym junkie, so I decided to get my personal training qualification and do a bit of PT work on the side. I was blessed to be given a great trainer so reckoned it would be nice to give something back.'

'And I was lucky enough to be assigned Lucas when I joined the gym.'

So it is a coincidence. The trouble is, I don't believe in coincidences. Grant hasn't been going to the gym for long, so could Lucas have targeted him? But how would Lucas even know that Grant is my husband? Our family name, Morris, is hardly unusual, and I don't recall mentioning Grant by name.

'When's supper?' Tasia scoots into the kitchen, her hair

tied up on top of her head, wearing a little crop trop and leggings that leave nothing to the imagination. She stops when she sees Lucas. I notice her eyes widen imperceptibly, obviously as taken by his good looks as I am. That makes me even more uneasy.

'Hello,' he says, almost coyly. 'I'm a friend of your dad's.'

Tasia just nods. She's used to the flow of strangers in our house, and to my relief she turns around to face me. 'I'm starving,' she says.

'In which case, you can set the table.'

She groans but does what I ask. 'What time are we eating?' Tasia asks as she removes cutlery from the drawer.

I glance at the clock on the wall. 'About ten minutes.' She sets the table haphazardly before she's out of the room.

'Your daughter looks just like you,' Lucas says.

'We've got two non-identical twins.' Grant laughs. 'Double trouble.'

'Goodness. I didn't realize you had twins.'

So they don't know each other well—or did I mention the twins to Lucas, and is he feigning the lack of knowledge? I don't think so, but Peggy might well have shared information about the girls, in which case he's lying. And where's the grieving, broken man gone? Has he even told Grant about Jade?

'Have a seat,' Grant says to Lucas, waving his hand towards the table. 'Just need to pop to the bathroom.' Grant places his beer on the table on his way out of the room.

The tension between Lucas and me is palpable. Rather than sitting down as Grant suggested, he places his beer on the counter and steps towards me, reaching his hands around my waist, pulling me towards him.

'No!' I whisper, panic mounting in my chest. 'Not here!'

He murmurs into my ear, his breath hot and tickling, 'Don't worry, I won't cause any problems. But you are looking completely beautiful this evening.' He releases me and steps backwards; his face is so full of longing, it creates a crazy storm in my stomach, a mixture of desire and terror. I can't even formulate any words, I'm so shocked by Lucas being here.

Grant's heavy footsteps give us plenty of warning that he's on his way back into the room, and by the time he steps into the kitchen, Lucas is seated at the table, nursing his beer, as if he's been there all along.

Grant shouts upstairs for the girls to come to the table, and we're all seated a couple of minutes later. Except I'm jittery as I serve the food—spilling dishes, barely articulating one-word answers when questions are thrown my way.

I need to get Lucas out of our home, but how?

THE CONVERSATION MOVES to elderly parents. Grant talks about his parents, who live in Vermont, about how one day we might retire there. I feel a pang of nostalgia for my parents, who are so far away in England.

'My mom lives alone,' Lucas says. 'Fortunately, a lovely local lady has been helping her out recently. I'm not sure what we'd do without her. She's truly an angel, a good Samaritan. I've suffered a bereavement recently, and she's been my rock.'

I realize I'm holding my breath, my fork of food hovering in midair, shaking slightly. I put it down on my plate, unable to look at Lucas. Fortunately, Grant's and the girls' eyes are on our guest and not on me. And what does he mean about being his rock? We haven't spoken a word since he asked me to meet up after learning about Jade's death.

'It's almost like she's becoming like a daughter to Mom.'

'How do you feel about that?' Grant asks. 'Is it a bit weird?'

Lucas laughs. 'No, not at all. I work all hours, so I'm grateful for all the help I can get, and it's perked Mom up enormously. What are the neighbors like around here?'

This conversation is making me feel physically sick. Lucas is toying with me, and I've no idea how to stop him. It's such a relief when the conversation turns away from Peggy.

'Are you alright, love?' Grant asks, placing a hand over mine.

'Yes, fine. Just had a rough day at work.'

'What is it you do?' Lucas asks.

I hesitate because Lucas knows perfectly well what I do. Fortunately, Grant answers for me, and the conversation drifts to the girls.

'It's Tasia and Arlyse?' he asks. They nod. 'I'm sure you get asked this all the time, but what's it like being a twin?'

Arlyse rolls her eyes very unsubtly.

'Hey,' I mutter.

'Sorry.' Lucas laughs. 'It's just quite novel for the rest of us, especially someone like me who doesn't have any siblings. Your dad says you're on a gap year. What are your plans?'

'I'm going to study marine conservation and hope to do a master's in Australia when I've finished my first degree. Arlyse is the clever one; she's going to be a doctor.'

'Sounds to me like you're both clever, but I guess with parents like yours...'

'Mom's only a florist,' Tasia says, which is cutting but true.

'But she runs her own business, doesn't she?' Lucas says. 'Entrepreneurship is something special. What do you girls do in your spare time? Do you ski?'

'We do,' Grant replies. 'But we don't get to the mountains enough. And you?'

'I'm a snowboarder,' he says. 'It's my big passion. I'm hoping to go to Switzerland next year and take part in some amateur competitions. Sadly, I'm too old to compete professionally.'

'I want to snowboard,' Tasia says, scraping her plate with her knife.

'Yeah, me too,' Arlyse adds.

'I can teach you.'

'Really?' The girls seem impressed while my heart sinks. The last thing I need is Lucas inveigling his way into our family life.

'I go to Waterville Valley over in New Hampshire. Do you know it? It's a good size, and there are plenty of slopes ideal for beginners. Perhaps we could go up there all together one weekend.'

'That's a great idea,' Grant says.

'Dad's only saying that because he's too mean to pay for us to have lessons, and I assume you won't charge to teach us,' Arlyse says.

'Rude but true,' Tasia says with a snigger. 'So, will you teach us?'

'With pleasure. Just let me know which weekend you're all free, and we'll put it in the calendar,' Lucas says with a smile. 'The sooner the better from my side.'

'It'll have to be soon because Tasia and I are off traveling in three weeks,' Arlyse says.

'I think we could manage that, don't you?' Grant adds, looking at me.

I try to plaster a grin on my face, but it feels forced and fake. 'Sure,' I say, but inside I'm thinking this is the worst possible idea and there is no way that I can let this happen. What the hell does Lucas think he's doing inserting himself into my life? It feels like the things I hold the most dear are being kept together by a gossamer thread, and Lucas has it within his power to snap it with the slightest gesture or a few choice words. I need to get him out of my house. Now.

I clear the table and remove an apple tart from the oven. Arlyse heads for the freezer and produces a large tub of ice cream. I serve everyone except myself, because if I eat another morsel, I will throw up.

'Are you alright, sweetheart?' Grant asks.

'Not really. I'm feeling a bit under the weather.'

'Do you want to go to bed, and the girls can help me tidy up?'

I'm not sure what to do. If I go to bed, how can I be sure that Lucas won't let something slip about me? But then I reason he could say something to Grant at the gym, but why would he? I can't fathom what game he's playing. He says he wants me, but is that just as a sexual plaything, or is he hoping that I'm going to leave Grant to be with him? None of this makes sense, and frankly, it terrifies me.

'It's fine, Mom,' Tasia says gently. 'We'll clear up. You go to bed.'

'Alright.' I give them all a weak smile.

'It was lovely to meet you,' Lucas says, standing up. I edge away from the table so he's out of reach. 'I hope we can meet again soon, perhaps take that trip to the mountains next weekend or the weekend after?' His eyes are boring into mine, and I'm sure that Grant or the girls are about to sense something, but then he suddenly sits down and mentions his training schedule days to Grant. I rush out of the room, and when I'm at the bottom of the stairs, I grip the banister, if only to keep my shaking legs still, but my stomach heaves, and I propel myself up the stairs, reaching the bathroom just in time to throw up.

I'M STILL awake when Grant comes to bed, but I pretend to be asleep. Being physically sick hasn't made me feel any better, and the churning spasms continue through the night as I toss and turn, unable to stop dissecting the evening.

The next morning, Grant is up and out before I've emerged from the shower. I'm too tired to bike to the Silken Stem, so I take my car.

Lesley arrives all breezy with glowing cheeks, wearing a pea green dress. Her bright mood is diametrically opposed to mine. She places her overflowing canvas bag on the table and removes her laptop.

'So?' she says, her eyes wide.

I frown.

'You were going to think about our expansion plans, get back to us on Matt's proposals.'

'Yes, and the thing is, I really don't want to be involved in some big business. We always said that we'd be happy if the Silken Stem gave us a decent income and a gentle life, and honestly, that hasn't changed for me.'

Lesley's smile slips off her face. 'I think that's a mistake.'

'I realize you're taken by Matt, that he's impressed you.'

'He's not just my boyfriend, Daniella. He's a really intelligent, successful businessperson.'

'I don't doubt that,' I say, although if truth be told, I find him a little too smooth and pleased with himself and suspect that he might talk the talk rather than walk the walk. 'But it's not about what Matt wants; this is our business and our future.'

'I realize this came as a surprise to you, but Matt's coming over later this morning. He's got some more projections, and I thought we could discuss it again. We could be millionaires, Dani. I know Grant has a good, solid salary, and you live in a lovely house, but I'm all alone, and I need to secure my future. Don't take this the wrong way, but it's not just about what you want.'

I grit my teeth because it's evident that Matt is on a brainwashing mission and sees us as a pathway to easy money, or alternatively, he's just trying to impress Lesley. What I don't really get is why he sees so much potential in our business. It's a solid little business, but to take it from what it is today to some global conglomerate is, frankly, pie in the sky. Besides, I'm really not in the right headspace to make any major decisions on the business, not while my thoughts are so utterly consumed by Lucas.

CHAPTER TWELVE

DANIELLA

The girls are home for the evening, and we're eating supper in the kitchen. 'How do you all feel about going to the mountains with Lucas this weekend?' Grant asks. He actually looks excited, which surprises me, because he's never shown much interest in skiing.

Oh no. I'd assumed that Lucas's offer of teaching the girls to snowboard was just him being polite. 'This weekend!' I frown, mentally trying to recall if there's anything in our calendar. Please let there be something vital that we can't get out of.

'Don't worry,' Grant says. 'I checked the online calendar, and we're all free unless either of you girls have a party or something we don't know about.' The four of us have a shared online calendar, although the girls only tend to include their work commitments rather than their social lives.

The twins glance at each other. 'Layla was talking about going to some new nightclub, but I'd rather go snowboarding,' Arlyse says.

'Yay, me too. Is Lucas going to be teaching us like he promised?' Tasia asks Grant.

I feel physically sick again. This can't be happening.

'That's the plan,' Grant replies. 'He's got some mate who rents out his cabin, so I've told Lucas to go ahead and book it. Apparently, it's ski-in ski-out too.'

'I'm not sure it's a good idea,' I add.

'Why on earth not?' Grant says. 'The girls want to go, don't you?' he asks them.

'Ergh, yes!' Arlyse exclaims. 'It'll be awesome. I can't believe you're finally letting us snowboard!'

It's not that Grant or I have stopped the girls, it's just that we've taken other holidays and haven't gotten around to a trip to the mountains for far too long. Panic starts to choke my throat, and I rub it with my hand. How can I get us out of this weekend away? I can't possibly be staying in the same cabin as Lucas with my family. What if he looks at me in that heated way or attempts to pull me into a hug like before? Or what if he lets something slip that he shouldn't know?

And why is Grant so keen for us to go away for a weekend with Lucas? It seems to me that Grant has become as hyped on the man as me, and that is the strangest situation for us to find ourselves in. No, strange isn't the right description; it's nauseatingly terrifying. I wonder if I should be honest with Grant and tell him that I slept with Lucas, that it was a onetime awful mistake. Except that would be a sure way to destroy our marriage and hurt my husband. But how the hell am I going to get out of this crazy situation? I could not go, but if I feign illness, I'm sure that Grant will cancel the weekend for everyone, and I can see how excited the girls are. And this is the last time for us all to be together before the twins go off on their trips. I don't understand why Lucas is ingratiating himself with our family. What is he trying to achieve? It doesn't make any sense to me.

It's like he enjoys playing this game of high-stakes poker, except the stakes are my marriage.

The next day, I try calling Lucas, except he doesn't answer the phone, and I don't leave a message. I try every day, but he never answers. I consider going to Peggy's house in the hope of cornering him there, but what would I say? And what if Peggy is there? It's not like I can ask him what he's doing in front of his mother. As I get increasingly worried, the twins and Grant become more and more excited.

The day before the trip, Grant returns from the gym sweaty and upbeat.

'Was Lucas training with you?' I ask, trying to make the question as casual as possible.

'Yes. There's no way I would be making this progress without him. I'm actually beginning to get abs.' Grant lifts up his T-shirt, except all I see is blotchy skin and a beer belly. 'He's a great trainer,' Grant says, allowing his shirt to fall back down. 'Perhaps you could join the gym too, and he could train you.'

I have to restrain myself from shivering or laughing manically at the suggestion.

The day of the trip, I pick up my phone, intending to leave a message on Lucas's phone, telling him to back off, except I chicken out at the last moment. If I upset Lucas, he's more likely to drop the bombshell and destroy my marriage. And so, I say nothing. Once again, I consider falling ill with some sickness, but even that option seems fraught with danger. It's bad enough that Lucas and Grant are hanging out together at the gym, but the thought of him with Arlyse and Tasia is equally concerning. Eventually, I decide it's better if I go. At least I can keep some control of the situation.

At 5:30 p.m. on Friday evening, our bags are packed, and the doorbell rings. Lucas is standing there, a large duffel bag at his feet.

'Hey, y'all. Ready for our adventure?'

Normally we have to cajole the girls to be ready on time, but this afternoon they're dressed in ski jackets and beanies, eager to pile everything into Grant's Yukon.

'Hey, mate,' Grant says, patting Lucas's back. I can't stop myself from tensing, seeing how buddy-buddy they are with each other.

'Good to see you again, Daniella,' Lucas says, throwing me that dazzling smile. 'Ready to hit the slopes?' He's acting as if he hasn't seen my multiple missed calls, and that makes me even more uncomfortable.

Thanks to having to navigate the evening traffic, the journey takes a good three hours, but we have plenty of sandwiches and cookies to munch on. Lucas and Grant chat happily in the front while the girls are engrossed in their headphones, leaving me to fret about the weekend ahead.

The weather turns for the worse as we approach the resort, with thick snowflakes drifting down and quickly coating the road. Grant is hunched over the steering wheel, always nervous driving in harsh conditions despite having lived in Boston all of his life.

'Not far to go now,' Lucas says cheerily.

Ten minutes later, we pull up in front of a wood cabin, an oversized lantern hanging over the porch, casting an orange glow on the snow-covered drive, smoke drifting out of the chimney. It looks alpine and cozy, and I wish I could relax and enjoy the surroundings. Except I can't. Not when I'm in such close proximity to the tinderbox that is Lucas.

'This is so cute!' Tasia exclaims, swinging open the car door and letting in a blast of cold air. I follow the others up to the front door, our boots making prints in the fresh snow. Lucas produces a key from a key safe and opens the door.

'Your humble abode for the weekend,' he says, standing back as we traipse through into the wood-lined hallway.

'This is lovely,' Grant says, and I have to agree. The living room and kitchen are open plan, with a large roaring fire in a glass stove, accessible from all four sides. All the walls are covered in rustic wood, and there's a wide picture window, which I assume looks out onto the pine forest that surrounds the cabin. I try to peer through into the darkness beyond, the snow reflecting light into the glass, making it hard to see.

'There are three bedrooms, all en-suite,' Lucas says.

That's a relief, as I really wouldn't want to be sharing a bathroom with him. Completely inappropriate images of a threesome pop into my mind, and I shake my head to banish them. I need to get a grip.

'I thought we should get an early night so we can be at the ski rental shop first thing and then hit the slopes.'

'Good idea,' Grant confirms.

We all go to bed a short time later, but I can't sleep. All I can think about is how Lucas is lying in bed on the other side of the wall, how he could so easily destroy my world. Yet he seems completely benign and jovial, friendly with Grant, joking with the girls. I want to get up to make myself a hot drink except what if he hears me and comes out? What if he puts his arms around me and tugs me to his bed and ravishes me with my family just inches away? No, I can't think like that. It's shameful. I continue to toss and turn, and at some point, I must drift off to sleep because I awaken to the sound of the shower running and a pale light seeping into the room.

To my surprise, I'm the last one to breakfast. The girls, dressed in their base layers, are munching and chatting away to Lucas.

'Are you going to try snowboarding too?' Lucas asks me.

'Absolutely not,' I reply. I'm a mediocre skier, having only been on a handful of ski trips, and I've no desire to try something new—especially something that might leave me, at best, with a bruised backside and, at worst, with broken limbs. In addition, I need to keep my distance from Lucas. I try not to imagine his hands around my waist as he tries to get me to stand upright on a snowboard. No. I'm definitely sticking to skis.

'Go on, Mom!' Tasia says. 'Dad's going to give it a go.'

'Are you?' I turn to look at Grant. My cerebral husband has never been that interested in sports or trying anything new.

'Lucas has promised he'll get me boarding confidently down the green runs by the end of the day.'

I raise an eyebrow. My husband seems to be completely in Lucas's thrall, which is weird and disconcerting. Grant has always been the teacher in our household, and now he's submissively allowing Lucas to take on that role. It doesn't sit well with me.

THE WEATHER COULDN'T BE MORE perfect for our day of snow sports. It's cold, well below freezing, but the sky is blue and the air completely still. After collecting our rented gear, we head for the lifts, our breaths making little puffs as we join the line. Lucas suggests that we start on some green, beginner runs in the Lower Meadows, so we take a rather rickety two-man chairlift to the top of the slope. The four of them click their boots into their snowboard bindings. While the girls have no trouble standing up, Grant can barely stay upright. Lucas starts instructing them what to do and how to move their body weight. Meanwhile, I'm getting cold just standing and watching.

'I think I'll head down the slope and come and find you in an hour or so.'

'Sounds good, but go carefully,' Grant says.

'We'll still be on these slopes,' Lucas adds.

I do a couple of easy runs, careful to make regular turns and, as best I can, avoid other skiers. I love the sensation, breathing in the cold air as it rushes past, the weak rays of sun on my face and the crunching noise the snow makes underneath my skis. I'm a better skier than I remember, but still, I'm wary. Accidents can happen so easily. At the base station, I unclip my skis, leaning them up against a stand, and find a coffee shop, where I stomp inside with my heavy boots and order a hot chocolate.

After warming myself up and doing a bit of people watching, I'm ready to head back up the slopes.

I spot them halfway down the slope and wave frantically from the chairlift, but only Lucas sees me. He raises a gloved hand in greeting.

When I reach them, Grant is on his backside with Lucas trying to help him to stand up.

'Look, Mom!' Arlyse shouts. I watch her and Tasia make several confident turns as they head down the trail. I'm impressed. I thought the girls would pick up snowboarding easily, but this exceeds my expectations. Grant, on the other hand, is struggling.

Not sure what I can do to help him, I head down to join the girls.

'Lucas is the best teacher!' Arlyse says. 'He's really cool. Get him to show you how he jumps.'

Ten minutes later, the men still haven't appeared, and I'm getting cold. 'Are you happy to head down to the bottom with me and we'll wait for Dad and Lucas there?' I suggest.

The girls nod, and I follow them to the end of the run. Tasia falls over once, but otherwise they're confident and capable.

Twenty minutes later, the men still haven't appeared, and I'm getting nervous. What if Grant has seriously hurt himself? Or what if Lucas hasn't been the caring teacher he promised to be? I'm just about to suggest we head back up on the chairlift when I spot them. Lucas is boarding backwards, holding onto Grant's arms. There's a look of terror on my husband's face. Considering they're negotiating a super-easy slope, it's almost comical. Eventually, they are level with us, and Grant collapses onto the snow.

'Get this damn thing off me,' he growls. 'I'm returning to skis.'

The girls find this hilarious. 'Dad is really shit at snowboarding,' Tasia snorts.

'Some people find it difficult,' Lucas says, but he's clearly trying to stop himself from laughing at his new friend.

'My thighs and backside will be battered black and blue,'

Grant says. 'I'm going to have a hot toddy, and I'll exchange this board for skis. I'll catch up with you later.'

I don't want to be left alone with Lucas and the girls. 'Would you like me to come back with you?' I ask.

Grant gives me a confused look. 'No, you stay out and enjoy yourself.'

Lucas throws me his dazzling smile, and my stomach lurches.

LUCAS DECIDES that the girls are ready for a slightly harder slope, so we take another chairlift higher up the mountain. It's a three-person lift, so I'm hopeful that I won't be alone with Lucas, except when we shuffle forwards to get on it, the girls go first, and no one else appears next to us, leaving him and me to go alone.

'Well, this is cozy,' Lucas says once the lift has risen up above the trees. He edges closer to me, the chairlift wobbling a little too violently for my liking. 'Relax,' he says, giving me a shoulder nudge.

I don't say anything, too aware of his presence right next to me.

'I'm sorry I didn't answer the phone this week. It's been crazy on my end. The business with Jade, well, it hit me hard. Were you calling for any particular reason?'

'No,' I reply, and then, finding myself mellowing, I ask, 'How are you? After what happened with Jade?'

I can't bring myself to look at him, but I'm so aware of the heat of him, the way his upper thigh touches mine, that scent of aftershave mixed in with sunscreen.

'Trying to put a brave face on things, but truthfully, it's been horrendous. It's not like I loved her anymore, but we were together for a year, and all my exes mean something to me. I'm just sad for her, that's all.'

'Of course you are,' I say. I wonder if he feels guilty, whether I'm complicit in her death too, except I can't formulate the words to ask the question.

We're both silent for a while, until I feel Lucas's breath on my face and he whispers, 'Keeping my hands off you is one of the hardest things I've ever had to do.'

I flinch and edge away from him, but he still manages to find my gloved hand and gives it a squeeze.

'Don't worry. I would never do anything in front of your girls or your husband.'

But his just articulating that fills me with panic. I have no idea what to say next, so we dismount the lift in silence.

The girls are waiting for us, already clipped into their boards. 'Right,' Lucas says. 'Let's take this slope slowly and easily.' He rolls his shoulders and flexes his head from left to right. 'This is a step up from the previous slope, so I want you to follow me exactly. Turn when I turn, okay?'

There are a few tumbles on the way down, but we all make it. Lucas is indeed impressive on a snowboard, jumping over moguls on the side of the slope, boarding backwards to help the girls down.

'I'm starving,' Tasia says when we're at the bottom.

'Me too,' Lucas adds. 'Time to grab a bite?'

I send Grant a message telling him where we're going for lunch, and we find Grant outside the restaurant, leaning against a wall, his face slanted towards the sun.

'Hey,' Lucas says. 'Feeling happier about skiing?'

'I certainly am. You're not getting me on that board again.' Grant pats his pair of orange and white rental skis, and both men laugh.

As we lean my skis and their snowboards up against a stand, Lucas's phone rings. Strangely, he doesn't answer the phone, but then it rings again just a few seconds later. He sighs. This time, he tugs off his gloves and pulls out his phone, his forehead creasing when he sees who's calling.

'What's up?' he answers the phone curtly.

'Really? Hospital?' Now he looks worried. 'Right, keep me posted.'

'Is everything alright?' I ask as he shoves his phone back into his jacket pocket.

'Mom's not feeling well. We'll see.'

A flash of worry goes through me. I would hate for something to happen to Peggy.

INSIDE, the restaurant is heaving with people, and the line for food is long. It takes a while for us to buy our hamburgers and drinks and find a table. But as we start munching, Lucas's phone rings yet again. He scowls as he removes it from his pocket.

'What now?'

His face pales, and he stands up, pushing his chair backwards with a scraping motion, and he steps away before turning his back on us and striding quickly out of the restaurant.

'What's all that about?' Grant says.

'I think his mother is unwell.' I don't say anything about Peggy, about the fact that the woman I've been helping out is, in fact, Lucas's mother. That Peggy who came for Sunday lunch is Lucas's mother. I've left it too long. I should have said something when Peggy came for lunch, and I most definitely should have said something the moment Lucas walked into our kitchen. Except I was so dumbstruck, so consumed with guilt, I clammed up. And now? I've dug myself such a deep hole I'm not sure I'll ever be able to climb out of it. I'm so stupid. This awful situation is one hundred percent of my own making, and it consumes me with guilt and worry.

Lucas doesn't return, which is weird. Curiosity getting the better of me, I tell my family I'm heading for the toilets. I weave through the tables, avoiding helmets and poles, stray gloves and puddles of melted snow. I spot him standing outside. I hesitate for a moment, but then he swivels around and sees me. He stomps back inside.

'Is everything alright?'

His face looks like thunder. 'No. Mom is ill and going to the hospital. I need to head back to Boston.'

'Oh, goodness, I'm so sorry,' I say.

His eyes seem strangely cold, his lips pursed in a thin, pale line. I've only ever seen the relaxed, charming side of Lucas. I tell myself that this look is one of disappointment combined with worry. Of course he'll be worried sick about Peggy.

'I'll collect my stuff from the cabin before I head off.'

'How will you get back to Boston?'

'You offering to drive?'

I hesitate because the answer is clearly no. I don't see why the girls should have to cut their weekend short because of Lucas.

He rolls his eyes. 'Of course not,' he says sharply. 'I'll rent a car.'

'I'm really sorry, Lucas,' I add again.

His voice comes out gentler this time, and his face softens. 'Me too. More than you can possibly know.'

'Will you let me know how Peggy is?' I ask.

'Sure. You'd best be getting back to finish your lunch. Apologize to your...' He waves his hand at me.

I nod and return to our table. When I glance over my shoulder to look at him, Lucas has disappeared.

It strikes me when I'm nearly back at our table that he could have said goodbye to Grant and the girls, that he didn't even ask me to apologize. But then again, he's probably in shock, worried for his lovely mother. When I explain that Lucas had to leave suddenly, my family is genuinely dismayed.

'He's definitely the coolest of all your friends,' Arlyse says.

'It's a bit off that he didn't come to say goodbye,' Grant adds.

'I think he's in shock,' I explain, wondering why I'm covering for Lucas.

'And now we've lost our teacher,' Tasia moans.

'Maybe you could take a class tomorrow morning,' I suggest. But the mood has shifted, and we finish the meal in silence.

TWENTY MINUTES OR SO LATER, we're ready to hit the slopes again.

'Let's do another couple of runs, and then we'll call it a day. Don't want to overdo it,' Grant says.

The girls seem disappointed, but nevertheless, we pick up our equipment and head back up on the chairlift. The girls, with their boards, go on the chair in front of us, and I ease into the chair next to Grant, feeling so much lighter now that Lucas has gone.

'Shame about his mother,' Grant says, as if he can read my thoughts.

The chairlift moves upwards until we're above the tree-line. The sun rays are weak, but the view is stunning. 'This is lovely, isn't it?' Grant says unexpectedly, putting an arm around my shoulders. He's right, it is. I think about my conversation on intimacy with Linda and wonder whether in different circumstances, this weekend might have been exactly what we needed.

The chair is descending, and we're just yards from the end when Grant shifts slightly—and then, to both of our dismay, his left ski literally drops off the bottom of his boot, hurtling to the ground, narrowly missing a skier.

'What the hell!' Grant exclaims, staring in horror as the ski slams into the snow. We're approaching the end of the lift, and Grant shouts, waving his arms at the lift attendant, who quickly realizes what's going on. The chairlift slows down dramatically, and the attendant is right there as we come to a complete halt. Our girls are waiting for us just to the side.

'My ski fell off!' Grant exclaims. 'I've only just rented them from the shop. How can that have happened?'

'The bindings weren't on properly, I guess,' the attendant says, helping Grant to his feet. Grant shuffles off to one side, sliding his right ski and hopping with his booted left foot. We wait at the side as the lift attendant restarts the lift. He then strides over to join us.

'That could have resulted in a really serious accident. You need to be more careful.'

'But it's not my fault. I told you, I just picked the skis up from the rental place,' Grant says.

'Which shop was that?'

'Ski Rite down in the village.'

'My cousin runs that place. Did they check the skis, put your boots in, ask for your height and weight?'

'Yes, all of that. They did a proper check from what I can tell.'

'Then someone has tampered with your bindings.'

'But who would do that?' Grant asks.

The attendant shrugs. 'We'll have to send a patroller to collect your ski. You're lucky no one was hurt; otherwise, you'd be facing one hefty lawsuit. If you wait here, I'll call for assistance.'

It takes half an hour for Grant to be repatriated with his ski, and then another few long minutes for the ski patrol guy to adjust the bindings and make sure everything is safe.

'Do you really think they were tampered with?' Grant asks.

The patroller shrugs his shoulders. 'Said you hired them off Ski Rite?' he asks.

'Yes.'

'No idea what's happened other than, sure as hell, the guys at Ski Rite wouldn't adjust one ski properly and forget to do the other one. Did you watch them do the adjustments?'

'Yes, I did,' Grant says. 'But I wasn't paying that much attention.'

'There's just no way they'd let you out the way this baby has or, rather, hasn't been adjusted. Anyway, you're good to go now.'

By this time, we're all freezing cold and just want to get back to the cabin for hot baths.

All four of us tumble as we make our way down the slope. No major injuries, but that initial bravado and enjoyment has dissipated. All I can think about is... Grant could have had a serious accident.

Has someone tampered with his ski? My mind flits to Lucas. He wouldn't have done something like that, would he? No, surely not. He's only been kind towards my family, and besides, he was in too much of a hurry to get back to Boston.

CHAPTER THIRTEEN

PEGGY

I know how he'll be. Lucas will be bursting with rage and worry by the time he reaches home. He's tried calling me on multiple occasions, but I'm not answering the phone. I suppose he'll have visions of me wired up to equipment in intensive care or lying cold and dead in a hospital mortuary. He'll have called all the hospitals, and then, realizing there's no one called Margaret or Peggy Denman, perhaps he'll think I'm unconscious or dead on the living room floor, unable to call 911, waiting and waiting for him to get home. The thing is, I genuinely felt extremely unwell. I'm sure it's the diabetes, which causes problems when I forget to take my medication, and then I panic. I need Lucas. Of course, I wish I hadn't had to disturb his little weekend, but despite everything, I'm fearful of dying. Especially alone.

When I see the headlights turn into our drive, I stand to the side of the window to peek out. He's driving a cute little orange rental car, which no doubt he'll despise. It skids to a halt, and I hurry back to sit in my chair, the television on, my knitting on my lap.

'Mom!' Lucas shouts.

'In here.' My voice is strong but still wobbles slightly as I anticipate what's going to come.

'What the hell!' he exclaims, his mouth dropping open as he sees me sitting as normal in my favorite upright chair.

'Good to see you, dear,' I say.

'What the fuck, Mother! You called me to say that you're dying, about to go to the hospital, that I need to race back to the city to be with you, and then I arrive and you're sitting here.' He's waving his hands around like a lunatic, his face flushed bright red with fury, his eyes flashing wildly. My heart speeds up, but I remind myself to remain calm.

'I'm sorry, Lucas. I knew you'd be angry at first, but I really did feel very unwell.' I put my knitting on the side table and lever myself upright. 'Why don't I warm you up some lovely homemade soup?'

'I don't want any soup!' he yells. 'I want to know why you've ruined my trip.'

'Take a deep breath, Lucas,' I say.

I know my boy, and I sense that he wants to throttle me. I see how his fingers curl into fists and how all the color drains from his cheeks. I need to get out of here. Forgetting the pain in my leg, I scurry into the kitchen, leaving Lucas in the living room.

'They were all falling in love with me!' he shouts. 'And I was spending time with Daniella.'

Slowly, I pour the hot soup into a bowl and find a spoon, then I butter a piece of freshly baked bread. As I walk back into the living room holding the tray, hobbling without my cane, I see feathers scattered across the floor and on the sofa, and shreds of fabric from my pillow lie discarded on the carpet. Lucas sits on the sofa, his head in his hands.

'You ruined everything,' Lucas spits as I carry the tray to the table. I place it down gently and pop a napkin on Lucas's knee. He scrunches it up and chucks it to the side.

'Oh, love. No, I didn't,' I say, sitting down again and ignoring my son's temper tantrum. 'You'll have plenty of time to spend with Daniella and those beautiful, clever girls. I wouldn't have called you back if I hadn't felt really unwell.'

'Why couldn't you have just called the doctor?!' he hisses. 'Probably because you're an old hypochondriac. How will I ever trust you again when you cry wolf? Everything was going perfectly for me, and, as usual, you had to ruin it.' Lucas narrows his eyes at me, and for a moment, I see his father.

'Take a breath, love,' I say. 'You're my son, and I'd do anything for you; you know that, but you need to learn patience.' I glance at the scattered feathers and shreds of fabric on the floor and see the evidence of his uncontrollable fury. 'I can get you help. You've resisted it previously, or more to the point, I've tried to ignore it. Except it's not doing either of us any good pretending that everything's alright. I love you, my son, and I want to get you help. Make sure that you're choosing the right partner in life.'

He stares at me as if I'm a complete stranger, and I shiver involuntarily.

'Where the hell has all of this nonsense come from?' he scoffs.

'You can carry on getting angry, and heaven knows, you'll likely end up in jail for punching someone, or we can sort all of this out once and for all.'

'I'm not a project,' Lucas says.

'Of course you're not. You're the person I love most in the world, and I've spent all of these years trying to protect you. Except you hurt the people you claim to love the most. I know you don't mean to.'

'The thing is, Mom, I really love Daniella. She's my soulmate. I knew it from the moment I set eyes on her. And she feels it too. I already told you that. Don't you want me to be happy?'

I'm silent, my eyes on my house slippers.

'Do you believe me?' Lucas asks, his voice so very loud.

I find it hard to conceal a shiver. 'I believe that's what you think,' I reply eventually. 'And of course I want you to be happy, more than anything else in the world.'

'Me and Daniella are meant for each other. She's the only person who can make me happy.'

When I glance up, Lucas is staring at me with such hatred in his eyes. Veins are popping on his neck and temple, and his fists are tightly curled. I know all the signs. I have to get away. Now.

'It'll be alright,' I say in an artificially smooth voice. Inside me, my guts are knotting with terror. I stand up, nerves making me unsteady on my feet. Lucas also gets up.

'Let's take a deep breath and focus on that,' I say, except no words will calm my son now. I've gone too far.

Lucas's breath is coming out in short, shallow gasps, and every muscle in his body is wired. I've seen him bad, but not quite like this. I know he won't mean to hurt me, except that he is so big, so strong now, a result of all the time he spends in the gym.

I turn as quickly as I can, my slipper catching on the edge of the rug. I steady myself by gripping onto the back of the sofa, and then grab my cane before hurrying as fast as I can out of the living room. Lucas is right behind me, his breath hot and damp on the back of my neck, his body vibrating so much that the air is humming all around me. I glance over my shoulder and see that he's holding one of my knitting needles. Fear propels me through the pain in my ankle, and I'm running now, heading towards the bathroom.

'It'll all be fine,' I say breathlessly, although this time I really doubt my words.

'Mother!' Lucas yells. Normally, I'd come to a halt and turn around, my face contorted into a warm smile, my arms out wide to embrace the small child in my adult son. Except today, I've left it too late. I hurtle towards the bathroom door, praying, just praying that I can slip inside quickly and bolt it behind me, giving myself a couple of minutes at least to try to climb out the window. I hear a phone ringing from far away and just pray that will distract him. Except, as I throw myself into the room, I know in my heart of hearts that I've left it too late.

CHAPTER FOURTEEN

DANIELLA

Although the girls and Grant seem deflated, I can relax for the first time this weekend. It's a relief that Lucas has gone, that we're just the four of us again. We organize a lesson on Sunday morning for the girls, but both Grant and I have lost our mojo for skiing. His near-accident has made him nervous, and when he falls one time too many, having already got bruises galore on his backside and thighs thanks to the snowboarding, we decide to call it a day. By midday, the weather has turned, the clouds descend, and it's sleeting. Unanimously, we agree to head back home.

AFTER A LONG JOURNEY, none of us feels like cooking, so I take a large pizza from the freezer and put it in the oven. We're all weary, but the girls loved snowboarding, and I'm glad we took the time to go away, even if it was with Lucas.

We're seated at the kitchen table, tucking into the pizza and talking about the potential house move.

'Are you sure you girls won't mind?' I ask.

'So long as we've both got a bedroom wherever you move to,' Arlyse says. 'Where are you thinking, anyway?'

'Somewhere a bit further up the coast,' Grant says. 'Your mom would like to be by the ocean. I'd rather have some countryside, a few fields maybe for some livestock.'

'You keeping animals?' Arlyse roars with laughter.

Grant pulls a face.

'I think you should start talking to Realtors, get the ball rolling,' Grant suggests. 'We need to know how much this place is worth and how much cash we'll have to buy somewhere new.'

'I can do that,' I say, with a frisson of excitement. Perhaps Grant and I can really take advantage of this new stage in our lives. Just as I'm mentally working out which agents I could contact, the doorbell chimes.

'I'll go,' Tasia says, standing up. 'Maybe it's Lucas.'

I sincerely hope it isn't. I haven't received any message from him regarding Peggy, and the single message I sent him appears to be unread. I fear the worst. I did ask Grant if he'd heard from Lucas, but the answer was also no. Actually, I think Grant's nose is still slightly out of joint because Lucas didn't say goodbye.

A couple of moments later, to my great relief, I hear female voices.

'Oh, sorry to disturb.'

It's Lesley.

'Is everything alright?' I ask, visions of some catastrophe happening to the shop.

'Yes, fine. I've got something exciting I want to tell you, but I can come back when you've finished eating.'

I can't recall a single time Lesley has just shown up at

our house. Of course she's been here on numerous occasions, but always when I've invited her. Here in Boston, it's not like back at home in the UK when we had keys to each other's apartments. There's a formality, and it's unsettling that Lesley has broken that unspoken rule. Besides, it's a Sunday evening, a day neither of us work, and these days, we don't socialize much.

'Would you like a glass of wine?' Grant asks.

'No, it's kind of you. I'll just wait in the living room, shall I, until you've finished?'

'No need,' I say, looking at the morsels of pizza still on my plate. 'I've had enough. Let's go together.'

I lead Lesley into the living room, turning on the lights and indicating for her to sit down. With a jolt, I recall what Lucas and I did on the floor here, and shame washes through me.

'What's going on?' I ask, trying to sound bright even though I'm exhausted.

Her face lights up, and she wrings her hands together. 'Matt has the opportunity to sign a lease in New York.'

'A lease for what?' I don't follow her and knot my eyebrows together.

'He wants to invest in the Silken Stem, and he's found a storefront that's absolutely perfect on a crazily good value lease. It's a once-in-a-lifetime opportunity, Daniella.'

The hyperbole is too much. I shake my head as if I'm trying to stop the dizziness. 'New York? This is getting out of hand!' I say. 'I don't want to move to New York, do you? And where's the money going to come from? We're making a profit, but we don't have enough to set up a new shop in New York or anywhere.'

Lesley stands up and starts pacing the living room.

'Matt's going to put up the money in return for a third of our equity. That way we don't need to eat into our savings, and we'll find someone to run it, and train them up here in Boston first.'

'You're not listening to me,' I say. It feels as if Lesley is about to give away our shared child without allowing me the chance to explore whether I'm comfortable with it. 'I don't want to expand; I don't want an investor.'

'But it isn't always about what you want,' Lesley says, waving her arms around so that her multiple bangles clatter. 'You're all settled with your family and your lovely home. I've got no one.'

'Seems like you have Matt.'

She flushes. 'You know what I mean. I have to think about my future, my retirement.'

'And me too.'

'So why won't you consider it?'

'Because I'm happy with the status quo. I don't believe that there's some pot of gold at the end of Matt's rainbow. Rapid expansion is never sustainable.'

'Oh, you're the brilliant businesswoman now, are you? I think Matt has a little more experience than you do!'

That's cutting, and as I know nothing concrete about this Matt, I can't respond.

'Just sell your share to Matt, then,' Lesley says. 'I'll find someone else who can make pretty flower arrangements. I'm sure they're a dime a dozen.'

I stare at my friend, open-mouthed. Lesley has never been cruel to me before; in fact, I can't recall when we've had a major argument.

'And what if I don't want to sell?'

We stare at each other, but I'm the one to look away first. I can't believe my oldest friend and I are having this fight.

'I think we should do some more due diligence into Matt,' I say eventually. 'What do you actually know about him?'

'That he's a brilliant man with a great success record. You haven't even given him a chance.'

'Because you've sprung this on me. A week ago, we were pottering along quite happily, and then suddenly you want us to sell a third of our business to a stranger, to open a new shop in New York, like, tomorrow. This isn't sensible behavior.'

'I knew you'd twist things.' Lesley scowls. 'If this opportunity passes us by, I don't think I'll be able to forgive you. You need to do the right thing by me and by the business.'

I scoff. 'So why don't I count? Why doesn't my fifty percent matter and all the hours I've put into our shared venture?'

'This is typical of you, isn't it?' Lesley snarls. She opens her mouth as if she's going to say something but then, at the last moment, changes her mind. 'Sometimes I wonder why we're even friends, let alone business partners.'

'I don't recognize you, Lesley,' I say, which is indeed the truth. 'I don't know what this Matt has done to you, but I don't like the person he's turning you into.'

She narrows her eyes at me and then grabs her bag before stomping out of the living room. I listen as she slams the front door behind her. I watch from behind the curtains as she strides to the end of our drive and disappears.

A few moments later, Grant appears.

'What's going on?' he asks. He puts his hands on my shoulders. 'You're shaking, Daniella.'

'I've just had a massive bust-up with Lesley. She wants her boyfriend to have a third of our business in return for investing in a New York store. It's the last thing I want to do.'

'It sounds crazy. What do we even know about this man?'

'Nothing. I've met him once. That's exactly my point.'

'In which case, you need to stand your ground. You know I'll support you, don't you?'

'Yes,' I say as I throw my arms around my husband. I lean into him and count my blessings that I still have my rock. I feel like I don't deserve him, but I'm going to work to atone for what I've done with Lucas.

'If we're going to move away from Boston, then perhaps this is good timing. You could sell your share of the business and retire.'

'Retire!' I exclaim. 'I'm not an old woman.'

'No, I wasn't suggesting you were, but you could have an easier life.'

'Out of the question,' I retort. 'But perhaps I'll set up my own florist shop and move back into real flowers.'

'Then Matt could be good for you.'

I say nothing because I feel like Lesley is forcing my hand. And even if we do move away, it doesn't mean I have to sell my share of the Silken Stem. I could commute like Grant will or employ someone to take my place and just work a day or two a week. I want the future of our business to be on both of our terms.

CHAPTER FIFTEEN

DANIELLA

Everything feels so precarious. My marriage, which I'm in danger of breaking, and my business, which was my security, is now also in jeopardy. Since we got back from skiing, I've been busy with Realtors. Three agents valued the house within twenty-four hours of me contacting them. It seems that houses such as ours rarely come on the market, and there's a great demand for them. My only concern is I haven't started to look for somewhere new to live, but for now, I'm running with it.

Of the three valuations, I've chosen the agent who gave us the middle price. The Realtor, Andrea Johnson, is a similar age to me, and I warmed to her on our first meeting. She didn't eulogize over our house but exuded a quiet confidence. On top of that, she promised to show the house herself rather than palm it off on a junior member of her team. After agreeing on a listing price and the commission, I gave her the go-ahead. She said it would take a couple of weeks to get everything sorted, but then she called me to say that her photographer had a cancellation and would be ready to take photos sooner than she anticipated. So there I was, racing around the house, trying to tidy everything up, cleaning like a dervish.

The photos are great, and now she's planning an open house. It's my first experience with this, and I'm nervous.

On top of everything, the twins are getting ready to go away on their trip to South America. It's midmorning, and both girls are home, trying to pack for their trips. They've finished their respective holiday jobs, and tomorrow they leave for their adventures.

'Mom, where are my Lululemon leggings, the ones Gran gave me for my birthday?' Tasia shouts through the house. She's quite capable of looking herself, and under normal circumstances I'd tell her that, but it's tearing me apart to realize that soon the house will be empty. Sighing, I trudge to the utility room and look through the pile of clean laundry that I've just taken out of the dryer. I find the leggings, at least I think they're the right ones, and carry them upstairs to Tasia's room.

A huge rucksack is lying on her bed, with piles of clothes on either side. The mirror image is in Arlyse's bedroom, although she's the neater of the twins, and I doubt she'll need my help with packing.

'Are you taking all of this?' I ask, unable to quell the edge of disapproval in my voice. There isn't a hope in hell she'll fit it all in.

'Yeah.' She takes the leggings from me and rolls them up into a tight ball, wedging them deep inside the rucksack.

'Have you got your personal safety alarm and money belt?'

Tasia rolls her eyes at me. 'You need to stop worrying, Mom. We're going to be fine.'

It's easy for her to say that. I tell myself that I have to let them go, that they're young adults now who have worked hard through school and deserve the chance to spread their wings. Both girls are sensible and ambitious, enrolled in proper gap-year programs, so I'm sure they'll be fine. It's just hard not to think about all the things that could go wrong, how some young people go off on their travels and never return. We've had the chats about drugs and safe sex and only drinking out of their own water bottles, but even so, I'm finding it impossible not to worry. I won't see my daughters for three whole months—the longest by far that we've been apart.

'Let me know if you need any help,' I say lamely, and turn to leave Tasia to it.

'Don't you have to go to work?' she shouts after me.

I laugh and look at her over my shoulder. 'Are you trying to get me out of the house?'

She blows me a kiss. 'Something like that.'

'Who's coming over?'

'Just Patty and Laura.'

'Alright, but finish off the packing before they get here. And try not to create too much of a mess in the house,' I add.

Tasia blows me a kiss. How I'll miss this banter. The only upside is, we have our open house this weekend, and now that the girls have packed up, it will be easier to keep the place tidy.

GRANT and I take the twins to Boston Logan International Airport together. Their flights are within an hour of each other. We stand by as they check in their bulging rucksacks, making sure that they are both wearing money belts and have their phones and passports. My whole body is taut, and my heart feels as if it's cracking. I'm trying very hard to keep the tears in check. When it's time to say goodbye, I can't hold in the sensation of desolation anymore. I'm utterly bereft. Grant has to peel me off the girls, and with tears running down my cheeks, I'm barely able to speak through the sobs.

'We're only going away for three months,' Tasia says, laughing. That's both the blessing and the problem with youth. They're oblivious to all the potential things that could go wrong.

'I know,' I mutter through the tears. 'But this is just the first step, and you'll never really be living at home again. It's a big deal.'

'Your mom's a worrywart,' Grant says, flinging an arm around me.

'Please stay in touch,' I say. 'And don't switch off your tracking apps.'

'They might not work where we're going,' Arlyse replies.

'Well, just drop us a text every day that you can. But most of all, have a fantastic time.' Grant smiles at the twins. And then the girls turn their backs on us and stride through the security barriers without once looking back.

'It's a rite of passage,' Grant tries to reassure me. 'They'll be fine.'

The truth is nothing feels fine. The twins are gone, and my marriage is on shaky ground. I'm worried about Peggy too. It was so strange the way Lucas bolted, and I fear Peggy might have been taken ill or have fallen again. Although I want to keep my distance from Lucas, I've called Peggy a couple of times, and each time she doesn't answer her phone and it goes straight to voicemail. I leave messages. I worry about Bippie too. Lucas seems attentive around his mother but less so about the dog. I recall him telling me how he prefers cats to dogs. I would stop in on Ivy Street if I could be sure Lucas wasn't there, but under the circumstances, I can't take the risk.

I haven't been into work since my argument with Lesley either, so that's another concern. I've used the excuse of needing to help the girls pack, and having to tidy up the house prior to our open house, but the truth is I can't face seeing Lesley after our argument. Except I'm going to have to talk to her sometime soon, and I'm behind on making up orders.

ON SATURDAY MORNING, the house looks the neatest I've ever seen it. I put bunches of flowers from the Silken Stem in vases dotted around the house, a fire is roaring in the fireplace, and the scent of freshly brewed coffee weaves through the downstairs rooms. I'd buy this house if I saw it looking like this. Pleased with myself, I get changed and then wait for Andrea Johnson so I can have a word with her before I leave. She told me the first viewers would arrive around 10 a.m., and she was hopeful that she'd have a steady crowd during the next four hours. Except 10 a.m. comes and goes, and Andrea doesn't turn up. I don't want to leave our house unattended, so I keep an eye on the window that looks over the driveway at the front, and there's no one here. I check the date and double-check her last email to me. It definitely says the open house is this morning.

At 10:15, I call Andrea. She doesn't answer her phone, and it goes straight to voicemail. That's really weird. Feeling unsettled, I go onto her website. Except I can't find a listing for our house. It was definitely on her website a couple of days ago. I try calling her again, and still there's no answer. By 10:30, I sense something has gone very wrong. Either I've got my dates mixed up, or she has. I stomp into the kitchen and blow out the candles on the island. I try calling Grant, but he doesn't pick up either.

At 10:36, my phone rings. It's Andrea.

'Where is everyone?' I ask before she can speak.

There's a long pause.

'I'm sorry, what do you mean, Mrs. Morris?'

'I got this place looking spick-and-span for the open house, and no one is here!' My voice sounds shrill.

'I received a phone call from your husband canceling the open house and telling me that you were removing the property from the market.'

'What?' I exclaim. 'No, that can't be right!'

'Mr. Morris told me that...' She clears her throat before speaking again. 'You were having marital difficulties, and although you wanted to sell, he didn't. And as the house is in his name, you don't have the authority to sell it.'

I am dumbstruck. Grant wouldn't do that, would he? He knew I was manically cleaning for the open house when he left this morning, so he would have said something to me. This makes no sense whatsoever. 'You must have the wrong property,' I say eventually.

'No, I definitely don't.'

'I'll speak to my husband and get him to call you,' I mutter.

'Well, I'm sorry for any mix-up, but it would be helpful to get clarification from Mr. Morris. And if you wish to withdraw it from the market, then I need it in writing, please.'

'Yes, but no. We don't want to withdraw it.'

There's a long, awkward pause before I say, 'I'll be back in touch.'

I CALL Grant repeatedly until he eventually picks up about fifteen minutes later. He sounds breathless. 'What's up, love? I've got all these missed calls from you.'

'Did you cancel the open house and tell Andrea Johnson we're removing the house from the market?'

'No,' he replies. I can hear weights clanking in the background, so he must be at the gym. 'Of course not.'

'And is the house in your name only?'

'Um, yes, I think it is. But what is all this about?'

'Andrea Johnson says you called her and said we were having marriage problems and you didn't want to sell the house.'

'But that's nonsense. I haven't called her.' There's consternation in his voice now, which gives me an iota of relief. 'There must have been some mix-up, Daniella. Perhaps she's confusing us with another family.'

'She says not.'

'I can assure you I haven't spoken to the woman. Shall I call her and confirm that?'

'Just come home, and we can ring her together.'

'Of course. I need a shower, and then I'll come straight home. See you in about half an hour.'

This makes no sense. If Grant is telling the truth—and I have no reason to believe he isn't—then either Andrea has got her knickers in a twist, or someone has pranked us. What if someone rang her pretending to be Grant? Who might do that? Would Lesley have had Matt do it? Relations are so strained between us, but why would she try to undermine us selling the house? I assumed she wants me to sell my share to Matt, so surely it suits her for us to up stakes and leave Boston, right? This really doesn't make any sense.

When Grant comes home, he flings his arms around me. 'Tell me what happened. Exactly.'

I reiterate the conversation with Andrea, but all Grant can suggest is that the Realtor has somehow screwed up and that perhaps I should find another company to sell the house.

IT'S SUNDAY EVENING, and the house feels empty. The girls have both landed and sent texts to say they're fine. They may be, but I'm not. When my phone rings and I see that it's Peggy, I answer immediately.

'I've been so worried about you,' I say before she can speak.

'You're a darling,' she replies. 'But I've been quite alright. It was a worry about nothing, except I'm not feeling so good again.'

'I'm sorry to hear that. Can I do anything to help?'

'Actually, that's why I'm calling. It's dear Jade's funeral tomorrow, and I'm not up to going. As you know, Lucas is quite broken about her death…' That surprises me because Lucas didn't seem the slightest bit upset when we were skiing. In fact, I thought he was almost callous in his disinterest. 'The thing is, I was wondering if you'd go with him, in my place?'

'Go to Jade's funeral?' I ask, unable to keep the dismay out of my voice.

There's some fumbling in the background, and then Lucas speaks. 'I know it's a lot to ask, but Mom doesn't want me going alone. She thought you'd be able to hold my hand, so to speak. Please, would you consider it?'

I'm thrown. 'Um, yes, but I'm not sure I'm the best person. Haven't you got anyone else you can take?'

'No. That's the point. Everyone else I know is working tomorrow, or they've never met Jade. Please say yes, Daniella. It would mean so much to me and Mom.'

I hesitate. It's the last thing I want to do. After all, I only met Jade the once, and that was hardly cordial. There's more shuffling noise, and Peggy is on the phone again.

'It would mean the world to me,' she says. 'I feel terrible that I can't go, but I really can't. My diabetes is playing up again.'

'I'm not sure,' I say.

'Please, Daniella. You'll be doing this for me, an old lady not in the best of health.' She lowers her voice. 'Lucas could go alone but frankly I'm worried he'll have a bit of a breakdown. He's been pretending he's fine about Jade's death but he really isn't.'

I'm being backed into a corner, and I'm not sure how to get out of this. I think of how Peggy is becoming a kind of substitute mother to me and how my mom would react if I turned her down. 'Alright,' I say very reluctantly. 'Where is it taking place?'

More fumbling, and Lucas is back on the line. I hear footsteps, as if he's moved into another room. 'It's in Pittsburgh.'

'In Pittsburgh!' I exclaim.

'We'll have to stay the night but will be back home on Tuesday morning. And please don't worry about the cost. I'll pay for everything. Your hotel room, food, the flight.'

I'm completely silent. This is so strange. If the request

had just come from Lucas, then I would have flatly refused, but it seems that I'm doing this for Peggy.

'Thank you, Daniella!' Peggy shouts from somewhere within the room.

Lucas lowers his voice. 'Please say yes.' I hear his footsteps. 'Hold on a moment.' More footsteps and then he speaks in a whisper. 'I promise to behave. Separate rooms and no hanky-panky.'

I hate myself for the reaction, but I shiver involuntarily. 'Alright.' I sigh. 'Message me the details.'

I call Grant. It's not like I can disappear off to Pittsburgh for twenty-four hours without explaining why. Except I'm still going to have to lie because I haven't told Grant that Lucas is Peggy's son. I practice what I'm going to say.

'Peggy, the lady whom I've befriended, has asked me to go with her son to a funeral of a family friend in Pittsburgh. I know it's strange, but she hasn't got anyone else to go in her place. I've provisionally said yes but am wondering how you feel about it.'

There's a pause while Grant thinks. 'If you want to go, then you should go.'

'Are you sure?' I ask, rather hoping that Grant will say it's a bad idea.

'It's your call, love, but I certainly don't mind.'

THE TRAFFIC to the airport is horrendous, and I'm late. Lucas has already messaged me three times asking where I am, and that's doing nothing to ease my panic. I've only got a carry-on and am dressed all in black for the funeral, so I race through the terminal, arriving at the gate just as they're about to close it. Lucas is there, stony-faced and, to my annoyance, barely acknowledges me as we're ushered through onto the plane. He sits in the window seat and keeps his gaze away from me. I throw him glances, and I'm shocked by his facial appearance. He looks like he hasn't slept in nights. Perhaps Jade's death has affected him deeply. I try to imagine how I would feel if one of my exes took their own life because they couldn't live without me, and find it hard to conjure up my emotions.

When the plane takes off and we've reached cruising altitude, he takes a deep sigh and turns towards me.

'Sorry I'm like this. The last week or so has been rough, but thanks for coming with me today. I'm going to sleep. Wake me when we've landed.'

I read on my Kindle, although it's hard to keep my thoughts on the book. I'm acutely aware of Lucas sitting right next to me. He's also all in black, looking smart in a suit with a black overcoat stored in the overhead locker. Although I don't want him to touch me and don't want a repeat performance of our lovemaking, I still feel this unwelcome attraction towards him. Even with his stubble and rings under his eyes, he is a beautiful man. I find myself giving him clandestine glances and admiring those long lashes, which sweep down towards his sharp cheekbones. He shifts slightly in his seat, and I wonder if he can sense my gaze on him. I look away abruptly.

The flight arrives nearly an hour late, so we race towards the taxi stand. Lucas holds the door open as I climb into the taxi, and he gives the driver the address of the funeral home. The traffic is awful, and once again, Lucas seems uneasy and restless, perpetually glancing at his watch.

'We're going to be late,' he mutters. 'Can you hurry!' he says to the driver, impatience in his voice.

By the time we reach the funeral home, the hearse is already there, and the coffin is being unloaded. It's piled high with white and purple flower arrangements, and a group of people dressed from head to foot in black are gathered around it.

A nerve is pinging in Lucas's jaw, and his hand clenches his small overnight bag so tightly, his knuckles are white.

'We'll have to wait to go in after the family,' he whispers. 'A fucking nightmare.' I'm not sure why Lucas is so uptight, but now isn't the time to ask. I just pat his arm.

As we're standing there, an older woman glances towards us, her eyes hidden behind large dark sunglasses.

'What's he doing here?' she asks in a loud whisper.

The man with graying hair standing next to her puts his arm around her shoulders. 'Whether we liked it or not, he was Jade's boyfriend,' he says.

Goodness, this is embarrassing. I glance at Lucas, and his jaw is clenched shut, his fingers balled into fists. 'Bastards,' he mutters. I feel like a spare limb and wish I were anywhere else except here.

The family follows the coffin inside the building, and then we slip in behind them. The room is enormous and completely packed. There are people wedged into every pew and still others standing at the back and down the far side. Music blares out, and everyone stands up. We slip in next to a group of young women who are sniffing loudly, dark glasses covering their eyes, paper tissues stuffed up to their noses.

The service seems to go on forever. That sounds uncaring of me, and perhaps it is, but it's not easy attending a funeral of someone you've only met once and under awkward circumstances. There are numerous readings and poems and people sharing their memories of Jade. She was clearly much loved, and of course it's tragic that she took her own life at such a young age. Not that suicide gets a mention.

Eventually, the proceedings come to an end, and we follow the crowds outside, where it's sleeting and bitterly cold.

'Are you expected to go to the wake?' I ask.

'Ha,' Lucas snorts. 'I'm not welcome. Her parents never thought I was good enough for her. Too old, too poor, not from the same racial background, not Ivy League educated, and so the list goes on. They won't want me there. No, I'll call a cab.'

HALF AN HOUR later we're in the reception area of a Holiday Inn. 'I did as you asked,' he says, 'and booked two rooms.'

I nod, relieved. We both check in and are handed our key cards to adjacent rooms.

As we ascend in the lift, Lucas says, 'Let's meet for dinner in forty-five minutes. Does that suit you?'

'Yes,' I say. I hurry into my room, glad to be alone.

Dinner is a quiet affair. Lucas doesn't speak much, and the dynamics between us are fundamentally different to how they were previously. We both have a single course, and by 8:30 p.m., we're finished. He pays for the meal, and we head back towards the lift.

Inside, we're alone. 'I need a hug,' Lucas says. And before I can object, his arms are around me and he's hugging me so hard, I can barely breathe. I feel his whole body pressed up against mine, and despite wanting to hate this, despite knowing I need to pull away, I don't. I inhale his scent and enjoy that deep shiver that runs through my core.

It's so inappropriate at every level, but I want this man so badly. He rests his chin gently on the top of my head and then lowers it, so his breath is on my ear.

'Sorry, Daniella,' he whispers. 'But I can't help myself. I don't know what I'd do without you.'

That sentiment shocks me. I spring away from him just as the doors ping open. I hurry out of the lift into the corridor, but Lucas is right behind me. As I reach my door, he puts an arm out to stop me from reaching the lock with my key card.

'Don't,' he says. 'I need you, and I know you need me too.'

'I'm married,' I say.

'To a weak man. He's told me that you never make love, that your marriage is broken.'

I gasp. Surely Grant hasn't said that? Except the first part of the statement is true.

'I love Grant,' I say.

'Yet you crave me.' He runs his fingertips down the side of my face.

'No,' I say, determined to be strong. 'I am not having an affair with you.'

'I don't want an affair,' Lucas says. 'I want forever.'

I stare at him in horror. 'I am not leaving my husband for you,' I say. I try to sound firm except I fear my voice is trembling as much as I am.

'Let me make love to you again,' he says. He's staring at me so intently, I take a step backwards.

'No, this isn't right.' I reach for my door handle, except Lucas grabs my hand, his fingers grasping my wrist so tightly it hurts.

'Stop it!' I exclaim.

'You've made me wait long enough,' he growls. 'I love you, Daniella, and I want to be with you. If you didn't feel the same way, I wouldn't push it, except I know you do. Our lovemaking was exquisite, and I think about you day and night. I can make you happy in ways Grant could never dream of.'

'I don't want you,' I say quietly.

'You're lying. Not only to me but mostly to yourself.' His voice is raised now, and his eyes are flashing, the grip on my wrist tightening further.

'You're hurting me! Let me go!' I exclaim, a knot of fear wending through my sternum and up my throat.

'Everything alright here?' I hadn't noticed a large man exiting his room to our left. He's staring at us, his head to one side, a look of concern on his jowly face.

'All fine. Thank you for your concern,' Lucas says, releasing his grip on my arm. I take advantage of the distraction, swipe the door with the key card, and I'm inside, the door closed before Lucas can say another word. I lean against the door, my heart hammering, my body shaking.

What the hell was that? Lucas just scared me silly. Is this really the same man who set my body on fire?

There's a knock on the door, and I jump away from it.

'Daniella, let me in,' Lucas says. 'I would never hurt you, you must know that.'

Except I don't. I don't know this man at all.

'I'm sorry I reacted like that,' he says. 'Jade's funeral was difficult for me, and I'm not in a good headspace. Please let me in. I promise I won't do anything you don't want me to do. We just need to talk.'

'No,' I say, unsure if he can hear me through the heavy

door. Quietly, I lift the chain from the hook and slide it across. 'Please leave me alone, Lucas.'

Still shaking, I walk to the bed, open up my overnight bag and remove my toiletry bag. There's another knock on the door, but I ignore it. I walk into the bathroom, lock the door behind me and turn on the shower. Stripping off, I step inside and relish the hot water cascading over my skin. It takes several minutes to truly relax. Lucas scared me this evening. It's like he's become obsessed with me, and I can't stop thinking about poor Jade and her unborn baby. I get that Lucas is shaken up after her funeral, but his behavior towards me was completely unacceptable. After a long, welcome shower, I'm ready for bed. I can't hear anything from the hallway now and just hope that Lucas will leave me alone. When I'm snuggled under the duvet, I call Grant.

'Hi, sweetheart. How was the funeral?' he asks.

'Very sad. I wish I were back home right now.'

'Is the hotel not up to standard?'

'No, it's not the hotel. It's just that I don't feel like I belong here.'

'How is it with Peggy's son?'

'Honestly, a bit awkward. He's very cut up about things.'

'Makes sense. You sleep tight, and I'll see you tomorrow.'

It's such a relief to chat to my kind and safe husband, but even so, I'm not looking forward to the flight home.

CHAPTER SIXTEEN

LUCAS

Sweet, beautiful Daniella. She is my lifeblood, my reason for living. My true love. I am so grateful she was there at my side today, yet this evening was such a disappointment. And it was my fault. I should have been vivacious at dinner, asked her questions, shared my excitement for our life together, except my head was filled with Jade. Images of her lying there dead. The way her parents were so scornful of my very existence. Of course, Daniella was nothing but charming at the funeral and later over dinner, leaving me convinced that we were going to have a repeat of our lovemaking. For her to push me away is devastating. How could she? Was it out of respect for Jade, or does she genuinely not want to pursue our relationship?

That thought creates a surge of fury. I pace the hotel room, kicking at the baseboard, needing to yell, to feel pain. Except I don't have the funds to destroy this hotel room and pay for the damage. I try to subdue the anger, but it's such an overwhelming force. Stomping into the bathroom, I turn the tap to freezing in the shower. Perhaps an icy blast will quell my passion; otherwise, I might need to leave the hotel and wander into the Pittsburgh night.

The shower works. It quashes my desire and quells my burning for Daniella, temporarily at least. But I still need her. After brusquely drying myself, I return to the bedroom and send her a text.

> Forgive me for my overzealous behavior this evening. I feel such passion when I'm around you sometimes I can't help myself. Please know that my intentions are pure. I hope that one day the intense love I feel for you will be reciprocated. In the meantime, I will keep my distance and respect you. Sleep well, and I look forward to seeing you at breakfast.

I wait for a response to my message, but nothing arrives. Initially I feel some anger, but then I assume Daniella must be asleep. No worries. I will redouble my efforts to make her see sense in the morning.

SURPRISINGLY, I have a good night and awake feeling refreshed and excited about turning over a new leaf with Daniella. I'm in the hotel restaurant at 7:30 a.m. and wait for Daniella. By 8:15, she hasn't appeared, and I wonder if perhaps she's decided not to have breakfast, or maybe she's overslept. I return to the corridor of bedrooms and knock on her door. There's no answer. Horrific thoughts of her lying cold and unseeing on that hotel bed fill my head. I hammer on her door, except there's still no response.

And then I see a member of the housekeeping team pushing a trolley towards me.

'Excuse me,' I holler. 'I'm trying to reach my colleague in this room, but there's no answer. Can you check that she's alright?'

The woman looks confused, and for a moment I wonder if she speaks English. But then she picks up a clipboard from her trolley and runs her finger down it.

'The lady has already checked out,' she says. 'I'm cleaning her room now.'

I go very still before I realize Daniella must be downstairs in the lobby, waiting for me. We were due to take a cab to the airport at 8:45 a.m., but in her typically organized form, she'll be early. Hurriedly, I return to my room, shove my belongings into my overnight bag and rush back, past the housekeeper and into the elevator.

When I get into the hotel lobby, Daniella is nowhere to be seen. An icy fear settles over me as I hurry to the receptionist, interrupting her conversation with another guest.

'This is urgent. I need to locate another guest. Daniella Morris. Has she checked out yet?'

The receptionist gives the other guest an apologetic look and clicks a few buttons on a keyboard.

'Yes, Ms. Morris checked out at 5:45 a.m.'

'What? She's left the hotel?' I ask.

'I'm sorry, I can't say anything other than she's checked out. If you could excuse me, I need to—' I don't wait to hear the end of the sentence.

I can't believe Daniella has left without me! I pull up flight schedules on my phone and see that the first flight back to Boston was with Delta at 7:20 a.m. Did she take an earlier flight, or is she waiting for me at the airport?

I try calling her, except she doesn't answer her phone. Is that because she's turned it off to block me or because she's on a plane? The only way I'll know for sure is if she turns up for our flight.

At the airport, I search for Daniella everywhere. I still hold out hope that I'll find her at our gate, except she's not there. By the time we're boarding the plane, I realize that my love has thwarted our return travel plans. She must have taken the earlier flight. How could she do that? How could she sneak away without so much as a word? I'm seething with anger.

It's hard to contain my fury as the plane takes off. I think back over all our interactions and how wholly she has stolen my heart.

I was truly shocked when, a couple of weeks ago, Grant told me that he and Daniella were looking to move away. That would mean I'd have to go too, to wherever they choose to live. But that would be complicated, not least of all due to my lack of money, so my first plan of action was to sabotage the move. I had fun with the stupid Realtor woman. Grant is my source of information, happily bantering about his life as we work out together at the gym. It wasn't difficult for me to find out the name of his Realtor, and when he told me the date and time of their open house, all I had to do was ring her up and pretend to be him.

That morning, I lurked at the bottom of their road to make sure no one turned up for the open house, and barely a car drove past. The cancellation of the open house worked like a charm. Of course they're likely to appoint a new agent, but I'll find ways to sabotage those viewings too, except is that really going to be enough to stop them from selling their house? I doubt it. It's not physically possible for me to keep a permanent eye on their home, and a potential purchaser could easily come along without my knowledge for a private showing. No, I need another way to keep Daniella close.

As the plane soars over the clouds, I consider burning their house down. Obviously, I'd choose a time when Daniella was far away. With nowhere to live, perhaps they would accept my gesture of kindness and move into Mom's house, and we'd be able to live together. Except Grant would be there too. The thought of that makes me crumple up the menu in the seat pocket in front of me. The stupid cow sitting on the aisle throws me a strange look, and I scowl at her.

The more I think about it, the more I realize Grant is the single largest obstacle to my future happiness. Grant has to go. And I'm in an excellent position to make that happen. The man is my buddy, or at least he thinks he is. Most days we train together, except however hard he tries, he's so far behind me. Whereas my muscles are ripped, his are invisible through the layers of flab. He can barely bench 130 pounds, whereas at a push, I can manage close to double that. The good news is that I know his schedule, and more often than not, he shares what Daniella's up to as well.

I let a slow smile linger on my lips as I imagine comforting my love, getting her through the temporary heartache of losing the man she thought she once loved. We can comfort each other through our loss. Her husband, my best friend. We'll be bonded through grief.

MY OPPORTUNITY ARRIVES a mere two days later. This evening, as we're working out, Grant tells me that Daniella has gone to Rockport to look at a couple of houses, and she's staying overnight at a hotel. Rockport! There is no way I can let that happen. It's way too far out in the sticks. I consider getting in my car and driving up there, hunting her down and giving her the surprise of her life, except I have no idea where she's staying. No, I need to use this time more efficiently. She's going to be out of the house for at least twenty-four hours, and that means tonight will have to be *the* night.

'Do you want to grab a drink since you're home alone?' I suggest to Grant as we head for the locker room.

'Daniella's left me some food to heat up. Knowing her, there'll be enough for two. Perhaps you'd like to join me?'

'Sure,' I say, unable to suppress a wide grin.

When Grant is in the shower, I check my duffel bag. Hidden at the bottom, underneath my towels and spare clothes, is a black balaclava, a couple of pairs of latex gloves, a black hoodie, and a hammer. I've been keeping them in there for a while, just in case. It's important to be prepared. I'm already wearing black tracksuit bottoms. If the hammer isn't enough, I'll find another implement at Grant's house. When he's dressed, I swing the bag over my shoulder and strut out to the car park. I feel so powerful as I hurl the bag into Grant's trunk and slip into the Yukon next to him. *Enjoy the next couple of hours, Grant*, I think to myself. *Because they're going to be your last.*

IT'S dark when we get to Grant and Daniella's house. Grant turns all the lights on, and I leave my duffel bag in the hallway before following him into the kitchen.

'Beer?' Grant asks.

'Sure,' I reply.

He opens the refrigerator and takes out a couple of cans

and a ceramic bowl covered with cling wrap. 'Looks like a stew,' he says. 'Alright with you?'

'Nice. You're lucky. Daniella's such a great cook.'

'I'll heat this up in the oven. Won't take long.'

He turns his back towards me and switches on the oven, then places the dish inside after removing the cover. I debate when I should make my move but decide that Grant will be easier to deal with once he's got food and some drink in him. I'm going to savor the next hour or so.

We sit on bar stools at their island, nursing our beers. Grant finishes his quite quickly, and as the oven beeps to let us know the stew is heated up, he goes over to a cupboard and produces a bottle of red wine.

'How about a glass or two?' he suggests.

'With pleasure.' Not that I'm going to drink much. I need my wits about me.

We talk about nothing much in particular, mainly about the Sox and some new protein shakes I've been trying out.

The stew is delicious, as I knew it would be, and I compliment Daniella's cooking. Grant drinks a couple of glasses of wine and then announces he needs the bathroom.

Now is my time.

I head for the knife block that's standing next to the stove and select the biggest carving knife. It's a vicious-looking thing and perfect for my needs. And then I stand behind the kitchen door, my back to the wall, ready to pounce. Grant starts talking when he's in the hallway, except I don't hear a word of what he's saying. Blood is pounding in my ears, every nerve ending poised and ready to strike.

But just at the last moment, a phone rings, the sound coming from the hallway.

'Just need to get that,' Grant shouts.

Fuck.

That was so close.

But maybe it was a lucky break. Thinking about it, perhaps it's better if I leave the house. If there's video footage from their doorbell, I need to be seen leaving, and then I can sneak back in later.

Rather than shoving the knife back in the block, I wrench open the dishwasher door and place it inside, quickly collecting our plates and putting them in the dishwasher too. I can hear Grant's voice rising and falling, and that's when I spot a little rack of keys neatly positioned under a cabinet. I grab the first one. Bingo. It's labeled *back door*. I slip it into my pocket.

Grant wanders back into the kitchen. 'Sorry about that. It was the woman who runs the local neighborhood watch group. Apparently, someone has spotted a black van driving suspiciously slowly. Probably just doing a delivery. Goodness knows why she has to call everyone when we're all on the WhatsApp group anyway.'

I feel like doing a fist pump. This could not be working out better for me. There's a dodgy guy in the area, and he'll get the blame for what I'm going to do. It's perfect.

'Well, thanks for this evening,' I say, stretching out my right calf muscle. 'I'd better be heading back. Got an early start.'

'Good to see you, buddy,' Grant says. He follows me to the front door, where I pick up my duffel bag.

'You alright to walk home?' he asks.

'Sure, it's no distance. And thanks again.' I give him a wave and head out into the night.

AT HOME, Mom is fast asleep. I get dressed. I pull on the black hoodie, balaclava and black latex gloves and slip my feet into a pair of black sneakers that I picked up from a charity shop. They're a size too large, so I've stuffed the ends with tissue paper. If I leave a footprint, at least it won't be my shoe size. Clever, heh?

I wait three hours. The longest ever three hours. I literally count down the minutes, adrenaline pumping through me, excitement making me want to whoop out loud. With Grant gone, Daniella is going to be mine and mine alone. I do a few deep breaths as Mom taught me, because I need to focus. I know I've only got one chance, and I have to get it right. But I'm strong and confident, so I should be fine. I put a baseball cap on and push the balaclava down my neck. I don't want to be spotted out walking, looking like a dodgy burglar. I'm also wearing a small backpack that holds the hammer, a headlamp, and a knife.

Walking briskly, I arrive at Grant's house. All the windows are dark, both up and downstairs. Good. I slip into the shadow of a large tree and cover my face with the balaclava, stuffing the baseball cap into my bag and positioning the headlamp on my forehead, but keeping it switched off for now. Finally, I pull out the hammer. Letting my eyes adjust to the low light, I slip onto the driveway, stepping gingerly over the lawn, keeping away from the house so as not to set off any security lights. When I spot the back door, I run towards it. Still no lights go on. I'm surprised how lackluster their security is. When Daniella and I are living together, I'm going to install cameras everywhere. Can't take the risk of anything happening to her. With trembling fingers, I remove the back door key from my pocket and insert it into the lock. It turns easily and silently. And then I'm inside.

Holding my breath, I wait for a good five minutes. The house is still, with just the quiet ticking of some appliance creating the only noise. Then I switch my headlamp on and remove the hammer, clutching it tightly in my right hand. I tiptoe through the house until I'm standing at the bottom of the stairs. Pausing for a moment, I creep up the stairs and turn along the corridor. I was worried that I didn't know which bedroom Grant would be sleeping in, but there's only one door that is closed.

Here goes. I push open the bedroom door, and it creaks.

Grant makes a strange inhalation noise, and I fear he might be waking. I rush into the room, with the hammer held high. Everything goes into slow motion. His eyes open wide, startled, blinded by the sharp, dazzling light from my headlamp. His supposedly brilliant brain doesn't switch into gear, and he freezes just long enough for me to bring the hammer down onto his head. There's a strange cracking, squelching noise. I'm blinded too now, with the sheer brilliance of what I'm doing, at how bright my future is going to be, with this overwhelming feeling of power and strength. I bring the hammer down again and then step backwards. I want to view my handiwork, to make sure that Grant is dead, but I remind myself I have a lot of work to do first. There will be time to gloat in the coming days and weeks.

This house needs to look like a burglary gone wrong.

I START RIGHT HERE in the bedroom, pulling out drawers—first the nightstands, tipping the contents onto the floor, then the drawers from the large dresser facing the bed, chucking clothes and belongings onto the floor. When I've finished, I rifle through the built-in closets that span the full width of the room and chuck out clothes and shoes. The space is a complete mess now. Kicking belongings as I go, I head downstairs, into the living room, picking up photo frames and other decorative items, throwing them onto the floor. I consider taking some things, but there's nothing I want, until my eyes fall on the framed photograph of Grant and Daniella on their wedding day, taking pride of place on the mantelpiece. I grab it and shove it in my rucksack. I head back into the kitchen.

At the kitchen sink, I run the hammer under the tap, watching as a stream of red liquid turns to clear; then I wipe it with a tea towel, shoving the towel into my rucksack. Happy that the hammer is clean, I head for the back door, closing it behind me. I pause for a moment, ears straining in the stillness of the night. I hear nothing, so I lift the hammer and slam it against a glass panel in the door. It takes a couple of attempts to shatter, but when it does, I put my hand through and turn the handle. I chuckle as I look at the shards of broken glass.

I indulge myself for a moment and let out a joyous sigh, unable to keep myself from smiling. Grant is dead, sadly battered in bed during a burglary gone wrong, and I'm free to take my prize. Daniella. Happy with my handiwork, I turn, intending to return to the bedroom to make sure that he is dead, intending to gloat about a job well done.

CHAPTER SEVENTEEN

DANIELLA

The thought of moving somewhere new is what's keeping me sane right now. I'm missing the girls terribly, and it's giving me something else to focus on. The move will take us far away from Lucas, which is another added bonus. That night in the Pittsburgh hotel, unable to sleep, I booked myself on an earlier flight home, relieved that I wouldn't have to see him. It's all so confusing. My body yearns for his touch, but then I'm riddled with guilt, and at the same time, he scares me. That intensity of his supposed affection, the way he became angry so quickly. It's good that I haven't heard from him since we got back.

My other concern is my strained relationship with Lesley. We still haven't had a proper talk, and our conversations are curt and restricted to day-to-day necessities.

Grant has given me his blessing to scout out new areas, so yesterday I packed my overnight bag and spent the day driving around Massachusetts, visiting delightful towns such as Rockport and Manchester-by-the-Sea, scouring Realtors' windows. To be honest, I'm no clearer as to where I think we should go, but I enjoyed the first day of house hunting and had a large pile of brochures to look through at the hotel.

I stayed at a charming bed-and-breakfast, five minutes from the beach. My room was comfortable and quaint, with a large comfy bed and a bathroom with a tub big enough to fit several people. The landlady asked me what brought me to Rockport, and when I told her I was house hunting, she said she'd put in a call to her brother-in-law at Roundstone Realtors. He'd give me the best deal in town, apparently. She promised to get him to call me.

I lay on the bed and browsed properties on my iPad. When I came across a new listing with views of a small harbor and a garden that descends to a rocky outcrop, I felt as if I'd found the one. It's a three-bedroom, three-bathroom house but plenty big enough for us, and the girls could still have their own rooms when they come to stay. A buzz of excitement ran through me. Could we really live somewhere like this? And while, no doubt it's stunning in the summer, what would it be like at this time of the year when the waves crash against the shore and a vicious cold wind blows across the Atlantic? Today was a perfect winter day, but I'd need to come back when the weather was bad.

After supper at a sweet restaurant a few doors down, I called Grant.

'How's the house hunting going?' he asked.

'I've found a beautiful house right on the shore. I'll send you the details. I'll try to view it tomorrow. It's so lovely up here, Grant.'

'Look forward to seeing it,' he replied.

'How was your evening?'

'Great. Had a workout at the gym, and then Lucas came back to ours, and I shared that delicious stew with him.'

My heart sank. How can I stop my husband from seeing Lucas?

'Anyway, I'm exhausted now, so I'm going to sleep. Have a good day tomorrow. What time will you be back?'

AND NOW IT'S the next morning, and I slept surprisingly well. First thing, I arrange to see the three-bedroom house with views. I have a couple of hours to kill, so I mooch around Rockport. I'm on my way to the viewing when my phone rings displaying *No Caller ID*. Thinking it might be the Realtor to say he's delayed, I answer quickly.

'Is this Mrs. Daniella Morris?' It's an unfamiliar man speaking.

'My name is Sandy Briar, and I'm calling from the Boston Police Department.' My stomach contracts. *Please let the girls be alright. Please!*

'I'm calling regarding your husband, Grant Morris. I'm afraid that he's in the hospital. We need you to come as soon as possible.'

'Grant?' I exclaim. 'What's happened?' I have images of him battered after a car accident, or perhaps he was hit by a car. He often crosses the road, his head in the clouds deciphering some equation, not properly paying attention.

'We believe there was a burglary at your home, and your husband has been severely injured.'

'No,' I stammer. My body starts trembling violently. 'Is he going to be alright?' *Please let him be alright. Please.*

'He's currently in an induced coma in the ICU at the Beth Israel Deaconess Medical Center. He's receiving the best care, but the doctors will tell you more.'

I want to scream at this stranger: how do you know that?

Why are you offering me platitudes? And an induced coma? That only happens when a person's life is hanging in the balance, doesn't it?

'Where are you, Mrs. Morris?' he asks.

'I'm in Rockport.'

'Alone?'

'Yes.'

'Are you safe to travel back by yourself?'

'I don't know,' I mutter, wiping tears that are splattering my cheeks. 'I think so.'

'In that case, it would be helpful if you could return to the city as quickly as possible. We'll need to talk to you too.'

'Is he going to survive?' I ask.

'I hope so, Mrs. Morris. I very much hope so.'

I DRIVE IN A TRANCE, completely unaware of my surroundings. It feels like there's a vise around my chest, a permanent jagged stone of fear wedged in my throat. I say silent prayers for Grant. My husband cannot die. He cannot. How I make it back to the city without having an accident or being stopped by the police for speeding, I have no idea. I find a parking garage near to the hospital and run to the front entrance. I'm breathless as I race to the reception desk and say my husband's name.

As I hurry towards the ICU, my phone rings. 'Don't answer the phone,' I mutter to myself. It seems like every time I answer the phone, it's bad news. Except I can't stop myself from looking at it and realize that it's the same No Caller ID number.

'Yes,' I snap.

'Mrs. Morris, this is Detective Sandy Briar again.'

'I'm at the hospital,' I say breathlessly. 'I just got here.'

'In which case, I'd like to meet you there in thirty minutes.'

'Why?' I ask.

'I'd like to discuss the break-in. Is that alright?'

'Yes,' I answer. All I care about is seeing Grant.

IT'S A SHOCK. A terrible shock. I barely recognize my husband, the way he's linked up to so many tubes, bandages around his head, his eyes closed, his face terrifyingly pale. All of those machines and beeping sounds. I can't help myself and burst into tears. A kindly nurse puts her arm around my shoulders and ushers me out of the room into the corridor.

'It often looks worse than it is,' she says. 'It's always a fright when loved ones see their relatives hooked up like that. You take a seat here, and I'll get the doctor to come and have a word with you.'

'Thank you.' I sniff as I dab my eyes with an already soaked-through tissue.

A couple of minutes later, a young man dressed in a white coat arrives with a clipboard. 'Mrs. Morris?'

'Yes,' I say, jumping to my feet.

'Your husband has sustained a major head injury. He's currently in an induced coma to reduce the swelling on the brain, but the recovery is going well, and we expect to take him out of the coma within the next twenty-four hours. Only then will we be able to fully assess the extent of his injuries.'

I can barely bring myself to say the words. 'Could he have a brain injury?'

'We're not sure. At best, he's likely to suffer some

memory loss, but I'm afraid we're just going to have to be patient. We've stitched up various lacerations.'

'But he's going to live?' I ask. So long as Grant stays alive, we can cope with anything.

'We're hopeful, yes.'

The doctor leaves, and I return to Grant's bedside, placing my hand over his motionless hand. 'You're going to be okay,' I say to him, even though the words sound trite. 'We'll get through this. I promise.' Except I can't stop thinking about my husband and his brilliant brain. How will he cope if he loses his intellect or, worse, his ability to talk? It's too horrendous to consider.

And then I think of the girls. Should I be contacting them? They'll want to come home straight away, except is that the right thing to do? Should I wait until Grant awakens, until we know more about his prognosis? I let out a small moan, and the nurse, who had her back to me and was typing something into a computer, turns around and throws me a weak smile. I sit there, stroking the back of my husband's hand, listening to the machinery and the beeps. When there's a knock on the door, I start. The nurse walks over to it and speaks quietly; then she turns to me.

'There's a police officer here to talk to you. Are you up to it?' she asks kindly.

I stand up and nod.

Detective Sandy Briar has an open, warm expression, thick dark hair, and blue eyes. He's dressed casually in a navy corduroy shirt and navy pants. He shakes my hand.

'Let's go and talk somewhere private,' he says. I follow him down the corridor, and he opens the door to a small room, where, I suppose, relatives get told bad news. 'Would you like a coffee or a drink? There's a vending machine around the corner.'

'No thanks, I'm fine.' Although clearly, I'm not.

I sit down opposite him.

'What we can ascertain is that there was a break-in at your house last night. Fortuitously, one of your neighbors was walking his dog. He heard the sound of breaking glass and then saw the silhouette of a person running away. Unsure what to do, he walked around your house and saw broken glass at the back door. He then called the police. My officers found your husband and called the paramedics.'

'Oh, God,' I mutter. 'He probably saved Grant's life.'

'Indeed. Luck was on your side. If you're up to it, I'd like you to accompany me to your house so we can assess what was stolen. I have a forensic team there now. Before we go, please can you confirm where you were last night?'

'I was house hunting and stayed the night at a bed-and-breakfast in Rockport. I spoke to Grant on the phone before we both went to bed.'

'We will, of course, be checking his phone, which we've retrieved from the property. Do you know his passcode?'

'Yes, it's 0408, the date of our twins' birthday.'

He scribbles that down in a little notebook. 'And your twins. Where are they now?'

'On gap-year adventures in South America. Should I get them to come home?'

'Why don't we wait a few hours and see how your husband is. I gather from the doctor they're hoping he'll be out of the coma in the next twenty-four hours.'

I nod.

'Is there anyone, to the best of your knowledge, who might wish you or your husband harm?'

I stare at him in shock. No. Grant is one of the world's nicest people, and there is no one who would want to hurt us. Lucas's face flashes through my mind, but would he really hurt my husband? They seem to be great friends.

'Wasn't it just a random break-in gone wrong?' I ask.

'Quite possibly, but we need to explore all options.'

'There was that mugging on Ivy Street a few weeks ago. I went to the aid of the lady who was hurt.'

He looks at me with interest. 'Tell me more.'

I give him Peggy's details and search through my online diary to find the date.

'Would you like a lift back to your house, or would you prefer if we both make our way back there separately?' the detective asks.

'I'll take my own car, if that's okay.'

'Of course.'

AFTER MAKING the nurse promise that she'll call me the second Grant wakes up or if there's any change in his condition, I leave the hospital. My legs feel like jelly as I make my way to the parking lot, and I have to concentrate doubly hard as I navigate the short distance back to our house. It's a shock when I get there. Two police cars are parked on the road before our driveway, and another one is in the drive. At least they're taking this seriously.

Detective Briar is already there, standing in the open front doorway, talking to a uniformed officer.

'Would you mind putting on these shoe covers?' he asks, handing me some elastic paper covers. I wobble as I slip them over my sneakers and follow him inside. It makes me feel nauseous to see two strangers in my house, dressed in white paper suits. I realize with a start that if Grant dies, this will be a murder scene. I guess that's why they're taking it so seriously.

The detective puts a hand on my arm. 'I'd like to walk around the house with you to see if anything is missing. Jewelry, money, electronics, paintings, credit cards, or anything of value.'

My heart is hammering as we pace around the house. There's a terrible sensation of violation, knowing strangers have been inside. I gasp as we walk into the living room. The room has been ransacked. Vases and table lamps lie shattered on the ground, cushions are askew, and paintings hang precariously from the wall.

'I'm sorry this has happened to you,' Sandy Briar says. 'Can you take a slow look around and let me know if anything is missing?'

I try to take in the mess. Weirdly, everything seems to be here. Even Grant's laptop is lying on the floor, and the large television is untouched in the corner.

'Trinkets, pictures, all here?' he asks.

'I think so.'

'Alright, let's head upstairs. I'm afraid the primary bedroom where your husband was found is an even greater mess.'

'Was there a fight?' I ask, my legs trembling in anticipation of what I'm going to see.

'We think your husband was battered in bed. Most likely, he was asleep and didn't have time to defend himself. Hopefully, we'll know more when Mr. Morris wakes up.'

I shudder. I try to brace myself, to be prepared, but honestly, I'm terrified. The detective walks into the bedroom first, and as I step into the doorway, I let out my breath. It's bad but not as bad as I feared.

'The forensics team has removed your bedding for analysis. As you'll see, there's still some blood on the mattress.'

My eyes are drawn to the mess. Drawers have been pulled out and tipped onto the floor; it looks like all of my clothes are scattered across the room. Jewelry catches the light, and my bedside table has toppled over. I gasp as my hand flies up to cover my mouth.

'We found your safe in the closet. Would you mind giving me the code, as we need to check that everything is still there?' the detective asks.

He pulls on some latex gloves, and I read out the safe code. The door pings open.

'Have a look inside for me.'

I peer in, and everything seems to be there. Our passports, the folders with birth and marriage certificates, share certificates and an envelope of cash, along with my small jewelry box. 'I don't think it's been touched,' I confirm.

'Do you have any valuables elsewhere?'

I shake my head. The jewelry scattered on the floor are cheap costume pieces.

'And this is what's strange,' Detective Briar says, straightening up. 'The intruder appears to have taken nothing, yet he hit your husband and created chaos.'

'What was Grant hit with?'

'We're not sure yet, but initial suspicions are with a hammer. We haven't found one in your house, but we found one in the garage. It looks untouched, but it's been sent away for analysis.'

'It's the only one we've got.' As I glance around the room, I wonder if I'll ever be able to sleep in here again. It's a scene of such horror. 'Were the girls' rooms touched?' I ask. My throat feels like it's constricting.

'No. The only two rooms that were ransacked were in here and the living room. But it would be helpful for you to walk through the whole house to see if we've missed anything. Also, do you have any cameras or CCTV footage?'

I shake my head. We've been lax about security, only switching on the house alarm when we go away. How could we have been so stupid? The detective accompanies me as I walk into every room in the house. He's right; it all looks untouched. Even Grant's office has the normal piles of papers stacked on his desk and textbooks neatly piled on the floor. The intruder clearly wasn't looking for any scientific secrets.

It's as I'm slowly glancing around the living room that I notice it. The large photo in a silver frame that normally stands on the mantelpiece seems to be missing. It's a photo of Grant and me on our wedding day, looking impossibly young and carefree and so very much in love. There are other photos in frames scattered around the room: the girls from when they were babies to the young women they are today, family groups including both Grant and my parents. But the one that is just of him and me, I can't see anywhere.

'Our wedding photo is missing,' I say.

Sandy Briar's eyebrows knot together. 'It feels personal,' he says. 'Or maybe the intruder was disturbed.' There's a long pause, and I reckon I know what he's thinking.

'My marriage is fine, in case you were wondering.'

CHAPTER EIGHTEEN

DANIELLA

'Our marriage is fine,' I tell Detective Briar again. Except I wonder if my lie will completely wash. We are, after all, in therapy, and if he sees Grant's diary, perhaps he'll find out. I feel my cheeks flush. 'Although with our twins leaving home,' I add, 'we have had couples counseling once or twice. Not because there were problems as such.' I let the words peter out. This is embarrassing. 'I love my husband,' I add.

He stares at me in silence before saying, 'Is there anywhere else you can stay tonight?'

My first instinct is to think of Lesley, except we're hardly on speaking terms at the moment, and I can't face some artificial reconciliation and her look of pity. How I wish my parents were close by. And then I think of Grant's parents and realize I'll have to tell them about his condition, as well as getting the girls flights back home. 'I'll find somewhere,' I add, thinking I'll probably stay at a hotel if I'm not allowed to remain at Grant's bedside.

'We'll stay in touch, then,' Sandy Briar says as he accompanies me back to my car. 'And I sincerely hope your husband recovers quickly.'

I sit in my car for a while, mustering up the energy to call Grant's parents. I'm fond of them, even though I've always gotten the impression that they didn't completely approve of their prodigal son marrying a poorly educated Brit. But they adore the girls and have been doting grandparents.

It's a relief when Jonah, Grant's father's phone goes to voicemail. I leave a message telling them that Grant has had an accident, that he's alright and they shouldn't hurry here. I just hope I'm correct. A retired physicist and academic, much like his son, I know that he will be calm, unlike Betty, Grant's mother, who is likely to burst into tears upon hearing the news. And then I remember they're on holiday in Australia, and it'll be the middle of the night there. I bash my forehead with the palm of my hand. I shouldn't have worried them, and now it's too late.

I'm under no illusion that the phone calls to the girls will be easier. I try ringing Arlyse first, hoping that her desire to be a doctor might quell her panic. Except she doesn't answer. I send both girls messages, asking them to call me urgently.

Back at the hospital, they still haven't brought Grant out of the coma. This worries me, but the lovely nurse, who I know now is called Yvonne, reassures me that there is nothing further to be concerned about. 'Sometimes it's better if the patient remains in a coma for longer, as it gives the brain more time to recover.' I sit next to Grant's bed, listening to those dreadful beeps for a couple of hours until Yvonne tells me I should go home. I don't tell her that I'm not allowed to go home. Once again, she promises to call if there is any change.

I'm utterly exhausted as I drag my feet along the corridors and out of the hospital. There's a hotel literally around the corner, the foyer bustling with people dressed in somber suits. I haul myself up to the reception desk and book a room for the night. Once I've got the key card, I head back to the car and collect the overnight bag that I used last night in Rockport, which seems like years ago rather than hours. Back in my stark but clean room, I collapse on the bed.

Tasia is the first to call me.

She's tearful when I tell her that Dad is in the hospital and promises to speak to Arlyse. I suggest she stays put for a few days, but Tasia is adamant she's coming home on the next flight. I ask her to send me the details of her flight and promise to wire her the money. By the time Arlyse calls me twenty minutes later, it's obvious she's spoken to her sister. Her normally steady voice sounds weak, but unlike her sister, she grills me for details. I have to admit that Grant was the victim of an attack, a burglary gone wrong.

'You need to set the alarm all the time, not just when you go away. And put it on at night too,' she says. 'You need to be safe, Mom.'

'I don't think it's unsafe,' I say without conviction.

'Promise you'll put the alarm on. And buy one of those Ring doorbells and put cameras inside the house. It's probably a good thing that you're going to move. Have you found anywhere?'

I let out a snort. 'I've barely started looking, sweetheart. We need to concentrate on getting your dad well first.'

'Right. I'll talk to Tasia, and we'll both come home.'

'You don't need to,' I say weakly.

'Yes, we do.'

I SPEND the next hour ordering interior video cameras and a Ring camera from Amazon, selecting next-day delivery. I call the hospital but am told there has been no change. It's a new nurse on shift now, and she suggests that I don't return to the hospital but try to get a good night's sleep. As if. The girls message with details of their flights, both returning tomorrow evening. I wonder if the police will allow us home by then, and I just hope I'll have the chance to tidy up before they see the state of the house.

Of course I don't sleep. As soon as I drift off, images of Grant, bloodied and battered, sear my brain and awaken me with a start. It makes me realize how very much I love my husband and what a terrible mistake it was to sleep with Lucas. At least I haven't heard from him since Jade's funeral. I'm hoping that the whole episode of our evening together can be forgotten.

AT 6 A.M., I'm up and dressed, so I go to the hospital. I'm disappointed to be told that I can't see Grant for a few hours. At a loose end, I head back to the hotel.

My phone rings just after 9 a.m. It's Lesley, and I don't want to talk to her. I don't answer the phone, except she calls again. And again.

Sighing, I answer.

'Bloody hell, Daniella,' she says. 'I heard what happened. I'm so sorry. Is Grant okay?'

'How did you hear?' I ask.

'You've been avoiding me, so I stopped by your house, and there's a police officer on your doorstep. I got it out of him. Are you alright?'

'Trying to get my head around everything.'

'And how is Grant today?'

'Unchanged, apparently. I'm not allowed to visit him until later.'

'Why don't you come into the shop? I'll make you a double espresso and pick up some of your favorite muffins. Is there anything else I can do for you?'

I hesitate. I don't feel like going in to work, but I have nothing else to do. Perhaps it would be good to clear the air with my old friend.

AS SOON AS I walk through the front door of the Silken Stem, Lesley appears in front of me.

'I'm so sorry!' she says, flinging her arms around me.

I can't help myself from stiffening and stepping backwards, away from her. She looks hurt but almost immediately says, 'Coffee and muffins over here.' She picks up a paper cup of coffee and hands it to me.

The shop is looking a little bare. I really need to make up some more arrangements to sell, except I'm not in the right headspace to be creative. There aren't any customers, so I perch on a stool next to the counter where we wrap and serve, sipping my coffee.

'It might not be the best time to talk about the business, what with everything that's happened to you and Grant,' Lesley says.

'Actually, we need to talk about it,' I reply.

'Look, the last thing I wanted was for us to break up the company,' Lesley says. 'I would never have suggested the expansion if I thought that was going to happen.'

'But we both want different things,' I say, trying to

remain calm. 'I'm happy with the status quo, but you're reaching for the stars.'

'Well, not really the stars,' she says.

'Actually, we are reaching for the stars.' Matt appears in the doorway to the workshop. Damn. I didn't realize he was here. 'But if you want to carry on running an underperforming business, then that's your call.'

'Matt!' Lesley says, glowering at him. 'Daniella is under a lot of personal pressure.'

I can't stand this man and don't understand what Lesley sees in him. He's leaning against the doorframe, smirking, dressed in black suit pants that are slightly shiny and a starched white shirt. He looks completely out of place here, and although he surely must know that Grant is in hospital, he doesn't even mention him. Matt isn't good enough for Lesley. She deserves someone who loves her for who she is, not someone who wants to get his hands on our business. I can see that he's going to hurt her, and I wish I could do more to stop this inevitable car crash of a relationship.

'The very nature of business is to manage pressure, whether that's in one's home life or at work. Being able to compartmentalize and focus on the matter at hand is absolutely essential.'

'Oh, come on,' Lesley says, giving him an eye roll. 'Daniella's husband is in the ICU. In a coma. Give her a break.'

'Actually, this conversation is between Lesley and me,' I say. 'I'd be grateful if you didn't get involved.'

'But I already am involved. I'll be making you an offer to get out of the Silken Stem, which is a shame because it means I've got less to invest, but if you want to screw up the deal for your friend, then so be it.'

'Stop!' I shout. 'You need to back off. There are bigger things in life than your desire to interfere in our business. I can see that you want to cause problems for me; you're not exactly subtle about it.' I'm slightly stunned at my own reaction. I would never normally go off the handle like this. But it strikes me that Matt could be behind a lot of my current troubles. 'Are you the one who called off our Realtor? Yes, you probably did, didn't you? It's the sort of idiotic thing you'd do!' The moment the words are out of my mouth, I regret them.

'What the hell are you talking about?' Matt asks, narrowing his eyes.

'You just want me out of the way, don't you?' I'm not sure why this man is winding me up to such a degree, but I see red around him. I guess it's his complete lack of empathy towards Grant and his avarice about our business. Not to mention how much he's changed my friend in the short time she's been seeing him. 'Someone rang our Realtor and told her that we didn't want to sell our house after all. Was that you?'

'Why would I do that? I want you out of the way! It suits me that you're selling your house.' He smirks at me.

I turn to Lesley, waving my arms in exasperation. She looks horrified and stands up, turning to face Matt. 'You told me that we need Daniella, not that you want her out of the way!' she exclaims. Tears are welling up in her eyes. 'Was that your game plan all along?'

'We all need to calm down here,' Matt says, pumping his palms towards us. 'This is a business deal. It's not personal.'

'Not personal!' I exclaim. 'Lesley and I have been friends for years, and you've just walked in here and trampled all over me. You're the one who is acting out of order. And you haven't once asked about my husband, who might actually be dying right now!'

Lesley is crying, her cheeks red and wet with tears.

'I'm done!' I say, grabbing my bag and causing the cup of coffee to tip over, brown liquid dripping onto the floor. I turn on my heel and stride out of the shop.

CHAPTER NINETEEN

LUCAS

When I receive a phone call from a detective called Sandy Briar, it is quite the shock.

'Mr. Denman, I'm calling about Grant Morris. Is it possible to have a conversation?' he asks in a singsong voice that I don't like one little bit.

'Of course. Is everything alright?' My heart is thudding in my chest, and I'm grateful that this is a conversation on the phone rather than face-to-face. I dig my fingers painfully into my thigh.

'Unfortunately, Mr. Morris has been the victim of a home invasion, and he's currently in the ICU in an induced coma.'

'What?' The exclamation is real. What the hell? Grant should be dead! I was expecting the detective to tell me that they were opening a murder enquiry, not that Grant is still alive.

'I understand that you are good friends and that you were together at the gym the evening before his attack.'

I release some of the tension in my body, shaking out my

shoulders. If I was under any suspicion, the detective wouldn't be talking to me in this casual manner.

'Yes,' I say. 'Grant has become a good buddy. I can't believe he's been hurt. Is he alright? He will survive, won't he?'

'We're hopeful he will recover, but it's early days. After you left the gym, where did you go?'

'Grant invited me back to his house for a meal after our workout. His wife was away for the night.'

There's a slight pause. 'Which could mean you were the last person to see Mr. Morris before his attack. I'd be very grateful if I could take a statement from you.'

'Do you need me to come to the police station?' I ask, trying to keep my tone of voice light and accommodating while I pace up and down my bedroom.

'That would be very helpful,' he says. We agree to meet in a few hours.

Perhaps I should have prepared myself for this, except I didn't. I'm furious. No, beyond furious. Livid. I didn't do the job properly. It's because I was disturbed. There I was, having finished trashing my beautiful Daniella's living room, and having broken the windowpane in the back door, when I glanced out the window and saw the outline of a man holding a flashlight in one hand and the leash of a dog in the other. Although it was dark inside the house, he was standing at the bottom of the drive, staring straight at me. My heart nearly exploded out of my chest. I banked on the fact that his vision in the dark would have been poor, so I bolted.

I ran out of the house and disappeared into the backyard, jumping the fence and keeping to the shadows. I jogged all the way home. I was confident no one saw me, or if that person did, he wouldn't have been able to make out my features. But it did mean I had to leave in a greater hurry than I would have preferred. After destroying the living room and breaking the glass in the back door, I had intended to return upstairs to make sure Grant was well and truly dead and to remove some of their more valuable possessions. Alas, I didn't have the opportunity to do that. All the same, I'm confident I didn't leave behind any traces that it was me. After all, my DNA and fingerprints will be all over that house quite legitimately.

When we end the call, I'm about to punch my hand into the wall when I stop. I need to get myself under control. If the police officer sees me with a battered hand, he might come to the wrong conclusion. Instead, I let out a howl, relieved that Mom is out of the house this morning. After taking an icy-cold shower, I dress in a nice suit and consider my options.

I have to finish what I started.

Somehow, I need to kill Grant.

Even if he's brain-dead or brain damaged, Daniella won't be free of him. I know my love, and I know she'd feel a sense of obligation to stay with her invalid husband because of his incapacities. Yes, it might allow us to carry on a relationship, but I want more than that. I want us to be together in the eyes of the world, not hiding behind closed doors. I want it all.

The only way forward is for Grant to die.

I think of lovely Daniella and wonder how she's feeling. I'm tempted to call her, to offer my support at this difficult time, but decide it would be wiser to hear what the police officer has to say first.

Before heading downstairs, I go into Mom's bathroom. It's old-fashioned, with the bath, toilet, and sink in what she proudly calls Harvest Gold. In fact, it's a putrid yellow color that's quite revolting. She could afford to renovate all the bathrooms in the house, but Mom likes to penny-pinch.

I open the cupboard above the sink where she stores her medication and remove her box of insulin vials. I'm not sure how many I'll need, but I'm hopeful that if Grant is hooked up to an IV, I'll be able to inject several doses straight into his bloodstream. I gather up a large handful and carry them back into my room. I prepare the syringes, then find my leather messenger bag and put them into the zipped compartment, then shove in a folder of papers and a cardigan. I drive towards the police station, park in a garage a block away, and leave my bag hidden from view, pushed under the front seat.

DETECTIVE SANDY BRIAR IS UNIMPRESSIVE. I make charming small talk, asking after Grant with an expression of deep concern. I explain that we're great friends, so much so, I recently went away with the family on a skiing trip.

'Could you tell me how Mr. Morris seemed to you the evening of the attack?' he asks as we sit in an office-like interview room.

'Completely normal,' I say truthfully. 'We had a beer and a couple of glasses of wine and ate a delicious stew prepared by his wife. We chatted as we always do, and then I walked home. He seemed relaxed, and there was nothing out of the ordinary.'

'Are you aware of anyone who might want to harm Mr. Morris?'

I laugh. 'Grant is one of the most convivial people you are ever likely to meet. I can't imagine anyone holding a grudge against him, except perhaps a student he's given a low mark. He's one of life's genuinely nice people.'

'That's the impression I'm getting,' the detective adds. 'Now, I understand that your mother was attacked in the street a few weeks back. Peggy Denman. Is that right?'

I start slightly, surprised they've put the two together. I need to concentrate.

'Yes. In fact, we haven't heard anything as a follow-up to that. It's very concerning that crime levels are so high in our area. Do you have any further information?'

'Unfortunately not.'

'But surely the two can't be connected?' I ask.

'There's no reason to think so at this stage. How is your mother, by the way?'

'She's a tough old crow, doing fine, thank you. Except for her diabetes, which causes the odd problem. We were very thankful to Mrs. Morris for helping her out.'

'Is that how you got to know Mr. Morris?' he asks.

'Actually, no. He joined my gym, and I'm his personal trainer. We became friends there, so it was quite the coincidence.'

Briar frowns, and I realize I might have made a mistake. Police officers don't like coincidences.

'Of course, we live very close by, so perhaps it was inevitable we'd become friends,' I add. 'Will I be allowed to visit Grant?'

'I'm not aware of the hospital policy. What time did you leave Mr. Morris's house?'

I think for a moment. 'Probably around 9 p.m., but I can't be exactly sure.'

'And where were you for the rest of the night?'

'At my mother's house. I'm living there at the moment.'

'Can anyone verify that?'

'Just my mother. I sent a few emails, which I could forward on to you if you wish.'

'No, that won't be necessary.' He closes his notebook and stands up. 'Thank you for your time, Mr. Denman. If you think of anything that might be relevant, please let me know.'

'I certainly will.'

'Oh,' the police officer says just as I'm about to walk out the door, 'which rooms were you in when you spent time at the Morrises' house?'

'The kitchen, the living room, and I used their downstairs powder room.'

'I don't suppose you recall whether there was a wedding photograph of Mr. and Mrs. Morris positioned on the mantelpiece?'

I try to hide the shock I'm feeling. How do they know it's missing? 'Um, no. I'm afraid that's not the sort of thing I'm likely to notice.'

'Indeed,' he says. 'Well, thank you again for your time.'

THERE IS nothing I want to do more than throw my arms around Daniella and comfort her. I know I could quickly banish any grief she has for her husband, and of course, he was my friend too, so my commiserations would be genuine. Her affection would switch rapidly as I prove what a loving partner I can be. Except I need to consider the long-term strategy and rein in my impulsivity. I'm having to tread a fine line here, because it would be heartless indeed if I didn't reach out in these circumstances.

As I'm sitting in my car, considering my next steps, I

decide to send her a text message. It takes a few attempts to work out the best wording.

> Dear Daniella, I was incredibly shocked to learn about your home invasion and Grant's injuries. Please know that I am here for you, and if there is anything at all that you need, please don't hesitate to reach out. Our very best wishes, Peggy and Lucas.

The text is formal, but I can't risk the police finding out that Daniella and I are in a passionate relationship. I hit send.

I know what I need to do next, and my body tenses in anticipation. I have to finish off what I started. My plan is fraught with danger, but I thrive on pressure, and I'm convinced I can do this. I am going to go to the ICU.

I stride into the hospital, my head held high, full of confidence. I have every right to see Grant. The man at reception directs me, but I approach the place with caution. Although I want to be there with Daniella, to feel her gentle tears on my neck and to soothe her worries, I know that I can't. The frustration is almost overwhelming. I've no idea if she's there with Grant right now, but I can't risk her seeing me. I accept that I could be waiting for hours, but it will be worth it. I position myself behind a pillar near the entrance to the ICU department. Not only do I need a fix of my love, even if I'm just setting eyes on her from afar, but I also need to be sure that she's actually left.

I open a newspaper and pretend to be reading it, except I don't absorb a word. I watch visitors and medical staff enter and leave. At some point, someone might question why I'm spending so much time hanging around there, but I'll deal with that if I have to.

To my relief, I spot Daniella about fifteen minutes later. She's wearing a thick coat that dwarfs her. My love is looking so pale and wan, with dark rings under her eyes as if she hasn't slept for a week, her hair tied back in a tangle of curls. She's on the phone as she walks past me to the elevator, completely oblivious to anyone and everything. I pace a few steps behind her, straining to listen to the conversation.

'No, he's woken up from the coma, but he's asleep. They still can't fully assess the damage until he wakes, but it's looking positive.' She pauses and then starts to speak again. "Yes. He'll be in the hospital for a long time, I imagine. I'm just so relieved he's survived. Don't fly home just for this. When he's well enough, you can speak on the phone.'

And then she's in the elevator, and with one last yearning glance, I double back on myself.

I walk confidently into the ICU department, confident in my business suit with the messenger bag over my shoulder. I stop a harried-looking nurse.

'Hi. I'm here to see Grant Morris. Could you point me in the direction of his room?'

'Of course. Can I take your name?'

'It's Brody Morris.'

'Ah, a relative.'

I smile but don't confirm or deny it.

'Grant is doing really well. He's out of the coma now but hasn't regained consciousness.'

It's a shock to see Grant lying in that bed, attached to tubes, looking diminished. He's asleep, as I hoped he would be, but he's not intubated. I sit down on the chair next to the bed, aware of the nurse behind me, rustling around in the supply cabinet.

'Hello, buddy,' I say, wondering if he can hear me. 'I'm here to make you feel better.' I have no doubt that death will be a considerable improvement on the condition that he's currently in. The syringes are in my hand the moment the nurse leaves the room. I have to work quickly. I stand up and lean over Grant, trying to work out which tube I need to insert the syringe of insulin into.

'Hello.' The shock makes me jump backwards. Two syringes slip out of my hand and roll under the hospital bed.

'Hey, Lucas. It's good to see you.' Grant's eyes are wide open, and he's looking right at me, even though his eyelids are swollen and the surrounding area is black and blue.

Fuck.

He was not meant to wake up.

'Hey,' I say, rapidly sitting back down in the chair.

A nurse bustles into the room.

'Well, hello there, Grant. How are you feeling?'

'Sore,' he says. His voice sounds raspy. 'Where's Daniella?'

'She's left for a bite to eat, but she'll be back soon.' The nurse plays around with a couple of the IVs, but my eyes are focused on the syringes lying under the damn bed. I have to get to them.

'Good of you to come,' Grant says, but he's unable to turn his head to look in my direction.

I could explode. Right now, I would like to punch his face and wring the nurse's neck. I knew my plan wasn't foolproof, but it's completely blown apart now.

'That should ease the pain,' the nurse says as she steps

away from the bed and writes something on a tablet. 'We want you to sleep as much as possible.'

'Can you look after Dani for me?' Grant's words slur, and his eyes close.

'It was lovely for you to visit, but Grant really needs to sleep now,' the nurse says. 'Perhaps you could come back tomorrow?'

I clench my teeth together. I cannot afford to make a scene, but I'm raging on the inside. I debate whether to make a lunge for the syringes of insulin or leave them under the bed. Standing up, I let my messenger bag slide to the ground.

'Damn,' I say. It gives me the chance to lean down for the syringes, to fumble around. I sense the nurse's eyes on my back. 'My pen rolled out of my bag,' I say as I lunge for one of them, quickly palm it and slip it into my bag. But now I can't see the other one. Perhaps I only dropped one.

I hurry out of that hospital as fast as I can, darting between staff and visitors, my heart hammering in fury. How could I have failed again? I want to let out an enormous roar, to release all of that pent-up anger, but how can I? I'm not stupid. I know I'm on borrowed time here. What if Grant remembers the attack? What if he recognizes my footsteps or the faint scent of any aftershave? And Daniella. How can I have my sweet Daniella now that she'll be caring for her invalid husband? I push a woman out of the way as I step from the sidewalk and run towards the parking lot. Someone shouts, but I'm out of there, darting inside the concrete building, waiting for a moment in the shadows.

And then it hits me.

I can make this work.

I have to get hold of Daniella and take her far away from

Boston. To a place where it'll just be me and her. A place where we'll both be safe.

CHAPTER TWENTY

PEGGY

My Lucas has been out of sorts the past couple of weeks. That red fury of his, the one I always used to be able to manage, is growing into an uncontrollable monster. The other week, when I was convinced he was going to hit me, I made it into the bathroom by a whisker. He put his fist through the door, and now the wood is patched up with an ugly piece of plywood, but at least Lucas avoided hurting me. He bought me a bunch of red tulips to say sorry for the mess.

I might come across as a naive old woman, but I'm not really. I know that my son's heart is lost to Daniella, and that's why he's been behaving so erratically. I haven't seen or heard from her recently, and Bippie is missing his walks. I do hope everything is alright. I daren't ask Lucas how things are going between him and Daniella. I assume not well, as he hasn't mentioned her. I fear I made a terrible mistake encouraging that relationship, but I'm only acting like any other loving mother. I want my boy to be happy. And goodness, Daniella really would be the perfect daughter-in-law. Such a kind-hearted lady and so very pretty too. Of course I wouldn't have a grandchild of my own, but those lovely twins, I'd happily be a step-grandmom to them. After my initial reservations, mainly because I hate to see the breakdown of a family, I changed my mind. If Lucas is so sure that Daniella is the love of his life, who am I to get in the way? I was hoping that trip to Pittsburgh would bring them together, but Lucas has been so hard to manage since then.

Lucas was out of the house early this morning, all dressed up in his work clothes. Not that it fools me. But now he's back, and from the look on his face, the interview or whatever he attended didn't go well.

'Shall I make you a chicken pie for lunch, love?' I ask.

'Did you hear about Grant?' he replies, throwing his leather bag onto the floor by the door.

'Grant, as in Daniella's husband?' I ask.

'He was attacked in his home.'

'Goodness,' I reply, sitting heavily in my armchair, shoving my knitting bag to one side. 'I heard about a home invasion on the radio but didn't realize it was at Daniella's home. How awful. Are they okay?'

'Grant was hit on the head, but he's alive.' Lucas talks through gritted teeth, and it strikes me that he's rueful that Grant is still alive. And then a terrible, terrible thought hits me. No. Surely not.

I listen to Lucas stomping around the kitchen. There's the sound of broken glass, and I sigh heavily. Do I let this one go or confront him? Lucas has a temper, but would he actually try to murder a man? Bippie is cowering at my feet. He hates it when Lucas is in one of his moods. There's the sound of something else smashing. Sighing, I push myself to my feet.

'Stay here, Bippie,' I say. The dog does as he's told.

Lucas is standing in the kitchen in front of the patio door, his hands on his hips.

'Is she really worth it?' I ask quietly.

He swivels around, his eyes narrowed at me. 'If you're talking about Daniella, then the answer is yes.'

'Oh, Lucas,' I say, wondering whether I should articulate my fear. 'Did you do anything?'

'What do you mean, Mother?'

I'm scared of actually looking at my son, so I bustle around at the sink, reaching down for the dustpan and brush to clean up the shattered glass on the floor.

'Are you really sure about Daniella? Sometimes infatuation can masquerade as true love. It's not like you know her very well. Perhaps you're imagining she's something she's not. Love isn't an obsession; it's deep-rooted and sustainable.'

'What the hell do you know about love?' he scoffs. 'You've never known love or passion, not like what I have with Daniella. You and Dad hated each other. He had no respect for you, and frankly, I don't blame him. You're just an old, pathetic, wet rag. Shame you didn't die when Dad did.'

Lucas's words sting. Except I know he doesn't mean it, not really. He's lashing out at the one person in the world he can lash out at without consequences. I mustn't take it personally.

'I know you're hurting, love. But is Daniella really worth it? Perhaps you could find someone who isn't married, a less complicated situation.'

'I love Daniella!' Lucas roars. 'I love her! Don't tell me to back off or find someone else. She's the woman I've been waiting the whole of my life to find, so why do you want to destroy my happiness?'

'I don't. I want to protect you, because I think you're hurting.'

'Of course I'm fucking hurting.'

That shocks me. Lucas rarely swears and never swears at me. He knows how much I hated it when his father used foul language.

'I will do anything, absolutely anything to prove my love for Daniella, to make sure that she and I are together for the rest of our lives.' Lucas is so tense, it's a wonder his insides don't erupt straight out of his body. Every muscle is defined, the veins in his neck are engorged, and his eyes are flashing.

The question slips out of my mouth before I can stop it. 'Did you try to kill Grant, love?'

'What if I did?'

Lucas darts across the room so he's standing in the doorway to the hall, his bulk filling up the space so there's no way I can get past him.

'Did you try to murder Daniella's husband?' I can't stop the shock from showing on my face, the tremble of horror in my words. Surely my son wouldn't have done that?

He takes a step towards me, and I cower. I'm an idiot. Normally, when we have difficult conversations, I position myself with an escape route. But today, I'm stuck in the kitchen with both the back and garage doors locked and Lucas blocking the kitchen door.

'Let's take a deep breath and calm down, shall we?' I say.

His eyes are flashing as he steps towards me. I glance around wildly, cursing the fact I'm so tidy, that there's nothing within reach to use to protect myself. I cower as

Lucas's hand rises into the air, and I close my eyes, readying myself.

CHAPTER TWENTY-ONE

DANIELLA

I cannot describe the relief when Grant woke up. My only regret was not being at his bedside. When it happened, his nurse rang me right away. By the time I reached the hospital, he was asleep again, and only woke briefly to say hello to me before drifting back to sleep. But at least he recognized me. At least he knows where he is, and the doctor says that it's extremely likely Grant will make a good, if not complete, recovery. I pray that his brilliant brain has been unaffected. I was tempted to sit at his bedside, waiting for him to wake up again, but the nurse strongly encouraged me to go home and rest so that I would have the energy for all the tough things coming in the days ahead. I reluctantly did as she suggested.

The girls were due home tonight, but I spoke to both of them, and we canceled the flights. As much as I'd love to see them, Grant is safe now, and I'm positive he wouldn't want them to ruin their adventures. They can come home when Grant is home, and in the meantime, they can FaceTime him daily. Both girls were tearful. I suppose at their tender age they assume their parents are invincible, and it's quite the shock to realize they're not.

It also means I haven't been in a crazy rush to clean up the house. The police have gone, and although I've tidied up our bedroom, I can't bring myself to sleep in there until a new mattress arrives. I'll stay in the spare room until Grant is home.

I'm vacuuming the living room and initially don't hear my phone ring. When I realize I've missed a call, that fear returns to grip my chest, especially when I see the message: *Missed Call, Caller ID Withheld.* Please let Grant be alright, I think. I'm just about to call the hospital myself when my phone rings again. I answer immediately, sinking onto the sofa in case my legs give way.

The male voice on the other end is indecipherable. It sounds like the person is sobbing, great big hiccups and slurred words. A wave of fear rushes through me. Is it Grant? Has he awoken confused or been given bad news? Or has something terrible happened to the girls?

'Grant?' I ask, sitting bolt upright on the edge of the sofa; my fingers are clutching the phone so tightly, I'm worried I might break the screen.

'No. It's Lucas.' His voice sounds hoarse and shaky. I puff out a breath of relief.

'Lucas?' Other than receiving his message, I haven't heard from him since the disastrous trip to Pittsburgh. To be honest, with everything that's been going on with Grant and the house, I've barely thought about him. 'What's happened?' I ask.

He lets out a sob and speaks again, but it's almost impossible to make out what he's saying.

'Lucas, you need to take a deep breath,' I say. 'I can't understand you.'

The phone goes quiet for a moment, and then I hear him blowing his nose. 'I'm sorry, Daniella. But I didn't know who else to call. It's Mom. She's dead.'

'Oh no,' I say as my chest constricts.

'I was away on business, and I didn't get home in time. She wasn't even that old, and she was getting better...' His voice cracks again, and a wave of sadness rushes through me. I didn't know Peggy well, not really, but I've grown very fond of her. She was on track for becoming a mother substitute, and I felt we had a deep bond. Ironically, I've shared more with her than I have with my therapist.

'I really am sorry. When did Peggy pass?' I ask.

'They think it was complications following her accident.' He sobs again. 'And she probably mixed up her medication. She was just there, lying on her bed, cold. I don't know what to do, Daniella. I only found her today.'

'Have you got anyone who can be there with you?' I ask.

He sniffs. 'Not really. A few mates, but they're not those kinds of friends. You know? I can't talk to them like I can to you. And you knew Mom. She adored you.'

'It's a really difficult time for me at the moment,' I say, 'with Grant being critically ill in hospital.'

'I know,' he says, which surprises me. 'I visited him.'

That surprises me more than anything. Was he really that good a friend of Grant's, or does Lucas have an ulterior motive for going to see my husband?

'Sounds like we're both going through tough times,' he adds. 'Bippie is completely lost, just wandering aimlessly around the house. It's as if he knows he's lost his mistress. It's pitiful to see.'

'The poor dog. And poor you,' I add.

'I know you must be spending a lot of time at the hospital, but is there any possibility Bippie could live with you for a while until I find a new home for the dog? It's just I have to go away for work, and I have no one else to leave him with.'

I hesitate. It is extremely inconvenient. I want to be at the hospital as much as possible, and having a dog at home is hardly conducive to that.

'Don't worry,' Lucas says. 'I'll take him to the pound.'

'The pound?' I ask, taken aback.

'I'm away too much. It wouldn't be fair to Bippie to keep him here all alone with no one to feed or walk him.'

'Well, of course I'll have him,' I say. Perhaps it'll do both Bippie and me good to have each other for company.

'That's so kind of you. Can I bring him over later?' Lucas asks.

'I'll come and get him from you.'

After the call with Lucas, I'm trembling at the shock of his news. Poor Peggy. And there I was thinking she was doing so well after the mugging. I feel guilty that I haven't been to see her recently, and now I never will. I wonder whether the police have made any progress in tracking down who might have attacked her. Does this become manslaughter now, or is it impossible to show cause and effect since we're many weeks on? Life is so unfair. It's been one shock after another the past few weeks.

And Lucas sounded really shaken up. I've now seen a vulnerability to him that makes him more endearing. At that thought, I bump my fist to my forehead. I cannot think like this. I cannot. I remember how aggressive he was at the hotel, and I never want to experience that again. I hope he won't use Bippie as an excuse for seeing me more regularly. I have enough on my plate without worrying about Lucas.

CHAPTER TWENTY-TWO

LUCAS

The last few days have been like living in a cauldron. I can't think straight, and the only constant is my overwhelming need for Daniella. I can't live without her. I think of her every waking moment, and I dream of her at night. Sometimes I see the two of us on a sandy beach, hand in hand, walking barefoot as the sun sets; other times she's in my arms and we're making passionate love. During the day, I wonder what she's doing. I've taken to spying on her, not just at the hospital but at home and, before that, in her shop. Yes, I know that sounds creepy, but she's like oxygen to me. I need to see her, even if it's just little fleeting glances as she drives past in her car or appears as a silhouette in her bedroom window.

I was so angry with myself for failing to dispose of Grant, but now I wonder if it was a blessing in disguise. It was too risky, trying to inject him with insulin at the hospital. There will be another occasion for that, I'm sure, and in the meantime, I can start planning for my new life with Daniella.

I'M UTTERLY DEVASTATED that Mom is dead. The past hours have been some of the worst of my life. First Jade, and now Mom. Then Daniella's rejection, and now Grant. It doesn't seem possible that everything has unraveled so quickly. My heart feels literally shattered at the thought that I'll never see my mother again, that she'll never tell me to take a deep breath and will never bake me another cookie. And how quickly the image of her dead has replaced the million memories of her alive. My grief goes so much deeper than most people's. Yes, we know at a visceral level that our parents will die at some point. We try to prepare ourselves for the inevitable, except most people by the time they reach my age have a family of their own. They are independent of their parents and have taken steps to unravel that deep bond. But not me. I know we were co-dependent, Mom and me. I needed her. She needed me. I still need her. And honestly, I'm terrified that my life will spiral out of control without her calming influence. And that's what makes it so impossibly hard.

The only positive thing in my life is Daniella. Sweet, beautiful Daniella.

Tears spill down my cheeks for the woman who gave me life and from whom I took life, and the only thing that binds me to life is knowing that I'll be seeing Daniella later today.

I TIDY the house in preparation for her arrival. As I knew she would, she rings the doorbell at 5 p.m. on the dot. Bippie goes berserk when he sees Daniella, licking her, his rear end wiggling backwards and forwards. I can't stand the dog, but he does have good taste.

'Hi,' I say, and we both stand there awkwardly. 'I'm sorry about Grant.'

Daniella busies herself hugging and stroking the dog.

'Please come in,' I say, but she hesitates. Oh my word, this woman is utterly luminescent.

'I'm very sorry about Peggy. She was a wonderful woman.'

'I was lucky to have her,' I say, sniffing loudly. 'Do you still have both your parents?' I ask her.

'Yes, fortunately I do. Although they live in England, so I don't get to see them often. I suppose that's one of the reasons I bonded with Peggy so much. She reminds me a little of my mom.'

'I'm an orphan now,' I say.

She pauses as we both let that statement sink in. 'Please just come in,' I repeat, standing back and beckoning for her to pass me. I breathe in her glorious scent as she moves just inches from my body.

'It is such a shock,' she says. 'I thought Peggy was doing well, although you did have to come home from skiing early.'

'Mom was doing well. That's the irony of the whole situation. One moment life is sweet; the next, it's snuffed out forever. Thank heavens Grant is alright. We suffered a lot these past days, haven't we? You and me.'

Daniella wraps her arms around herself. How I wish I could pry them away from her gentle curves and wrap myself around her instead, except I don't. I'm the epitome of politeness.

'Come through into the kitchen, and I'll find all of Bippie's stuff.'

She hesitates but follows me into the house. When she's

standing in the kitchen, I turn around and walk up to her, gently stroking her cheek.

'I've missed you,' I say, my voice husky.

'No, Lucas.' Her body is rigid, and she steps away, edging backwards towards the hallway door. 'I already told you. I'm married, and what happened was a mistake. I love my husband, and he's seriously ill in the hospital. I'm only here because I'm sad Peggy died and I'm willing to look after Bippie.'

'It's not like Grant is loyal to you,' I mutter. 'He also had affairs.' If she was rigid before, now she freezes. Good.

I don't go to her because I'm not the sort of man to force myself on a woman even if I know in her heart of hearts she wants it as much as I do. She's slightly breathless now, her cheeks flushed pink. God, she's beautiful.

'Please, can you get Bippie's things?' she asks, her voice high-pitched.

'Of course.' I open the cupboard where Mom keeps the dog's belongings. I grab bowls and a sack of kibble along with his bed. 'Let me put these in your car,' I say. I follow her outside, where she opens the trunk of her car, and I shove the dog's belongings inside, wedged up next to a small suitcase.

'Can I cook you supper one evening?' I ask.

'No, Lucas. I know things are difficult for you right now, but we can't see each other anymore. Grant needs me. You can message me about Bippie, but that's it. You must respect me and my marriage.'

'Respect?' I chortle. 'What we have is—'

She cuts me off. 'I'm sorry, Lucas. I can't. It was a mistake. If you insist on this behavior, then you'll never see me again.'

There is a fraction of a second when I consider

punishing Daniella for her vicious words, except I manage to stop myself. I love this woman, and at this stage, love means being gentle with her. And patient. Daniella opens her car and calls Bippie, who jumps up onto the back seat. For a moment, I think about changing my mind. As annoying as the dog is, he's my last living link to Mom. But Daniella clearly wants him to stay with her, and he will provide us with a reason for staying in touch.

'Please let me know when Peggy's funeral is,' she says. And then she's in her car, starting the engine and driving away. I watch until her car is out of sight.

Returning back inside, the house feels so empty. To begin with, I mope, wandering from room to room, restless, kicking at doorframes, throwing open cupboard doors and wondering what the hell I'm meant to do with all of the junk that Mom collected over the years. I go through every room. Every room except her bedroom.

Because that's where she died.

That's where I had to kill her.

Mom gave me no choice.

I FIND a crate of expensive-looking wines in the basement, covered in dust, so they've probably been there since Father died all those years ago. I heave them upstairs and uncork a bottle. Giving it a sniff, I pour a large glass and savor the rich aroma. The good news is that now I'm rich. All those years of worrying about money, demeaning myself by begging Mom for cash, are over. I've no idea what this house is worth, but it's a lot, and I'm pretty sure that Mom has healthy bank balances. I just need to get access to them.

I take my glass of wine and the bottle to her desk. It's an

old oak bureau desk that belonged to my grandfather, ugly and dark. I open it up and attempt to open the top drawer. Frustratingly, it's locked. I hunt around for a key, but I don't find one. Instead, I use brute force and pull it open. Bingo. Here are her bank statements and letters from her financial advisor and attorney. I'm right. She's loaded, or more like, I am. I grin widely and take another swig of wine. Really, I should be drinking champagne. I think about all the things I can do with the money, starting off with buying Daniella a beautiful ring. Perhaps I'll visit Tiffany's tomorrow, or maybe she's a Cartier kind of woman.

The phone rings. It's Mom's attorney, an annoying, pedantic man whom I last saw a decade ago when Father passed. 'I'm very sorry for the loss of Margaret,' Philip Morton says in his nasally voice. 'As you may be aware, I am the executor of your mother's will, and it would be helpful if you could come by my office so we can discuss the contents of her will.'

'What's there to discuss?' I ask. 'I'm her only son.'

'Her will isn't completely straightforward,' Morton replies.

'What do you mean?'

'It would be helpful if you could come to see me. Would tomorrow be convenient?'

He's acting like this is some power game, so I hesitate for a long time before saying, 'I can only do 11 a.m. tomorrow. I trust that is convenient?'

'Indeed, it is. I look forward to seeing you then.'

What the hell is all that about? I assumed that Mom had left everything to me, but now a flicker of nerves makes my stomach clench, and the wine on my empty stomach makes me feel queasy. Perhaps she's put it all in a trust so that I can't access it until I'm sixty or some such nonsense. No, Mom wasn't bright enough for that. But even so, it's unsettling.

THE NEXT DAY, I arrive at Philip Morton's office, a brownstone not unlike Jade's house from the exterior, but completely different on the inside. The rooms are shabby and dark, lined with numerous bookshelves all holding old-fashioned tomes. I'm late. On purpose, of course, because Morton thinks he's important, and I have no desire to add to his misplaced self-importance. Heaven knows why Mom stayed with this guy; he must be at least a decade over retirement age. I'll need to check if there are any laws against attorneys practicing beyond a certain age.

'If you could follow me,' the receptionist says. 'Mr. Morton is waiting for you.' The woman reminds me of Mom a little, in her tweed skirt and sweater set. She knocks on a dark wooden door and pushes it open to let me pass through. Philip Morton stands up from the other side of his desk, dressed in a pin-striped suit with a ridiculous yellow bowtie at his neck. It's only as his bespectacled eyes flicker away from me that I notice a woman seated in a chair next to the vacant one that's presumably for me. And then she stands up too and turns to look at me.

I'm not sure whether to faint with shock or sweep her into my arms.

What is Daniella doing here?

I'm thrown and just stand there for a moment, staring at her. To give her credit, she also looks like she feels awkward, although that could be a feigned expression, I suppose. I sit down.

'What's Daniella doing here?' I ask Philip Morton.

'I'll get to that,' he says, pushing his glasses farther up his nose. He lifts up a manila envelope and withdraws a formal-looking document. Perhaps Mom has left Bippie to Daniella; that would make sense, as she knows I'm not the greatest fan of the dog.

'As I said yesterday, I'm very sorry to learn of your mother's passing. She was a lovely woman.'

I wonder how he knows that.

'She, ergh, redid her will quite recently, in fact. I believe there are no legal grounds on which to object to it, as she was very much of sound mind and was quite clear what she wanted to happen to her estate. If I may, I will read the will and then a letter that she wrote to you, Mr. Denman.' He clears his throat and removes another smaller piece of paper, in pale blue. I recognize it as Mom's stationery with her address printed at the top.

'I, Margaret Denman, resident in the City of Boston in the County of Brookline, State of Massachusetts, being of sound mind, not acting under duress or undue influence, and fully understanding the nature and extent of all my property and of this disposition thereof, do hereby make, publish, and declare this document to be my Last Will and Testament, and hereby revoke any and all other wills and codicils heretofore made by me. I direct that all my debts, and expenses of my last illness, funeral, and burial, be paid as soon after my death as may be reasonably convenient, and I hereby authorize my Personal Representative, hereinafter appointed, to settle and discharge, in his or her absolute discretion, any claims made against my estate. I further direct that my Personal Representative shall pay out of my estate any—'

I interrupt him. 'We don't need all the legal stuff. Just skip to the bit I'm here for.'

'Right.' Philip Morton clears his throat. 'Your mother appointed me as the executor to her will. I'll skip forwards.' He clears his throat yet again, and it sets my nerves on edge. 'I devise and bequeath my property, both real and personal and wherever situated as follows: The first beneficiary is Lucas Denman to whom I bequeath all of my estate with the exception of my house at 1184 Ivy Street and its contents, which I bequeath to the second beneficiary, Daniella Morris.'

Sorry? What?

Did I just hear that correctly? That Mom has left the house and the contents to Daniella? Why the hell would she do that? The redness swarms in front of my eyes, and I feel my breath quicken and my muscles tense. This can't be right. The house must be worth nearly two million dollars, even though it's run-down. That should be mine! Rage quickly burns into a cauldron of fiery fury.

'No, I can't accept it,' Daniella says, breaking into the frenzy of my thoughts. 'It's not right. The house belongs to Lucas.'

And it's as if a fire hose has been directed straight at me. The rage dissipates instantly, and I look at this woman whom I love so much. Because at some point in the near future, what is mine will be hers and what is hers will be mine. So does it matter who owns the house? I can see now what Mom has done. She's giving the house to Daniella so that the two of us can be together. It's her final legacy, and her very greatest. How blessed am I?

'I realize this will come as a surprise to you both, but may I suggest that you go away and think about it.'

'But Peggy barely knew me, and Lucas is her son,' Daniella exclaims.

I lean across to Daniella and pat her knee. Fortunately, she doesn't recoil from me. 'If Mom wanted you to have the house and its contents, then it should be yours.'

Both Philip Morton and Daniella stare at me, but I know I'm right. This is my mother's final and greatest gift. A way to bring Daniella and me together forever.

CHAPTER TWENTY-THREE

DANIELLA

I walk out of Philip Morton's office in a state of shock. Fortunately, the attorney asked Lucas to stay behind to sign some papers, so I didn't need to speak to him further. To be fair, with so much going on, when I received the phone call from Morton's secretary, I was disinclined to attend his office. But as he is located just around the corner from the hospital, and they were washing Grant when I arrived, I had some time to kill. I'm stunned that Peggy left me her house. I'm also rather confused. If she was childless, it might make sense, but Lucas appeared to be a loving son, frequently at her house, hurrying home when she fell ill. As I stroll back to the hospital, I wonder if maybe she was very wealthy or even whether Lucas has such a large property portfolio himself, meaning he doesn't have the need for yet another house. Although that is also odd, because I imagine there are sentimental reasons for keeping the home in the family.

What is even stranger is how, after the initial shock, Lucas seemed keen for me to have it. Who in their right mind happily gives away an asset worth a couple of million dollars?

My next problem is what I'm going to tell Grant. I've hated how I've been lying to him, not just for sleeping with Lucas, which was completely indefensible, but also for not telling him that Lucas is Peggy's son. I dug myself such a deep hole there seemed no way out of it. It's so true that one lie spawns many more. Yet now I have no choice but to tell him about the Lucas-Peggy connection. I feel doubly awful that I'm going to be taking advantage of my husband's brain injury and confusion, but so be it.

I'm still in a daze as I walk into Grant's hospital room.

He's been moved out of the ICU and is now in a small room with a view of an internal courtyard. To my delight, he's propped up in bed. Not sitting fully by himself, but definitely awake and alert. He grins as I enter the room.

'How are you feeling?' I ask, hurrying to his bedside.

'As if I've been walloped over the head so hard it feels like my brain is going to explode.'

I grimace, but that is the longest and most complex sentence my husband has said to me since he was attacked, and my shoulders relax with the relief that he is most definitely on the mend.

'I'm sorry,' I say, squeezing his hand. 'I've had the most extraordinary news.'

He tries to turn to look at me and grimaces.

'Do you need some more painkillers?' I ask.

'No, I'm woozy enough as it is.'

'So, you remember the lady I helped after the mugging? Well, she passed away last week. This morning, I was contacted by her attorney. She has left me her house and all the contents.'

'What?' Grant frowns, but that clearly hurts him, and he lets out a sigh.

'There's more. I discovered that Lucas is Peggy's son.' I can't bring myself to look at my husband as I'm saying this, and I take advantage of the fact that he finds it hard to turn his neck.

'Lucas is Peggy's son?' he asks.

'It's the weirdest coincidence. What are the chances of that?'

'I'm not following.' His voice sounds a little slurred and weak now.

'Do you remember that I helped a lady when she was mugged on Ivy Street?'

'My memory is blurred, so no, not really.'

'Do you recall Lucas?' I ask, hoping for a second that perhaps the whole gym friendship thing has been erased from my husband's memory.

'Of course I know Lucas.'

'Well, I've been left his mother's house in her will.'

I can see that I've lost Grant now. His eyes close again, and his breathing deepens, and I'm left alone to ponder everything that has happened. I stay at the hospital for a couple of hours. Lesley sends me a message, asking how Grant is, how I am. I don't reply. Instead, I think about what I might do with the funds from Peggy's house. We can pay off the girls' college fees and living expenses so they won't enter the workplace with any debt. I still want to sell our house, but maybe we could buy them an apartment so they get a foot on the property ladder. And then Grant and I can take a holiday somewhere exotic when he's better. A second honeymoon.

I NEED to get home for Bippie. Despite the cameras and the burglar alarm, I'm relieved to have the dog, not just for much-needed company but also as extra security. Our home doesn't feel safe anymore.

Lucas calls me. I consider not answering the phone except it feels mean, especially as I feel I've been given his inheritance. Briefly, I wonder if he's calling to tell me he's going to contest the will. If that is the case, I won't fight him.

'Hey,' he says gently. 'How are you? How is Grant, and how is Bippie?'

'All doing fine, actually,' I reply. 'I'm sorry about earlier. It was such a shock.'

'I want you to have the house,' he says. 'If it's what Mom wanted, then so be it. The only thing is Mr. Morton has suggested we go around the house together so that I can create a list of the things that I'd like to keep. You know, sentimental things that have no monetary value, but mean something to me.'

'Is there a hurry for that?' I ask. I know nothing about probate, but I assume it will take months for me to become the legal owner of the house, and it's not like I'm going to chuck Lucas out of his old home. 'Couldn't you just take the things you want. I don't need to be there for that.'

'According to Mr. Morton, unfortunately, you do need to be there. I know it's not a great time for you with Grant being ill, but could you spare an hour?'

I hesitate, uneasy. But then reckon it would be churlish of me to decline. There is definitely something strange about Lucas. That easy-going, articulate, extraordinarily good-looking man has morphed into something else. Someone who makes me uneasy, scares me slightly. Yes, he's still handsome and self-assured, but I didn't like the anger he displayed in the hotel, and I'm uneasy about being alone with him. I tell a white lie.

'I could pop over shortly, but I can't stay long. I have a friend coming to my place for supper, so I need to get back.'

'Thank you, Daniella,' he says. 'See you soon.'

I call Grant to find out how he is.

'Doing well, I think,' he says, his words still slurring a little. 'When are you coming over?'

'A little later. I'm popping over to Peggy's house first, but I shouldn't be long.'

PEGGY'S HOME feels different without her. She used to keep the house extremely warm, but now there's a coldness, and the chill isn't just from the temperature. Lucas is polite and doesn't make any attempt to touch me, for which I'm relieved. He's holding a pen and a notebook.

'Philip Morton said we should go through the rooms, and I should document the items I wish to keep, with your permission, of course.'

'This is all very quick,' I say.

'He's a lawyer.' Lucas laughs. 'Everything has to be aboveboard, and honestly, it'll make me more comfortable to do things properly.'

'I'm still in shock,' I say.

'Mom loved you. It's what she wanted.'

And yet so much has gone wrong in my life since I first rescued Peggy. The unresolved argument with Lesley and the hideous Matt; Grant's attack and Lucas's largely unwanted attention. Being bequeathed her house, does that make up for it all?

'Shall we start in the living room?' Lucas suggests, breaking into my thoughts. He is surprisingly relaxed considering the awkwardness of the situation and the recent death of his mother.

It's weird being here without Peggy. Her favorite upright chair still has a half-knitted sweater on it.

'I'd like to keep all the photos,' Lucas says, pointing to the one on the mantelpiece. It reminds me of how our wedding photo was taken, and I shiver involuntarily. 'And some of the books, if you're okay with that.'

'Of course,' I say. He bends down and opens a cupboard underneath the bookshelf. 'Photo albums,' he says, pulling out a few yellowing albums. 'You can have all the china. Can't stand those little porcelain figurines. They creeped me out as a child.'

I laugh. They're not to my taste either. Lucas opens the doors of the tall cabinet.

'Good heavens, more yarn,' he says. 'You're a knitter, aren't you?'

'I am,' I confirm. 'I've always got a sweater on the go.'

'In which case, take everything out of Mom's knitting bag,' he says, pointing to the felted bag that was always at her feet. I lift it up and look through the skeins of mauve yarn. And then I see an envelope. Removing it from the tangled yarn and pairs of knitting needles, my heart quickens when I see my name on it. Daniella Morris is handwritten in ink. Fortunately, Lucas isn't looking at me as he rifles through a drawer full of silver cutlery. Hesitating at first, I quickly open the envelope and remove a piece of pale blue paper. I read it quickly.

Dearest Daniella,

If you are reading this, it means I'm dead. Probably killed by my son, Lucas. Rightly or wrongly, he adores you. At first, I was worried about him breaking up your family, but then I realized that you two could be happy together. I adore you, too. You're like a daughter to me, so it made me happy. But now, I've realized that Lucas is no good, even for the people he loves the most. Please, my dear, stay away from him for your own sake and the sake of your family. I don't want him to get into trouble with the police. Jail would break him. I changed my will recently and hope that the gift of my house will give you the funds to move you and your family far from Boston. Far from Lucas.

With love, Peggy.

P.S. I hid this in my knitting bag because I know this is the one place Lucas won't look!

My hands are literally shaking as I finish reading the note, and when I look up, I see Lucas is standing right in front of me, his face stony.

'What's that?' he asks.

I try to shove the letter back into the envelope, but Lucas has certainly seen the shock on my face, the fear of him, the horror of those words. He grabs the letter. I know I need to get out of here, except I'm frozen with fear. My breath is shallow and audible.

Lucas's face is impassive as he reads the letter, and then he lets out a loud snort.

'You don't actually believe this, do you?' His laugh is harsh as he rolls his eyes. 'You do know that Mom had diabetic ketoacidosis?'

'What's that?' I ask.

'One of the symptoms is, in basic terms, brain fog. She would get confused and say the most ridiculous things. It's due to years of not keeping her diabetes under control. Look it up if you want.'

'But she seemed completely with it whenever I was with her, except when she was in the hospital, and that was because of a head injury.'

'Oh, she was good at pretending, but you never saw her in the evening, did you? They were always the worst. She'd talk nonsense and genuinely believe it. For a while, I thought she had dementia, but no. The doctor said it was a result of her diabetes. It's what killed her eventually, too.'

Lucas is speaking with such conviction, except I'm not sure that I believe him. I know nothing about diabetes, but this sounds strange to me. That letter is well written, the handwriting neat. There is nothing about it that suggests confusion.

'I think I should go,' I say, stepping to the side to get past Lucas.

'Oh no, you don't,' he replies. 'We need to talk.'

'Whatever that letter is, I'm not comfortable. I think we should communicate through the attorney.'

Lucas puts his arms out and grasps my shoulders. Once again, I freeze.

'You don't get it, do you? Daniella, I love you. I want to be with you for the rest of my life. I would do anything, absolutely anything, to make that happen. You can sell this house, and we can move somewhere else, or we could do it up and live here together.'

What?

'But I don't want to be with you!' I exclaim, trying and failing to wriggle out of his tight grip, his fingers digging painfully into the muscles of my shoulders. 'I'm married to a man I love, with whom I have daughters.'

'You don't love Grant!' he spits. 'And Grant doesn't love you. He's been cheating on you anyway. You're just with him because you feel guilty. Let him go, Daniella.'

I know now with absolute certainty that this man is deluded. And scary. It's as if a switch goes off in my head, and I completely lose it. Grant, cheating on me? That's ridiculous, isn't it?

'Get your hands off me!' I try to wriggle away from him, except he puts a foot out, and I stumble over it, landing in a heap on the sofa. An arm snakes around my neck, his breath hot in my ear.

'Don't make me hurt you.'

I lash out at him, limbs flying everywhere. Except Lucas is strong. Too strong. 'Let me go!' I scream. A hand clasps around my mouth and nose, making breathing impossible.

'You're so beautiful when you're angry,' he murmurs, his mouth on my neck. I kick backwards, and I must hurt him this time, because he yelps. 'You bitch.'

He releases his grip for just a second, but I'm not quick enough.

My world goes black.

CHAPTER TWENTY-FOUR

LUCAS

I'm in Macy's, shopping. It's really rather thrilling spending time choosing the perfect things for my love. I'm currently in the lingerie department, and no, I'm not some cheap pervert. I'm only interested in buying beautiful items: a lacy nightdress, silk underwear in taupe. Nothing gaudy for my classy love. In my basket is a cashmere sweater and a pair of warm pants—functional clothes to keep her warm. I go to the cosmetics department, but here I'm completely out of my depth. Plastering on my most charming smile, I select a pretty blonde assistant.

'I was wondering if you could help me. My fiancée is coming to stay, and her luggage got lost. I promised I'd stock up on everything. We have a long-distance relationship at the moment. Any chance you could help me buy all that's needed?'

She flutters her eyelids at me. 'Of course, sir.'

After answering a few questions as best I can, I purchase shampoo, conditioner, soap, makeup remover, toothpaste, and an electric toothbrush. I think of all the accouterments that Jade had and then hand my basket to the shop assistant. 'Please fill it up with everything a woman might need,' I say.

Ten minutes later, the basket is heaving. When she rings up everything at the register, I'm shocked to be spending several hundred dollars. But then again, I have the money now, and my beloved is worth it.

On the way home, I stop at Target and purchase cozy bedding and a couple of fluffy blankets. I also pick up a bottle of champagne and a lovely bouquet of roses. Daniella will love those.

Yes, it's unfortunate that I'm having to keep her in the basement. It's dark, cold and dank down there, but it's the only place in the house that is fully secure. It's just a temporary measure. After knocking her out—which, believe me, was quite definitely the worst thing I've ever had to do—I carried Daniella downstairs. Then I dragged a mattress into the basement and gently laid her on it. She's covered up with two comforters, her head on the softest pillow I could find. Fortunately, the basement is largely empty. Mom cleared it out after Dad died, announcing that it reminded her of him and she never wanted to go down there again. I don't blame her. The basement has too many terrible memories for both of us. I've had to secure Daniella, which is unfortunate but necessary. At least there are no implements down there with which she could hurt me or herself, and there is only one way in and out—up the concrete steps, with a door that only locks from the outside. There is no window, and it's impossible for anyone to hear her shouting. All in all, it's perfect, other than it's not heated and stinks of damp and decaying rodents. To cover up the acrid smell, I sprayed a healthy dose of my aftershave. I know she likes the scent; she told me so.

Daniella was still sleeping when I left. I used Mom's

hairbrush to gently brush her hair, worried about any bumps or bruises I might have caused when I knocked her out. Initially, I was concerned I might have caused her damage, except her breathing was regular. I even used Mom's blood pressure monitor, carefully winding it around Daniella's upper arm, and her blood pressure, although on the low side, was normal. I hope she doesn't wake up when I'm not there, because she might be scared to find herself in a strange, bleak basement. But once the initial shock has passed, I will be able to soothe her. We may not be married yet, but I promise to care for her in sickness and in health.

BACK AT HOME, I make sure that there are no snooping neighbors around as I take the copious shopping bags from the trunk of the car. I hope that Daniella will approve of my purchases. I want to make the basement as cozy and romantic as possible. It's far from ideal, but I remind myself that this is a temporary measure. Inside the house, all is quiet. There's still the lingering scent of Mom, her sickly-sweet perfume with a hint of violets and burned dust from the electric heaters she kept running day and night. It's off-putting because I know in my heart of hearts Mom wouldn't approve of me keeping Daniella captive. But what other choice do I have?

I unlock the basement door, locking it again behind me and, lugging some of the bags of purchases, descend the steps. I left a low light on, and when I reached the bottom, Daniella is sitting up on the mattress, her hands still secured as I left her.

'How are you feeling?' I ask, hurrying towards her. 'Would you like water, a tea, some Tylenol perhaps?'

She's staring at me, her face deathly pale. 'What are you doing to me?' she asks in a hoarse whisper.

'I'm sorry about putting you down here,' I say, placing the bags at my feet. 'But I need to keep you somewhere safe.'

'You need to let me go, Lucas.'

I shake my head sadly. 'I can't. You'll see that this is for the best, and I'll find somewhere much nicer for us to live, where we're away from everyone.'

'You're demented!' Daniella shouts at me and tugs at the fastening around her wrists. 'Let me go!'

'Hey, hey,' I say. I'd like to put my arms around her, mutter sweet nothings into her ear and calm her down, but in this feral state, she might try to bite my ear off.

'How long do you plan on keeping me here?' Her voice echoes across the bare brick walls. 'I'm going to be missed! Grant will wonder where I am, as will the girls. Don't you think they'll start looking for me? Call the police?'

Fortunately, I thought of that. I remove Daniella's phone from my back pocket and wave it in the air. 'You're going to send some messages to everyone who might miss you. Let's start with Grant first, shall we?' I hold her phone up in front of her face, and she tries to lurch towards me, but with her wrists tied together and from a seated position, she does no damage. The phone opens up.

I navigate to WhatsApp and see that she hasn't sent Grant a message since before his accident, but prior to that, they'd send each other messages at least a couple of times a day. Messages about who will pick up the dry cleaning or when Grant is returning home after work. They're mundane and rather depressing. Certainly, there are no loving words here.

'Has Grant got his phone with him in the hospital?' I ask.

'I think the police gave it back, but he hasn't been well enough to use it.' Daniella seems deflated now, shoulders hunched, refusing to meet my eyes.

'In which case you're going to call the hospital and tell them you've come down with a bug so you can't see Grant for a couple of days.'

'I'm going to tell them you've captured me and they need to call the police.'

'Oh, Daniella,' I say, shaking my head sadly, 'if you do that, I'll have to hurt you, and it will be bad. That's the last thing I want to do. After that, I'll head to Belize and Costa Rica and find Tasia and Arlyse. It would be so sad if tragedy struck at the prime of their lives. I've been following them both on social media, and we've been messaging, the three of us. I've promised to take them snowboarding again, and sailing, too. What you need to do is be sensible, and then the four of us can live happily ever after.'

'The four of us?' Daniella asks. Why is she being so obtuse?

'You, me, Tasia, and Arlyse.'

'And what about Grant?'

'Right, enough talk. I'm sending everyone messages, and I'll call the hospital on your behalf, as I don't trust you.'

'Why are you doing this?' she yells at me. I wish she wouldn't raise her voice because it's enormously triggering, and I really want to stay calm around Daniella. 'Is it because your mom left me this house? If so, you can have it. I've already said I don't want it. The second you let me out, I'll sign an affidavit relinquishing the inheritance, and we can never see each other again.'

'And that is exactly what I don't want to happen. I'm fine with you owning this house. It will be our home. You can redecorate it in any way you like. Mom has left me plenty of funds. And if you prefer, we can even knock it down and build a new house to your exact specifications.'

'You don't get it, Lucas! I don't want to be with you. Never.'

'Oh, come on, Daniella. I know you don't mean that. I love you. And I know that you love me too, deep down. You can't deny that you showed me your love when we were together?'

'I don't love you, and I never will!' Daniella shouts. 'You're crazy.'

I smile wryly. 'Crazy in love. I accept that it's difficult for you to show your true feelings, but I know you will eventually. You need to calm down. I'm in this for as long as it takes. I want us to have a wonderful life together, Daniella. I'm going to leave you here while I message your family, and when I return, you are going to be calm, and you'll have thought through what I've said. You and I are blessed. Most people never know true passion, true love.'

She turns away from me, and I realize that she's sobbing. But I can't let her display of emotion unravel me. I click on her phone to ensure it doesn't lock, leave the bags near the steps and return to upstairs.

I see that she's set up a three-way WhatsApp group including herself and the girls. The recent messages have all been about Grant's recovery.

I start typing.

I've been to see Dad, and he's doing really well, so there's no need for you to worry.

I wonder if I need to add something else to stop them

from hopping on a flight home, but decide the least said, the better. Then I call the hospital.

'Hi, I'm a friend of Daniella Morris. Is it possible to get a message to Grant, her husband?'

'Of course. How can I help?' the kindly-sounding nurse asks.

'Daniella has got a nasty stomach bug, so she won't be coming in to see her husband for a couple of days for fear of passing anything on. Can you please leave messages on her phone with any updates?'

'Sure. Tell her we hope she gets better soon, and yes, it's important she doesn't visit the hospital until she's fully recovered.'

I do a little fist pump. I've just bought myself a couple of days, at least. I just wish that Daniella could see sense. But I'm not giving up. I'm in it for as long as it takes. I'll show my love for her every second of every day, and I'm sure that soon enough she'll recognize she feels the same.

CHAPTER TWENTY-FIVE

DANIELLA

You read about crazy men keeping young girls captive in their basements for years at a time. There is the occasional story in the press and plenty of similar narratives in thriller books. But you never think it's going to happen to you. It's not like I'm some young kid. I'm a middle-aged woman living a normal life. So how the hell did it come to this? I blame myself. Of course, I should never have slept with Lucas. I should have backed right away from him and never seen him again. Except how could I avoid that with Peggy leaving me this house? I go back through all of our encounters, and I shiver at the thought that I found this man alluring; no, more than that. Gorgeous. I wasted hours of my life daydreaming about him. Yet he's a delusional crackpot. How could I have not seen that?

I look around this basement, and it's apparent there is no way for me to escape. He's secured my hands together with plastic zip ties, and there's a rope around one ankle that's attached to a hook on the wall. I am a prisoner. I recall how he told me that he'd hurt me if I try to escape, and then I think of Grant. Did Lucas attack him? Was everything a ploy to get my husband out of the way so he could swoop in as my savior? And then I think of the one item that was missing from our house. Our wedding photograph. Did Lucas take that? I shiver as I curl up tighter despite the warmth from the many woolen blankets. Will Grant believe I'm sick, and what if he takes a turn for the worse and I'm not there?

And then I think of Bippie, all alone in our house with no one to feed him or to take him out. Lucas is clearly a violent man. I know for sure he hit me and knocked me out. I can lift my hands high enough to feel the lump on the side of my head, and the pounding headache confirms it. So I can't risk angering him. Maybe I need to do what he wants. Pretend to be in love with him. It sickens me. No, worse, it's repulsive, but if it means I can get out of here alive, then that's what I'll do.

I've no idea what time it is or how long I've been here. I need the toilet, and I see he's left me a bucket. I'm hungry too.

Some time later, I hear the unlocking of the door and his heavy footsteps descend to the basement. Lucas appears holding a tray.

'I've made you some supper. How are you feeling?'

I shrug my shoulders. He places the tray on the floor next to the mattress and turns up the electric heater, which is on the other side of the room.

'We need to talk,' I say, trying to sound calm, as if this were a perfectly normal conversation.

'You're right. We do.'

'I'm sorry if there has been a misunderstanding,' I say. 'I didn't want to hurt you or Grant.'

'You need to forget about Grant,' Lucas says.

I try not to show my dismay. 'Was it you who attacked him?' I ask.

Lucas chortles. 'No. I want to win you over in a fair fight not by default.'

'What does that mean?

'I want you to choose me, Daniella, like you did when we made love on your living room floor. Do you think you can do that?'

'Um, yes. Perhaps.'

'You know that Peggy adored you,' he says. 'At first, she didn't want me to break up your family, but then she realized that you were my soulmate. That's why she left you the house, to help us be together.'

We're both silent for a while.

'Have you ever been married?' I ask.

'I've been engaged twice but never married. You're the first woman I'm completely sure about. I think I'd rather spend my life alone than accept second best to you.'

I almost want to burst out laughing at the absurdity of this situation. Lucas is sitting on the floor, his arms wrapped around his long legs, chatting as if this were all perfectly normal.

'Have some food,' he says, nudging the tray towards me. I notice that he's laid out plastic cutlery and the food, which looks like a fish pie, on a paper plate. I'm starving, and my mouth waters.

'How am I meant to eat with my hands tied together?' I ask.

He obviously hasn't thought that one through. Lucas hesitates. 'I can feed you, or you can promise not to do anything stupid,' he says. 'I'm strong, Daniella, and the last thing I want to do is hurt you, but if there's any silly business, then I won't hesitate to break one or more of your limbs.'

He says this through a smile. He is completely crazy, but now isn't the time to try to overpower Lucas, who is two or three times as strong as me. I'm going to have to be cleverer than that if I'm going to get out of here.

'I promise not to do anything,' I say. 'I'm genuinely hungry.'

He nods, produces a pair of scissors and cuts the ties on my wrists. Then he reaches forward and pulls my ankles together, wrapping a tie around them instead.

After eating a few mouthfuls, I try to think, try to come up with a plan. I turn to him. 'You know, we've never really talked. You haven't told me about your childhood, what you do, or whether you went to college. It would be good to get to know you better.'

His face morphs into a broad smile, the one that used to make my stomach do butterflies but now leaves me cold; no, worse than that, it repulses me.

'I've lived here my whole life. I was the eldest, and Louise was my little sister. Mom is a wonderful woman.' He swallows hard. 'Was. She kept our family together. Father was cruel to all of us. I know he beat Mom, but what could I do? I was just a kid. Once I tried to stand up to him. I must have been ten or eleven, and he whipped me until I bled, then locked me down here in the basement. I was here for days until Mom got me out. She paid the price for doing that. As I got older, I started going to the gym, and before long, I was physically stronger than Dad. He kept out of my way then. At sixteen, I left home and only returned after he died. From the outside, we had it all: this big house, lots of money, he was a successful banker, Louise and I did every after-school activity there was, and my parents entertained loads. No one would have guessed what went on behind closed doors.' He looks wistfully off into the distance.

'And your sister?' I ask, recalling how Peggy told me she had died.

'Louise. Little Louise. It was a terrible accident. None of us truly recovered after what happened.'

'What did happen?' I ask. My heart is thudding now, and I wonder if I really want to know.

'She fell. I got the blame, of course, but it was just child's play.'

I consider asking more probing questions, but the last thing I want to do is anger Lucas. 'And these days, what do you do? You said you were a property developer.'

'That's boring, Daniella. Who wants to talk about work? Not me. Let's talk about our hopes and dreams. Our plans for the future.'

I know I should be looking at Lucas, but the more he talks, the more I realize he has completely lost his mind. Does he really think that my future is tied up with him? This man belongs in prison or in a psychiatric hospital. Yet I know I need to play along.

'I fell in love with Rockport,' I say.

'You'd rather sell this house and move up there?' he asks.

'Maybe. What do you think?' I ask.

'I'll go to the moon and back so long as I'm with you.'

There's a long pause.

'Are you going to hurt me?' I whisper.

'Of course not. I'm not a violent man,' he says. Except I don't believe a single word that's coming out of his mouth.

'All I want is for the two of us to be together. When I'm

convinced that you love me as much as I love you, we'll be out of here. That, I promise.'

CHAPTER TWENTY-SIX

DANIELLA

'Wake up, Daniella.' Lucas is crouched down next to me, and I cower away from him instinctually. I can see from the flash of anger across his face that he doesn't like that.

'You gave me a fright,' I say. 'I was fast asleep.' I've no idea what time it is, as Lucas has removed my watch and, of course, I don't have my phone.

He stands up, and I see that he has several shopping bags at his feet, all emblazoned with either the Target or Macy's logo. 'I've bought you some clothes, and I'd like you to try them on.'

'Now?' I ask. 'You'll have to cut the wrist ties.' He put them on again after I was done eating.

'I will, but don't do anything stupid,' he says as he cuts the plastic ties. 'I don't want to hurt you.'

It's such a relief to be able to move my hands and arms, and I stretch and rub them to ease the soreness.

'I've bought you some lovely items. I hope you'll enjoy them.' He pulls out a silk negligee, and I shiver at the thought of having to put that on.

'I'm not getting undressed in front of you,' I say.

'I'll turn my back, but I need to trust you, Daniella, and I'm not sure I do yet.'

'In which case, I can't try on the clothes.'

He sighs loudly. 'Fortunately, we have thirty days in which to return them, so I'll just put them back in the bags.'

That's a relief.

'Has there been any news from the hospital or my girls?' I ask. I can't stop thinking about Grant. He must be worried that I haven't called him. He would know that even sick I would at least call to check in.

Lucas removes my phone from the pocket of his jeans and holds it up in the air. 'Nothing,' he says. 'Relax, Daniella. It's all good.'

Of course I don't trust him.

He's just putting the phone back into his jeans when it rings. We both jump.

'Are you going to answer it?' I ask.

'Lesley. Who's she?'

'My business partner and she'll be really worried about me. I go into work every day, and if I don't contact her, she'll start to investigate.' Of course, that isn't true, especially since Lesley and I aren't really on speaking terms.

To my dismay, Lucas doesn't answer the phone. A moment later, the phone pings, indicating I have a message.

'Can I listen to it?' I ask.

'Hold your hands out in front of you first.' He slips a plastic tie around my wrists once again, and I'm annoyed with myself that I lost an opportunity. When he's sure that my wrists are tightly secured, he holds the phone in front of my face, and it unlocks. Then he presses play.

Tears spring to my eyes as I hear Lesley's familiar voice.

'Daniella, what's going on? I know you're still pissed with me, but I've been around to your house several times, and there's a dog there, trapped inside, and he's going ballistic. I got really worried, so I went to the hospital to see Grant, and he said that you haven't been in touch for twenty-four hours, other than a message left with a nurse to say you've got a bug. I'm really worried. If you don't call back within the next hour, I'm going to call the police, and we'll break into your house. Call me, okay?'

I have never felt such relief. I'm going to get out of here. My lovely friend has realized something is horribly wrong. Except when I look at Lucas, it's obvious he's really agitated. He is pacing around the cellar, his fingers clenching and unclenching, his jaw thrust forwards and a vein pulsing in his neck.

'Why the fuck does your business partner have to stick her nose into your affairs?' he growls.

'They'll be able to track my phone and see I'm here, in your house,' I say, relief coursing through me.

'You're going to have to tell them that you're fine. That you went away for a couple of days,' he says.

This is my chance.

'Your bitch of a friend cannot go to the police. Once they're involved...'

He spins on his heel and stands in front of me, his hands on his hips. 'This is what is going to happen. You will call Lesley and tell her that everything is alright.'

'And if I don't?' I ask quietly.

'I'll kill you, and then I'll kill myself,' he says. 'Stay here.' And then he's running up the steps. I move to run after him, but I am jolted from the rope around my ankle. I trip and graze my knees. My heart is pounding again; what is going to happen? Why has he disappeared?

I have to wait a mere thirty seconds before Lucas is running down the steps. I swallow hard. He's holding a handgun in his right hand.

I'm trembling now. I'm not used to guns and have never even held one.

'What are you going to do?' I ask, my voice quivering.

'You are going to call Lesley. You are going to tell her that you're sick and that your neighbor is coming over to help with the dog. That she has nothing to worry about.'

'And if I don't?' I ask.

'This gun is loaded.' He lifts it up and points it at my head. I think I'm going to throw up. 'I'm not scared of dying. Are you?'

I can't speak. Yes, of course I'm scared of dying. Not the act itself, but because my girls still need me; Grant needs me. There's still a lot I want to do with my life.

'Shall we do a practice run?' Lucas asks. I'm shocked at how calm and composed he is now. He lowers the gun. 'I'll pretend to be Lesley. Hey Daniella, what's going on?'

'Um, sorry I didn't answer the door. I'm sick.'

'Oh no,' Lucas says in a fake, high-pitched voice. 'Can I come over and help?'

'Ergh, no. I'm staying with Grant's parents.'

The gun rises up, and he points it at me again.

'No!' he roars. 'You're at home. If you say you're with Grant's parents, she might double-check and discover you're not there. Get it?'

I nod. 'Sorry,' I say, lowering my eyes.

Before we can do another practice run, my phone rings

once more. He looks at the screen and tells me it's Lesley again.

'I'm going to answer it and put it on speaker. If you say a word wrong, you're dead. Get it?' Lucas says.

I nod. He presses answer.

'Daniella?' Lesley's voice blares out from my phone, and I have to stop myself from bursting into tears at the sound of her familiar voice.

'Sorry,' I say. 'I've been sick. I couldn't get to the door.'

'It's such a relief to hear your voice. I was really worried. Can I come over, maybe get you some medicine on the way?'

'No, I'm fine,' I say. But then I've no idea what to say next. Lucas glowers at me and taps the gun against his thigh.

'Look, we've got loads to talk about,' Lesley says. 'I could pop over, and we could watch a film together, chat over everything.'

'Um, no. I don't want you to catch this. I'm fine. I've been watching back-to-back episodes of *Friends*.'

'*Friends*?' Lesley asks, confusion in her voice. She's going to think that's very weird indeed, as I'm one of the tiny handful of people in the world who never got into the series. I need her to pick up on the sense that something is horribly wrong.

And then I remember all of those years ago when we were young and going out together to nightclubs. Lesley and I had a safe word. If either of us rang the other and said the word *sunflower*, we knew the other one was in trouble. Sunflowers were both of our favorite flower, and we reckoned it wasn't a word that would easily come up in conversation. It's been over two decades since I've thought of that, but Lucas has made a mistake. Lesley and I know each other too well.

'Anyway,' I say quickly, 'did you remember to order the sunflowers? I'll need them to do that big order.'

There's a long pause. Lucas narrows his eyes, but he can't possibly know that there was a double meaning to that sentence, can he?

'Right,' Lesley says eventually.

'Oh, and can you possibly look after the dog? I thought the neighbor was coming over, but maybe she forgot. You can get the house key from her. Mrs. Bladon lives in the house on the left of ours. I'm not well enough to take him for a walk.'

'I didn't know you had a dog,' Lesley says. I can tell that she's really confused about this entire conversation.

'It belonged to Peggy, the lady who died.'

Lucas makes a motion to tell me to stop talking. I open my mouth to speak further, but he raises the gun and points it at my face. I fall silent.

'Sorry, I've got to go. Going to be sick,' I say. Lucas ends the call.

'Now that wasn't so hard, was it?' he asks in a singsong voice.

I just pray that Lesley has worked out I'm in trouble. I'm sure she will. If the shoe were on the other foot, I'd certainly take action. She doesn't know that I've inherited this house, but Grant does. When she discovers I'm not at home, will she come here?

'We're moving,' Lucas says. 'You and I are getting out of this house.' He hurls my phone against the wall, and it tumbles to the ground with a clatter. Then he stomps his booted foot on it over and over until the screen is completely shattered.

'No,' I say. The gun is pointed at me once more. I can't let him take me away. So long as I'm at Peggy's house, there's a chance that I might be found. But if he shoves me in the trunk of his car and drives me to some unknown location, there will be little hope.

I'm cowering on the mattress now, completely at a loss as to what I should do. Lucas paces around and around, scratching his head, chewing his lip with concentration. Eventually he stops, puts the gun in his back pocket and turns to face me. 'This is what is going to happen. I'm going to fill up the car with stuff that we're going to need over the next few days, and then we'll take a drive. We'll find Airbnbs and go on a road trip, far from here. You'll act like my loving girlfriend, and if you don't, I'll kill you. Got it?'

I nod. Surely this plan is fraught with danger for him. What's that sign that women do when they're in trouble? It's where you tuck your thumb into the palm of your hand, fold your four fingers over it and lift and rewrap your thumb to indicate danger. Surely I'll have the opportunity to do that at some point? He kicks one of the Macy's bags towards me. 'Get dressed in these clothes while I'm upstairs packing the car. Tuck your hair up under the baseball cap.'

'You'll need to untie me.'

First, he checks that the tie around my ankle is secure; then he unties my wrists. 'No silly business. Got it?' he asks. I nod.

And then he's running up the stairs. I do as Lucas says and get dressed in the clothes in the bag. They're nice clothes too, a couple of cashmere sweaters, some thick navy pants and a pair of leather boots. There's no mirror in here, but I'm sure I look a mess despite the quality clothes.

A few minutes later, he's back.

'We're going to walk to the car, and you're going to get into the passenger seat. Remember we're in love, Daniella, so do as I say.' Clearly his idea of love is subservience, but I guess that shouldn't surprise me.

He bends down to undo the tie that attaches my ankle to the rope, enabling me to pull on the pants properly. For a moment, I wonder if I could bash him on the head, but then I see the gun slipped into the back of his jeans. I'm no match for a man with a gun.

'You're going to walk in front of me, and if you attempt to run away or do anything stupid, I will shoot you. Do you understand?'

I nod.

'Walk slowly towards the stairs.'

I do as he says, and I can feel the metal of the gun pressed against my back. I climb the stairs, my knees trembling, feeling unsteady on my feet. 'Go slowly,' he says.

'Where are we going when we reach the top?' I ask.

'You will open the door, then walk very slowly through the kitchen and into the garage.'

I wonder if I could make a run for it, grab a knife from the block in the kitchen.

'We are going to be happy,' Lucas says, his breath hot on my neck. 'Don't make me hurt you.'

I slow down as we enter the kitchen, but he shoves me in the back. 'Keep walking.'

I haven't been into the garage before, so it's a genuine question when I say, 'Where should I go? I've never been in this part of the house before.'

'Straight ahead. There's a door next to the back door. Open it,' he commands. Except I realize I have a choice. In that nanosecond, I make a grab for the handle of the back door, wrenching it towards me.

'Wrong door!' he hollers as I discover the back door is locked. I deflate. Of course it is. He's not that stupid.

'Sorry,' I murmur. Although the only thing I'm sorry for is that I can't make a run for it. I open the door in front of me, and he pushes me into the garage. It's a double-car garage with a workbench running down one wall. The main garage door is closed, an old-fashioned up and over type, and there's another door on the far wall. Lucas's Honda is parked in the middle of the space.

'Are we going far?' I ask, remembering how captives always try to keep their captors talking in films.

'I've already told you. You're going to get in the trunk, and then when I'm sure that you're not going to do anything stupid, I'll let you sit in the front. But not until we're far out of state.'

I hadn't been expecting that. How the hell will I escape if I'm bundled into the trunk of the car?

'I get carsick,' I say, which isn't true.

'So you'll just have to throw up,' he replies. He's still standing behind me, and there's very little space between the rear of the car and the closed garage door. The car is old, and I realize that he will physically have to open the trunk, rather than it pinging open with the click of a remote control. This could be my chance. I turn around to look at him just as he slips the gun into the waistband of his jeans again.

'Please, Lucas,' I beg him. 'Let me sit in the front.'

He ignores me and opens the trunk with one hand, the other heavy on my shoulder.

'I'm scared,' I say, shivering melodramatically.

'Of what?'

'I'm claustrophobic. Being trapped in the trunk is going

to be horrible.' I take a huge risk and lean up to give him a kiss on the lips.

'What are you doing?' he asks suspiciously. I push my body up against his, trying to swallow the revulsion.

'Giving you a kiss,' I say. In the millisecond that he relaxes into me, I bring my knee sharply upwards and get him straight in the groin. He yelps, but I'm faster. I grab the trunk of the car and bring it down as hard as I can. It catches him on the side of the head. Lucas roars with pain and releases me.

I have to get out of here.

Except I don't have the remote control for the garage door.

And I don't have any time.

I race around the side of the car, back the way we came, tugging at the door to the house, except it's locked. Did he lock it behind us? The other door. I need to get out the other door. I skid around the car and grab the handle to the other door, and to my utter relief, it turns.

I'm outside.

I hesitate for a second. I've never been in Peggy's backyard before and have no idea where to go. How to get out of here. And that second is too long because Lucas is right behind me.

CHAPTER TWENTY-SEVEN

LUCAS

'Louise! Come back!' I shout. We've done this so many times. Playing hide-and-seek, her running from me. Me finding her. Because I always find her. But she's never kicked me in the groin before, the little bitch. And it hurts, a lot. She's ahead of me, but only by a fraction of a second. I've got much longer legs, so I'll be able to catch her, so long as I can ignore the throbbing of my head and the gut-wrenching pain in my groin.

She looks over her shoulder at me, and I realize it's not Louise. It's my love. Daniella. Her eyes are wide with fear, and her legs are pumping up and down as she runs. Except unlike Louise, Daniella doesn't know where she's going. She's skirting around the edge of the yard, the overgrown borders filled with tangled hydrangea and thick, untamed boxwood. Mom used to care for her yard with such tenderness, except the past few years, she hasn't been able to bend. She had a gardener until I fired him.

The treehouse is still there. I thought they'd pull it down years ago, but it became a memorial to Louise. It was her treehouse. Father made sure we knew he'd paid a fortune for it, with its two little turrets and Rapunzel-like steps that wrap around the trunk of the huge European beech tree. And how Louise loved it. She cried when she looked out her window on her seventh birthday. It was the perfect present for a treasured little girl. She took her dolls up there and sat them on the floor, having endless tea parties with her imaginary friends. And somehow, despite all the gales and the harsh winters, the treehouse remains intact, forty years on.

She's running so fast now, glancing over her shoulder at me, stumbling and hauling herself up again.

'I'm going to catch you!' I taunt. I hear Mom's laugh. How she loved seeing the two of us playing together. 'My perfect family,' she'd cry. Except we never were a perfect family. It was always a facade.

The yard is much too small for the house, and these days it's even smaller with all the overgrown plants encroaching onto the pitted muddy lawn. Most houses around here have large plots and open-plan yards, perhaps with some picket fencing to divide the properties up. Not our yard. This has always been self-contained and private. It's why Father liked it. He could do whatever he wanted in our backyard without fearing prying eyes. And it's why Louise loved her treehouse so much. With his enormous feet, Father never ventured up those narrow steps. But my feet were small back then. Sometimes she invited me up, but mostly it was her refuge from me.

She's doubled back now, clearly realizing there's no way out. If she's looking for a secret gate buried in the thick branches, she's going to be disappointed. The only way out of this yard is through the door we came through, the side door in the garage. Or the back door, but that's locked.

I'm laughing. 'Coming to get you!' I yell.

'Help!' she cries, the sound piercing and hurtful. That's not part of the rules. Except Father is at work, and Mom is baking, so no one will hear us. She's circling the trunk of the treehouse again, and now I'm so close, I can touch her. I reach forwards, making a grab for her sweater. She shrugs me off, but she has nowhere to go.

Silly girl. She's starting to climb the steps, up and up. Doesn't she know how dangerous it is? It might be the cutest treehouse in Boston, but it's high.

'Be careful!' I hear Mom's cry.

There's the sound of splitting wood and a yell, but I don't care. It worked all those years ago, and it'll work again today. She kicks her foot out but misses my forehead by an inch. I could grab her foot now and pull her down, except I'd rather face her in that turret, just like last time. I don't like mean girls. I don't like girls whose parents love them more than they love me. I don't like girls who don't do what I tell them to.

She's up there now, on the ledge. More cracking of wood and a step falls down, the plank spearing into the soft, muddy lawn below.

'Leave me alone!' she shouts, but I laugh.

Of course I'm not going to leave her alone. I'm going to push her, and she's going to die. Just as I like it.

CHAPTER TWENTY-EIGHT

DANIELLA

'Louise, don't be silly,' Lucas says.

I stare at him, wide-eyed. I'm trapped. It was so stupid to come up here, except where else was I meant to go? This yard is fully enclosed with thick, tall hedges and no way out. Does he still have the gun? I can't see because he's crouched down in front of me. There's barely enough space for the two of us up here, and the wood is rotten. One false move and we both might tumble down.

'Don't be scared, LouLou,' he says. Lucas's eyes are glazed over, and I see that I'm no longer Daniella in his mind. He's regressed decades. I assume he thinks I'm his sister. I'm not sure if this scares me more or not. 'Everything will be alright if you do what I say.'

'What do you want?' I ask. I barely recognize my own voice.

'For Daddy to love me like he loves you, of course.'

I freeze. What the hell is going on in Lucas's fractured mind? One push and he could shove me out of this tree-house. I might survive, but I'd surely break a limb or two.

He's staring at me as if he's expecting me to answer. 'Of course Daddy loves you,' I say.

Lucas slams his hand down, and it goes straight through the wood, leaving large, painful-looking splinters in his palm, but he doesn't seem to notice.

'He loves you,' Lucas says, jabbing his forefinger at me. 'And he hates me. Lucas, you're ugly. Lucas, you're dumb. Lucas, why can't you be more like your little sister? She has such a sweet nature, unlike you. You'll never make a success of yourself. You're a pathetic mommy's boy. Your mother is a whore anyway; you've got whore genes. On and on and on he goes. And look at you, all pretty in your cutesy dresses and pigtails. Top of the class and oh so pretty. The perfect little girl.' He scoffs. If this were any other situation, I might feel sorry for Lucas. His mind is clearly shattered, and for sure he's not seeing me, but his little sister.

'And you know what's going to happen now, LouLou? You are going to die.'

I flinch and edge backwards, but there's nowhere to go with Lucas blocking the entrance. The only way down is to jump, and it's too far. What the hell am I going to do?

'I am going to take away the only thing that Father loves. And that is you.'

Oh my God. Lucas clearly did kill his sister, and now it looks like he's imagining that I'm her, and he's going to kill me. Where's the gun? Is it still wedged in his waistband? He lunges for me, his muscular arms reaching out, hands grabbing my neck. I kick out and once again catch him in the groin. He groans but doesn't let go. I hear the crack and splinter of another board, and I think how the ground far below is weirdly green for this time of year. I do everything I can, kicking with my feet, jabbing my elbows backwards.

'You little bitch,' Lucas cries.

And then I hear the clatter of metal on wood, but I'm faster than him. I lunge for the gun, my hand clasped around it. Lucas's fingers are squeezing my neck, harder and harder. I pull the trigger. There's a deafening shot.

'You're dead!' he shouts. His fingers let go of my neck, and I lose my balance, but not before I fire the gun again. Then I'm grappling with air and I'm falling. Falling. The green ground comes rising up to meet me. So quickly. And in an instant, green turns to black.

CHAPTER TWENTY-NINE

DANIELLA

'Hey,' I say. 'How are you feeling?'

Grant yawns and rubs his eyes. 'I should be asking you the same question,' he replies as he tries to sit up in bed. This hospital room feels so familiar now.

'It's not too bad,' I explain. 'Just a bad sprain.' My arm is in a sling, and my shoulder is battered blue with bruises, but extraordinarily, nothing is broken. The winter ground was sodden from a recent thaw, and the softer ground eased my fall. My head is sore from getting a concussion twice in as many days, and that's the reason I was kept in the hospital overnight.

'You were so brave, darling,' Grant says.

I shrug. I don't think I was brave. I just did what I had to do. The person I owe the most to is Lesley.

There's a knock on the door, and Detective Sandy Briar pops his head in. 'Any chance I could have a chat with both of you?' he asks.

'Sure,' I say. 'How is Lucas?' I can't stand the man, but I

do feel an iota of pity for him. He's clearly broken, physically and mentally.

'Two fractured legs and a gunshot wound in the shoulder,' he says, pulling a gray plastic chair from the side of the room and positioning it next to me. 'He's having a second surgery, but we'll be questioning him properly tomorrow.'

'And he's in custody?' I ask. I can't bear the thought that he's here in the same hospital.

'Don't worry,' Detective Briar says. 'He's going nowhere. He's secured to the bed, and there's an officer positioned in his doorway twenty-four seven.'

'Am I in trouble?' I ask.

'You've already explained that you shot him in self-defense. We'll need to take some more statements from everyone, but you shouldn't worry too much. Now, Mr. Morris, you said you have something to tell me.'

Grant looks at me and then at Sandy Briar. 'I've remembered something from when I was attacked.'

'Go on,' the detective urges.

'Lucas and I had spent the evening together, and he left to go home, probably around 9 p.m. I went up to the bedroom quite early, had a chat with Daniella on the phone and then went to sleep. I was definitely asleep by 11 p.m., but something woke me just before 1 a.m. I went to the toilet and was back in bed, my eyes closed, when I heard a creak at the door. My eyes were wide open in the dark, and I froze with terror when I heard footsteps. A flashlight was shone in my eyes, but not before I saw the eyes peering at me through the slit in the balaclava. I know those eyes. It was Lucas. And I smelled his distinctive aftershave. I'm absolutely positive about it. Except you'll probably just think I'm making this up because of what happened to Daniella.'

Detective Briar gives us both a slow smile. 'I don't think you made it up, Grant. We have the evidence now. First, we found your wedding photograph in Lucas's room at his mother's house. Well, half of it anyway. He'd replaced your head with a photo of his own, Grant, so it looks like he and Daniella are in the photo. And we found your backdoor key in his bedside drawer. I'm assuming you never gave that to him.'

Both of us shake our heads.

'And the final bit of evidence was the balaclava. We can't be sure he wore it that night, but it matches what you're telling us. As soon as he's well enough, we're going to question him again. In the meantime, I gather you're being discharged from hospital,' the detective says. Grant smiles broadly and reaches across to squeeze my hand.

'We will be charging Lucas with your attempted murder, as well as the false imprisonment and attempted murder of Daniella.'

'Lucas came to visit me here in the hospital,' Grant says. 'It's a bit hazy, but I remember him leaning over me, and then a nurse came in, and he left quite quickly after that. Except the nurse found a syringe of insulin under the bed after he left. She asked me about it, but honestly, I was too out of it to put two and two together. Do you think Lucas tried to kill me a second time?'

I gasp.

'Possibly.' Detective Briar clasps his chin in his hand. 'The question is, why did he want to kill you?'

'I've no idea,' Grant says. 'I thought we were friends. He helped me at the gym most evenings, and we always had a good banter. It doesn't make any sense. He even came on a skiing trip with us.'

Except I know why he tried to kill Grant. But can I bring myself to say anything? The shame courses through me. This is all my fault. Everything that has happened is because of me.

Detective Briar stands up.

'I'll come by your house after we've interviewed Lucas Denman,' he says. 'In the meantime, take care, both of you.'

He's walking out the door when I quickly stand up and hurry after him. 'Detective,' I say, 'can I have a quick word?'

'Of course.' I close the door to Grant's hospital room behind me, and we walk in silence to the end of the corridor. When I'm sure I'm not going to be overheard, I murmur, 'It's my fault.'

The detective pauses, one eyebrow lifted.

'I slept with Lucas. It was just once and was a terrible, terrible mistake. Except after that, he became fixated on me. He seemed to think that I was going to leave Grant and we'd be together happily ever after. Except that was never going to happen. When I rejected him, he turned on me. That's why he tried to kill my husband. That's why he captured me and then tried to kill me too.'

'It's always about love or money,' Sandy Briar mutters.

'And I think you need to investigate two other deaths. Are you aware that his girlfriend, Jade Larson, took her own life?'

'Yes, we are looking into that. Bearing in mind everything we know now, there could be cause for further investigation.'

'Are you aware that Lucas found her?'

'Yes, it's suspicious.'

'And the insulin. Peggy Denman, his mother, passed

away last week. Lucas said she died as a result of her diabetes. Do you think she died from natural causes?'

Detective Briar lets out a whistle of air. 'Seems like we have a lot more investigating to do. Thank you for all of this, Daniella.'

'Oh, and there's something else,' I add. 'Peggy told me that her daughter died when she was young. When Lucas was chasing me, it was like he regressed into a child, and he was going on about how their father preferred me to him. I think in that moment, he thought that I was Louise. He basically admitted to pushing her to her death.'

'Wow, this is quite something,' Sandy Briar says. 'If I may, I'll come and take a statement from you tomorrow. But for now, I think you and your husband need to get home.'

'Thank you,' I reply. 'One final thing. Please, can you leave it up to me to explain everything to Grant? He deserves to hear about my infidelity from me and not from you.'

'Of course. And good luck.' He turns on his heel and walks away.

AN HOUR LATER, Grant and I are in a taxi on our way home. I know about the surprise that is waiting for him there, and it's hard to contain my excitement. He's still a little unsteady on his feet, so we clasp each other as we walk up the steps to our home. Before I can put my hand on the doorknob, the door flies open.

'Welcome home!' Arlyse and Tasia hurl themselves at us, with Bippie nuzzling at our legs.

'Careful, girls,' Lesley says as she stands behind them, a broad smile on her face. 'Your parents are still invalids.'

Arlyse immediately goes into caring mode, slipping her

arms between both mine and Grant's, while Tasia holds Bippie, whose tail is whipping all of our legs. I'm not sure I have ever been so happy to see the twins, and even Grant has happy tears in his eyes.

'Come into the living room,' Arlyse says. 'We've got the fire going.'

The room is cozy and homey, and for a moment I forget the chaos that Lucas created. The girls cluck around Grant while I follow Lesley into the kitchen.

'How's the shoulder?' she asks.

'Not too bad. I owe you a huge thank you,' I say.

'And I owe you a huge apology.'

I raise an eyebrow.

'You were right about Matt. I got completely swept along in his grandiose ideas. I've told him that I don't want to expand the business, and guess what?' She sighs. 'He's ghosting me. So much for being a loving boyfriend.'

'I'm sorry,' I say. And I genuinely am. Fortunately, Lesley remembered our safe word. It was fortuitous that sunflowers are very much out of season at the moment, and there is no way that I would be asking her to order any, fake or real. After sending the police around to my house and realizing I wasn't there, she called Grant at the hospital. It didn't do much good for his blood pressure, but he told Lesley about Peggy's house and how I mentioned I was going there. She called the police back and told them to hurry to Ivy Street. As it happened, with his broken legs and gunshot wound, Lucas wouldn't have been able to catch me, but fortunately the police arrived shortly after I regained consciousness.

'Before all of this happened,' I say to Lesley as I lean against the kitchen counter, 'Grant and I were talking about moving away, and that was before this house became tainted. If we move up the coast, I could become a silent partner in the Silken Stem, or maybe we could organize some kind of management buyout. But that's something we can discuss in the future.'

'Or we could sell the business altogether,' she adds.

'Maybe. But there's no need to make any decisions in a hurry.'

'You're right. First of all, you need a cup of tea and to spend some time with your girls. I'm going to leave you to it, but if you need anything, anything at all, don't hesitate to call me.'

'Thank you, Lesley,' I say, throwing my one good arm around her. I'm relieved we seem to be repairing our relationship.

THAT NIGHT, Grant and I lie together in bed, his arms tightly around me. I haven't told him why Lucas did what he did, and weirdly, he hasn't asked me. But I know I need to be honest. Taking a deep breath, I say, 'It's my fault, everything that happened. I let Lucas into our lives and then...' I squeeze my eyes tightly in the dark, and the words slip out in a whoosh. 'I slept with him. I'm so sorry, Grant. It only happened the once, but I should never ever have let him seduce me. I betrayed you. And then Lucas became obsessed with me, and he wouldn't leave me alone.'

I wait, tense, bracing myself for Grant to release his grip on me, to switch the light on, to tell me that he wants me out of this bed, out of this room, out of this house.

Except he doesn't.

'I know,' he says.

'What do you mean, you know?' I ask, leaning over and putting the bedside light on. Grant shields his eyes from the light and edges up in bed. He still has bruises around his neck and shoulders.

'It's not your fault,' Grant says.

'But it is!'

'I saw Lucas in the gym, and I knew he'd be your type. I thought perhaps if I encouraged Lucas to sleep with you, you'd get it out of your system. Maybe you wouldn't feel that I was letting you down so badly. I thought it could be a bit of fun for you, and then we could return to normal.'

I stare at Grant, my jaw hanging open.

'Except then I realized that was the stupidest of ideas and a terrible mistake. I suspected that you'd slept with him. You were different afterwards, riddled with guilt, I suppose. And Lucas was all swagger, so full of himself. He acted like we were best buddies, but now we know he came back later on and tried to kill me.'

I am so shocked, I can't speak.

'Why did you want me to sleep with him?' I ask eventually, hugging my arms around my torso under the duvet.

'Because I thought I couldn't give you what you needed and reckoned it might be best if you got it elsewhere. I love you so much, Daniella, and the thought of losing you is terrifying.'

'Except you nearly pushed me into another man's arms,' I say.

'The stupidest thing I've ever done,' Grant mutters.

'We've really screwed up, haven't we?' I murmur.

'Yes, except we still have each other. Can you forgive me?' he asks.

'Me forgive you? It should be the other way around. I'm the one who broke our marriage vows.'

'Except I encouraged it,' Grant says. 'I avoided counseling because I didn't want to face up to my lack of libido and the cracks in our relationship that I guess are normal after twenty years. But that was a mistake. I want to fight for our marriage. I want to make things right, and I want to attend counseling with you. What do you think?'

'What do I think?' I ask. I throw my arms around his neck, and we both flinch, but then laugh out loud. 'The state of us,' I murmur into his ear.

'Who love each other,' Grant says.

'I love you so much,' I say. 'I was completely terrified I was going to lose you. I never want to give up on you, Dr. Grant Morris.'

He smiles and gently kisses my lips. 'I'm going to go to a real doctor and see if there's a physical reason why I have such a low libido.'

'Honestly, it's not that important.'

'Except it is. And we need to be completely honest with each other. Promise?'

I snuggle back down under the duvet and lie with my face against his chest, listening to the strong, steady beat of his heart. 'I promise,' I say.

IT'S A WEEK LATER. The girls, reassured that we are both on the mend, have flown back to South America. The day after we left the hospital, Detective Sandy Briar came over and took a formal statement from me. And now, he's at the front door once again.

'Good afternoon, Daniella. Is it convenient for me to have a quick word?'

'Of course,' I say. 'Except Grant isn't here. He's returned to work.'

'That's fine. It's you I want to talk to.'

I lead him into the kitchen, and he accepts a cup of coffee. We both sit down at the kitchen table.

'We've been tying up some loose ends,' he says. 'Lucas Denman has admitted to attacking Grant. He also admitted to being in the hospital with some insulin syringes. It's not like he could deny either accusation, as there was CCTV and evidence. In light of that, we have had another look at the death of his mother, Margaret Denman. It seems too much of a coincidence that she died as a result of an insulin overdose.'

'I wasn't aware that was the cause of death,' I say.

'Lucas hasn't admitted to killing his mother, but we're working on the premise that he did. Based on your statement as to the death of his sister, we also talked to him about her death. However, he flatly denies killing her. Unfortunately, with no evidence and with the passing of so much time, we can't pursue that. What we can pursue is the death of Jade Larson. Lucas told us that he was on a skiing trip with you at the time of Jade Larson's death, except we're now aware that he returned home early. Is that correct?'

'Yes,' I say.

'We believe that Jade Larson died on that Saturday sometime between 10 a.m. and 2 p.m. and that it was homicide and not suicide.'

'Except Lucas was with us then,' I add. 'We were skiing together. He didn't return home until late afternoon.'

Detective Briar goes very still. 'That doesn't add up,' he murmurs. 'Are you aware of the Denmans' history?' he asks.

'No.' I frown.

'Peggy Denman admitted to killing her husband some fifteen or so years ago.'

'Peggy?' I gasp. Lovely, sweet, gentle Peggy.

'I've had a good read through the case files. She spent three years in jail, but there were many mitigating circumstances, not least of which is years of coercive control at the hands of her husband. At the time, the killing was considered to be in self-defense.'

'But she seemed like such a lovely woman,' I say, shocked.

'A woman who has acted rather strangely though, don't you think? She left you her house, didn't she? Do you know why?'

'Yes. In fact, she left me a note. I completely forgot to tell you about it. I'm not sure what happened to it after Lucas hit me and kept me locked up. Peggy wrote that she saw me as a substitute daughter. Initially, she thought Lucas and I could be together, which is ridiculous, of course, but then she realized Lucas was dangerous, and she told me to stay away. She wanted me to have the house, to sell it and use the money to move far away from him.'

'It's all very strange,' Detective Briar says. 'I'm wondering whether Peggy was the sweet old lady she appeared to be. If what you're saying is correct, her son, Lucas, could not have killed Jade Larson. The forensics don't match up. But Peggy could have done it. My theory is that she's spent years protecting her son. I think she knew there was evil in him, but perhaps there was evil in her too. Or perhaps not. Maybe she was delusional and thought the only way to make her son happy was to facilitate the two of you getting together, and for that to happen, Jade needed to die.'

I sit there in shock, trying to imagine Peggy taking Jade's life.

'It's grim, but we've had to exhume Jade's body. We've found traces of insulin.'

'Was Jade pregnant?' I ask, suddenly remembering how she told me she was pregnant with Lucas's child.

Detective Briar tilts his head to one side and frowns. 'No, she definitely wasn't pregnant.'

I let out a sigh of relief. It's hard to absorb everything that the detective is telling me. 'So what you're saying is Peggy killed her husband and Jade.'

'I think it's highly likely she killed Jade, although maybe Lucas killed his father and she covered for him. I will need to reread the case notes.'

'And Lucas probably killed his sister based on what he told me, and he tried to kill Grant and me.'

He nods. 'Quite the family, hey?'

I lean back in my chair. 'And what about her mugging, that very first day I met Peggy?'

'I'm afraid we have no concrete evidence; however, we did find dark clothes in Lucas's possession that matched your description. So perhaps he attacked his own mother. I'm afraid we're unlikely to prove that one way or another.' Detective Briar stands up. 'I know this is a lot to absorb. I'll be in touch again when we've decided exactly what charges we're going to bring against Lucas Denman.'

'What should I do about the house Peggy left me?'

'That's a matter for your attorney, but it seems it's yours to do with whatever you like.'

'We'll sell it as soon as possible.'

He laughs. 'I'd do the same in your shoes.'

I see the detective to the door. I'm shaking as I return into the house, Bippie at my feet.

The phone rings. I pause before answering it, thinking of every other call I've had recently and how they've invariably been the harbinger of bad news. But then I see that it's Grant calling.

'Everything alright?' I ask.

'Sure is. Would you like me to pick anything up on my way home?'

'Actually, can you come home early? Detective Briar has been to see me.'

CHAPTER THIRTY

DANIELLA – A YEAR LATER

'Hey, Mom!' It's Arlyse.

'How did the exams go?' Naively, I'd thought that with the twins away at college, my role as Mom would be lessened somehow. That is certainly not the case. Both girls call most days, and the only time we don't hear from them is when their lives are going so swimmingly they forget Grant and I exist.

'I passed everything!'

'That's such a relief,' I say. I knew she would, but my goodness, she's been stressing these past weeks.

'How's the unpacking going?'

I turn around to look at the sea of boxes. 'It's a challenge.' I laugh.

'Can't wait to come and see you at spring break. Gotta go now.'

That first house I saw the details of in Rockport sold quickly, but we found another one, bigger, and with a yard large enough for Grant to keep chickens. Whether or not he'll get around to it is debatable, but we both love it here, as does Bippie. Grant has taken a step back from work, although he still seems to have his head in research papers day and night.

He wanders into the living room holding his mobile phone. 'Detective Briar on the line.'

A jolt runs through me. We've put so much behind us this past year. Selling our house, selling Peggy's house, helping the girls settle into their colleges, attending Lucas's trial, and of course, repairing our marriage. I rather thought we'd never hear from the detective again.

Grant presses the speaker button.

'How are you both doing?' Sandy Briar asks.

'Well, thank you,' Grant replies. 'We're settling into our new house in Rockport and trying to unpack.'

I raise an eyebrow because Grant is most definitely not doing his fair share.

'I have some information, and I wanted you to hear it from me rather than on a news bulletin.'

I tense, and Grant flings his arm around me, holding my shoulders tightly. I thought anything to do with Lucas was firmly in our past.

'The new owner of Peggy Denman's house has demolished it. When they were digging up the yard, they found some human bones. I'm afraid to say that they are the bones of an infant, probably around four months old.'

'But Louise Denman was eight when she died, wasn't she?' I exclaim.

'Yes, I've been through the death records and associated paperwork. Louise died due to an accidental fall. The investigating officer at the time was suspicious, but the statements from all family members confirmed it was a tragic accident, so that was deemed the official cause of death.'

'Do you believe that?' I ask.

'Based on what we know now, no. But we will never be able to prove it.'

'So who was the infant?'

'The birth of a third child was registered. A Daniella Denman.'

'Daniella?' I gasp.

'Yes. Perhaps that's another reason why Peggy bonded with you. It was the name of her third child. Except I haven't found any further records for Daniella Denman. No active social security number, no health records, no digital footprint. So we carried out forensics on the DNA from the bones, and it has been confirmed that the infant was Lucas Denman's sister and Peggy's daughter.'

He pauses.

'I'm afraid there's more. The forensic pathologist believes the infant died from a broken neck.'

I gasp. 'Was she murdered?'

'We will never be sure, but it looks that way. We've questioned Lucas Denman, but he refuses to talk about either of his sisters. This is going to blow up into a big story, so I'm just glad you're not involved. We'll be doing our best to keep your names out of the press.'

'That's horrible,' I murmur. 'Who would have killed her?'

'Unless Lucas confesses, I fear we'll never know. Anyway, I wish you both well, and if there are further developments, I'll be sure to let you know.'

Grant and I stand there staring at each other after he hangs up. 'What a family,' he mutters.

'You can never know what goes on behind closed doors,' I say.

'Indeed.'

We're startled by Bippie barking. 'I'll go,' Grant says, releasing me. I perch on the edge of the sofa, shaken by Detective Briar's news. Grant returns to the room, holding a pile of mail.

'All junk,' he says, sifting through the envelopes. 'Except this one.' He hands me a postcard.

I smile. It's from Lesley. She's traveling around America on a big tour, visiting all of those cities she dreamed of seeing, and this postcard is from New Orleans. We sold the Silken Stem, and although we didn't make the millions that Matt promised it was worth, we both came away with a healthy bank balance.

I'm still deciding what to do next, but if I can find a suitable storefront, I'll likely open a flower shop. A real one this time.

'How is Lesley?' Grant asks.

'Having the time of her life.'

'And I think we can have the time of our lives too, living here,' Grant says, squeezing my hand.

I smile. We're still having regular couples counseling. We make love from time to time. Our marriage isn't perfect, but whose twenty-year-old marriage is? We've been through a lot together, Grant and me, and one thing I know for sure, together we can face any storm that blows our way.

A LETTER FROM MIRANDA

Thank you so much for reading *Don't Answer The Phone.*

For the first time, I've set a book in the USA. Our daughter spent four glorious years at Berklee College of Music in Boston. As it's a city I've visited and love, I decided to set this novel there. I hope I haven't made too many mistakes.

Some novels write themselves; others are a little harder. This one fell into the latter category. I got thinking about how one good deed could set off a chain reaction and alter the course of a person's life. Lucas and Daniella came to life in my head quite quickly, but then took many circuitous journeys before I settled on the current story. It's been a while since I've created a really troubled, unpleasant male character so I hope you both despised and pitied him.

I've dedicated *Don't Answer The Phone* to Pippa Bugby. To those of you who follow me on social media, you might be aware that we recently gutted and renovated a very old house. My talented friend Pippa managed the whole process, and I simply couldn't have got through the last year without her vision, design skills, calm demeanour, and acute eye for detail. I certainly wouldn't have had the time to write four books these past eighteen months. A huge thanks to Pippa, who incidentally is one of my most loyal readers!

Recipients of my newsletter have the chance to name characters in my books. Thank you to the following people who suggested the names I used in *Don't Answer The Phone.* I'm so grateful for your support.

Daniella Blowitski, Arlyse DeLoyla, Phyllis Fried, Peggy Haas Denman, Suzan Larson, Diane Martin, Linda Mehall, Deb Morris, Lesley Rennie, Bob Riley, Sherri Hamilton, Jill Sutheran, Jade Lee Wright.

Thank you as well to my editors Jan Smith and Claire Milto. Claire went above and beyond with this book, and I'm hugely grateful. And my thrillers would be a confused mess without Jan. The team at Inkubator Books is the best and it's a joy working with them. Thank you to Brian Lynch, Garret Ryan, Stephen Ryan, Jan Smith, Alice Latchford, Claire Milto, Elizabeth Bayliss and everyone else.

I'd like to extend a special thank you to all the awesome book bloggers who take the time to review my psychological thrillers and share their views on social media. I try my best to thank them on Instagram and Facebook but if I've missed a mention, please know that I'm grateful beyond words.

Most importantly, thank *you*. If you have a moment to leave a review on Amazon and Goodreads, I'd be massively grateful. It helps other people find my books.

If you would like a **FREE** copy of my novella, The Cheat, and the chance to name characters in my future books, please sign up to my newsletter at: **https://bit.ly/The-Cheat-Signup**

You'll also get exclusive access to new releases, giveaways and more!

My warmest wishes,

Miranda

PS – Here's that FREE thriller for you: https://bit.ly/The-Cheat-Signup

www.mirandarijks.com

ALSO BY MIRANDA RIJKS

Inkubator Books Titles

Psychological Thrillers

THE INFLUENCER

WHAT SHE KNEW

THE ONLY CHILD

THE NEW NEIGHBOUR

THE SECOND WIFE

THE INSOMNIAC

FORGET ME NOT

THE CONCIERGE

THE OTHER MOTHER

THE LODGE

THE HOMEMAKER

MAKE HER PAY

THE GODCHILD

EVERY BREATH YOU TAKE

THE HOUSE SWAP

VIOLETS ARE BLUE

YOU CAN TRUST ME

ONE LITTLE MISTAKE

DON'T ANSWER THE PHONE

The Dr Pippa Durrant Mystery Series

FATAL FORTUNE

(Book 1)

FATAL FLOWERS

(Book 2)

FATAL FINALE

(Book 3)

FATAL SERIES BOX SET

Titles Published by the Author

GASPS

I WANT YOU GONE

DESERVE TO DIE

YOU ARE MINE

ROSES ARE RED

THE ARRANGEMENT

THE VISITORS

Printed in Dunstable, United Kingdom

84242597R00170